KILLI

Affair with Murder Series

Book One

B.R. Spangler

TITLES IN THE SERIES

Killing Katie

Painful Truths

Grave Mistakes

ACKNOWLEDGMENTS

While working on this new series, I was aided by several individuals to whom I wish to offer my immense gratitude and appreciation. Thank you for reading early drafts of book one, and for offering critiques and encouragement. As always, your feedback has helped to shape the story.

To Chris Cornely Razzi, Don Shope, Monica Spangler, Linda Eighmy and so many others for providing invaluable feedback, and helping me recognize the potential of this book.

KILLING KATIE

1

MURDER. I'M OBSESSED. I can't stop thinking about it. Even as the sound of sizzling bacon fills our small kitchen, I imagine that it's something more tempting, something more sinister, something more lethal. And the dreamy thought of killing is more delicious than any food I've ever had. One problem, I've never killed a thing in my life. So why am I stuck on the idea?

I wish my obsession were simpler—maybe an attraction to someone else. I'd even welcome a housewife cliché, like filling my days with frivolous hobbies or getting lost in afternoon talk shows. But that isn't me. That isn't my passion—mine is dark and deep and seeded in every fiber of my being.

"I'm a murderer."

There, I said it. That is the first time I've ever confessed it aloud. I have a problem and there's no twelve-step program that can help me. I know. I've checked. I used to have hope that my problem could be solved by some random act that would shake it out of my system. If I'm being truthful, the real obsession, the greatest lie, is that I've been trying to be like everybody else most of my life. I'll never be like everybody else. I know I am different. I've known for nearly three dozen years. But one day, I'll finally become me—the real me. I just don't know when that will be. And when that happens, I'm afraid that I'll be like an alcoholic and won't be able to stop after the first one. *There might never be enough.* I worry I'd need a busload—if you get my meaning—the kind of murderous campaign that would spawn a storm of newly published books and even a movie or two.

My name is Amy Sholes, doting mother of two, impossibly in love with the most handsome man I've ever met, and living a life that makes some downright jealous. Sure, we have our moments—ups and downs, just like anyone else. From the busy mornings to the endless patter of tiny bare feet, there isn't much to complain about. But, like anything that is great, there is a catch—and that catch is me, and my preoccupation with murder.

The smell of the bacon rose from the stove. I took

in a deep breath and let it out. The familiar wish for something that could never be tugged at my heart while the scent tickled my palate. Sinful. Both of them. A rumble from our bedroom took my mind off this morning's fantasy. I looked up, waited. I heard another stir. Today was my husband's birthday. Steve's favorite way to start his new year? Breakfast. And then a little something else too. The thought of what was coming brought a flush to my neck and face. It had been a while.

I listened. One foot, then the other. I saw him in my mind, stretching and rubbing the sleep from his eyes and then pushing uncombed, salty grays against his head. But then I heard him falling onto our king-size bed and knew I'd lost him to that place where you could still remember your dreams. I shifted, feeling suddenly disenchanted. Steve had been working so hard the last month; I knew I should concede that he needed sleep more than he needed me. Breakfast could wait. Bacon always tasted great—hot or not. And so did I.

Cunning and powerful, murder crept back into my thoughts like a dark shadow. What would my friends and family think if they peeked inside my head and saw one of my fantasies? I'm sure they would lock me away, appalled, shuddering in disgust. But in my mind, my imagination seems normal. When I'm thinking about murder, daydreaming and playing out all the gory details, my heart jumps and my blood gets hot, rushing through my arms to my fingertips like an electrical charge. And, deep inside, a flutter of anticipation consumes and takes over, pulsing through my entire body.

If my family knew *who* I wanted to kill, though, they might look more mercifully on me. My prey? My fantasy? Killing the seediest of criminals that, frankly, we'd probably be better off without. That's what I tell myself, anyway. This month, I've been "targeting" the outcasts. You know the kind I'm talking about; you've seen their faces flash across the television screen during the evening news. You might have even covered your mouth in shock and awe, spit a few breathy words in disgust over what they'd done. I know that targeting the seediest of criminals is easy—it could even be considered a cop-out since the world won't lose anything when they die. But that hasn't always been my fantasy. There has been one murder fantasy which has haunted me for years. Killing Katie.

Katie Dawson is my best friend. As my mother tells it, we were thrown together in a tub one sweltering day, at the ripe young age of two, and we've been together ever since. Growing up, we did everything together. We went to the same schools. Made fun of the same teachers. Failed the same classes. And then there was college, where we pledged the same sorority and met our future husbands. An unexplainable, enchanted closeness kept us together from our first apartments to house hunting and then to having our children around the same time. Katie is my dearest and closest friend. So why do I want to kill her? Crazy, right? Don't get me wrong. For all the daydreams in the world, I'd never, ever harm Katie, let alone kill her. It's just my quirky fantasy—a role-playing game—like playing dress-up. I suppose the fantasies with Katie is helping me prepare for the real thing? And I guess I use Katie because she is the closest person to me, my person, and I have found no one else. Not yet, anyway.

My first memories of killing Katie—the fantasies, rather—had to be while we were in high school. Duran Duran and Prince and Boy George were on every radio station. They were playful and simple ideas at first, like spilling water on the floor at the grocery store where we worked part time so she would slip on it. Or fiddling with the brakes on her car like I'd seen in the movies. Truth is, I don't know the first thing about a car's brakes. Back then, before the Internet had Google or YouTube, we couldn't look up easy step-by-step instructions.

I daydreamed a lot during high school. But I didn't have the usual schoolgirl crushes. Instead of drawing little hearts on the covers of my notebook, I drew some rather sophisticated and elaborate designs for how to kill Katie. I felt like Wile E. Coyote planning a trap for the Road Runner—I loved that cartoon. And the more gruesome the plot, the more intricate the design, the brighter the murderous spark. Satisfaction. But it was a different kind of spark inside me, and not at all like the fluttery kind you get while staring at a cute boy. I'll admit though, the two went together great, like peanut butter and chocolate. And who doesn't like a little peanut butter with their chocolate?

I struggled, though. Especially after I'd finished each design. What I'd drawn wasn't exactly something I could tack up onto our fridge with a pineapple-shaped magnet, announcing: "Hey, Mom, look what I did!" Mostly, I felt accomplishment, a relief, but then I'd come crashing down. My emotions after were filled with sadness, confusion, a wonder about what was wrong with me, and why I was different. It was during those days I wished I were more like the other girls. It was those days I'd consider a murder—just one—to protect the rest of the world from who I believed I truly was.

But like an autumn rain, my gray days always passed. I tried to fit in. I'd listen to the other girls—the ones I'd call my friends—go on and on about their plans for a dance or an upcoming Friday night at the roller rink. I'd contribute a few words too—just enough to maintain some semblance of normalcy. The girls never suspected that I was different, but Katie picked up on it sometimes. I'd blame my being distant, and my blue moods on a girlish crush, carefully picking one of a dozen cute guys who were already spoken for.

I'd never acted on any of the *Katie* designs; I chose instead to pack them away in my secret box. I rolled up my blueprints tightly and safely tucked them next to a smaller collection of teen-girl memorabilia. Katie is still the closest person to me, and while I've never acted on my fantasies, I've never escaped the dreaminess of them. For some reason, the itch to do something about them has been getting stronger and stronger, almost urgent.

I jumped when Steve wrapped his arms around my middle—I'd gotten so lost in my thoughts I hadn't even heard him come downstairs. He held me tight, and I leaned into his warm embrace. He kissed the back of my neck and then pressed against me. And at once, I could feel just how happy he wanted his birthday morning to be. The earlier spur of excitement awakened. I moaned a sexy tone I knew turned him on, and as if on cue his hand wandered up my side, touching playfully before landing on my breast. Another moan slipped from my lips, and I felt my nipple harden beneath his fingers. A moment later, the stove's burners were off, and I was humming "Happy Birthday." We made our way to the couch. I came with him, thinking of my fantasies nearly the entire time. Like I said, some things just go great together—like peanut butter and chocolate.

2

MOST OF OUR mornings are nothing at all like our celebrated birthday mornings. I suppose that is why they are so special. That's not to say that Steve and I don't have a good sex life—we have a great one. Maybe we are just lucky and hit a relationship lottery of some kind, connecting on all the right levels. I'd like to think so, anyway. Or maybe we'd just become more comfortable with ourselves and each other in our middle age, which, by the way, I've found to be one of the sexiest things about us.

There was one moment, though, when I nearly ended us. It wasn't because of my quirky murder fantasies. I shook my head, remembering how young we were back then—hot, oversexed, and way too naive—I had truly thought we were over. Steve cheated on me. The memory of it aches like an old scar. I cringe and cover my heart when I think about it: a wound that never quite healed.

The extent of his cheating, you ask? As I'd been told by a friend who'd witnessed the indiscretion, she'd seen Steve wrapped up with a beautiful, tall redhead. Tucked away in the shadowy corner of a neighborhood bar, hidden in a bubble of lust, their heads turning, hips grinding. She'd said there was no mistaking what they were doing. She'd recognized Steve right away and even raised her hand to wave hello before she realized what was going on. "Heart-shaped tattoos," my friend remembered seeing. "A set of three between the skank's thumb and forefinger." There are some things you never forget.

And I remembered that night. I'd been home with the flu, too sick to go out. I'd thought it fortunate that Steve's friends were gathering at the bar for a guys' night to watch the Phillies sweep the Mets. That is likely how it started—buckets of beer, baskets of wings, and cheering or jeering the baseball game on the big screen. But when it comes to those sports-bar tramps, they're as easy and as free as the chips and peanuts.

A month before we were to marry, Steve told me everything. He spilled like a fountain. I'll never forget how he said it either—abrupt, like an accidental cut of a knife. My hand in his, walking to his car after a weekend showing of the original *Titanic*, and Steve blurted the words: "I was with someone." I had flinched as if slapped in the face, and then stopped in the middle of the road. I stood on the double yellow lines for what seemed an eternity, slipping one foot over to the other side, tempted to run from the small burst of hurt and jealousy that came with his confession. He pulled me close to him then, smelling of movie popcorn and cola. I gazed up, searching his eyes, my view clouded by the sting of disappointment. The moment seemed surreal—our magical fairytale ending in tragedy. I thought that I must have misheard him, that he must have said something else. In my mind I tried to reason with the confession, but the logical part of me would hear none of it.

And just exactly who had Steve been with? Who was this vixen with the long red locks thrown over my man's shoulders? I never did find out. I know that some women have to hear a name and to see the other woman's face, but I never understood wanting the torture of knowing. So I never found out—accidentally or otherwise. Steve offered me her name once—I could see it perched on his lips, the first syllable tumbling out and rhyming with *nah*. I had quickly raised my hand and pressed my fingers against his lips.

"No names," I'd told him, not wanting to know who this scarlet lady was, not wanting to add her name to my list. Up until then, my list had stayed short and safe and deep in my mind. Who knows how easily something could materialize later in my life? I'd kissed him long and hard then—sensually. I told him that he was allowed this one slip, this one mistake, and that he had the rest of our lives to make it up to me.

"I love you," he repeated later that evening, the agony still in his voice. We made love, and I never doubted him after that. The thought of who *nah* was has crossed my mind from time to time. Yes, I'm human too. But my gut told me never to try and learn her name. I trusted my gut, and it was a good thing for *nah* that I listened to it.

While the suddenness of Steve's words had stopped time and nearly broke my heart that day, what he did to us—to me—wasn't fatal. Why would I give him a second chance? Simple. I believed him. But more than that, because he gave me the opportunity to make a decision before I walked down the aisle. That is more than I can say for myself. After all, who was it who was *really* bringing the most baggage into our marriage? I already had plenty of secrets—a trunkful that I dragged with me and kept hidden in my nest of lies. But there was another reason I didn't break up with Steve. And with every part of me, I hope that I am right about him. Somewhere, deep inside me, deep in my heart where love *is* magical and comes alive, I believe that if Steve ever saw me—the true me—he wouldn't run. That is why I love him. That is why I married him.

Our busy and chaotic morning passed like a sudden tornado after that—the dog barking to be fed, bodies whipping around in the kitchen, eating breakfast, lunches being made, and the rush to get Steve to work and Michael to school. My boy is about to become a new teen. He's just beginning to hit that stage of awkwardness with that forever feeling of self-consciousness. Now and then, I'll catch him diving into an old bin of his Legos or watching cartoons, and I know that for the moment he is still a little more mine than the world's.

We were young when we had Michael, early in our marriage. I can still see the furled eyebrows and the curious looks from friends and family as they counted the months and tried to do the math. Steve and I called Michael our honeymoon baby, but secretly, we knew he was a few months older than that. Like I said, we were always horny and oversexed, and we didn't always play it safe.

That was early in Steve's career too—fresh out of the police academy, filling his evenings and weekends with work. I was alone most of the time and often felt like a single parent, but I think most new mothers feel like that at times. Steve's hard work eventually led to him being promoted to detective, which only meant that he was around even less. But no matter how tough things were, we'd made it work, even later, when life delivered one of its biggest surprises.

I'd mentioned the patter of bare feet . . . that would be our little girl, Jennifer, but we call her Snacks. "She looks funny and smells bad," her older brother told us the day we brought her home. "Can we send it back?" We had laughed nervously and kept her, in spite of his request. We almost never call Jennifer by her real name, preferring to call her Snacks on account of her endless need to snack between meals. Michael jokingly came up with the name one evening when Jennifer had been particularly naggy and bugging us for something to eat. She'd clopped around—a messy tangle of hair bouncing above her head—yelling "Snack! Snack! Snack!" The nickname stuck. I'm not sure Jennifer even knows what her real name is.

By the time Snacks turned four, her hair had grown as long as mine, dark blonde with just enough reddish highlights that it can pass for red in the summer sun. But my baby girl's face is nearly all Steve. I see him in her chin and lips and even her round cheeks. But I see my eyes in her eyes, an unmistakable deep hazel with a touch of green, like an emerald. I remember her fourth year because Steve had been promoted again, and the lost nights and weekends had become a little easier. On occasion, a criminal case would come across his desk that took him away from us. But by then, he'd staked out his office turf and learned the art of delegation.

I liked it when Steve brought home the popular cases—the ones that were on the evening news. He was never one who managed to work late into the evening. Not at home, anyway. I could always count on him falling asleep with at least a half-dozen case folders strewn open across our bed. That was my cue. That was my time to embellish some of my fantasies.

I gushed with anticipation whenever he fell asleep while working. *Take a breath*, I'd tell myself, trying to quell the urgent storm brewing in my mind. First, I'd open a bottle of wine, let it breathe before that first taste. Then I'd rush through each bedroom, silently making my way from bed to bed and tucking in the kids, kissing them goodnight. Next, I'd make sure Steve had no reason to get up. I'd pick off his round eyeglasses, place them on the nightstand. Sometimes, if he stirred, I'd rub his chest to coax him back to sleep. When I was sure the house was down for the night I'd carefully pull away the case files, clear the bed, and put them back together. But before putting them away in Steve's briefcase, I'd secretly spend hours at our kitchen table, reading.

With a glass of wine in my hand and the silent murmur of our sleeping house, my heart would thump out of rhythm with each page turn. I loved the touch of the folders' thick manila paper, the smell of the Xeroxed documents, and the smooth emulsion on the face of the crime-scene photos. I'd read every page and gaze at every photograph at least a half-dozen times. I'd even imagine myself as a hunter, prowling for my next victim, leaping like a cat, and pouncing, toying with a life.

On more than one occasion my studies had been interrupted, but I'd become used to it, expected it. I'd hear Snacks thumping down the steps, unable to sleep. I'd perch her on my lap and whisper sweetness into her ears while studying the case files. And as I'd finish with the cases, she'd tug on my shirt and hold her balled hands up, clutching at the air, wanting more to eat. She was closer to seven and growing faster and faster with each passing day. The mother in me still liked that she was needy, but I knew it wouldn't last forever. And as I filled her carry-cup with her favorite cereal, I couldn't help but wonder when Steve would have another set of case files. I hoped it would be soon.

3

"I DON'T WANT to be here," Steve said grimly. I wove my arm through his and stepped onto the grass, my heels sinking into the soft earth. Steve braced me, letting me lean into him as we made our way over the carpet of green. "Thank you for coming."

"Of course," I answered softly, though I tensed a little, hurt that he'd felt he had to thank me. "John was my friend too. I've known him as long as I've known you." He gave me a short nod and then struggled to say more, muttering words as grief hung over us, jabbing our senses at random moments.

The cemetery was solemn and absent of voices, leaving only the sound of jays and cardinals calling out while they skittered across the tops of tall evergreens lining the graves. A cloudless sky promised no rain on this sorrowful day, but broke in the center with the sun at high noon. The steely yellow eye watched while we slowly gathered to say good-bye to a friend.

And it was true. I'd known John for as long as I'd known my husband. I met them both on the same night, and at first, my eyes were for John. Tall and rugged, he was the best-looking man in the bar. Three drinks in, I knew I wanted him—until I saw Steve. And after meeting my future husband, I suddenly became blind to everyone else. Sounds sappy, but it's true.

The memory of John's sweet voice as he introduced me to Steve came back to me.

"Steve, this is Amy. Amy, Steve," John had said, patting Steve on the back and gently nudging him closer. "It was nice talking to you, Amy. You can trust that Steve is a good guy." But, after shaking Steve's hand, I only vaguely heard John. He left us alone then. It had been just the two of us, lost in a sea of dancing and drinking and hopeful chatting as everyone around us tried to find the same thing we were in search of at that age. I swayed to the music as we traded a few opening lines, both of us hoping each line lead to another one.

"What kind of music do you like?" Steve had asked, winking at John. But John had already gone—lost to the attention of a gorgeous blonde who'd slowed and stopped before passing us.

"All kinds. But nights like tonight, I want to hear

country the most," I had answered, feeling the first nervous flutters that happen when I'm attracted to someone.

"Country!" he said, cocking his head and looking hot. "We're a bit north for country music. Why tonight?"

"I like country songs best when I'm drunk—you know, a bit like now—sounds amazing when I can't understand the lyrics."

"So that's the secret," he answered, trying to appear surprised. "So you have to be drunk first."

"That's it!" I told him. I surprised myself when I quickly added, "Do you want to get drunk with me, Steve?" He had closed the distance between us and put his hand to my hip, joining me in my sway. "You're so beautiful," he said, looking at me as if I were the first woman he'd ever seen. The moment lifted me from the floor and put me into his life forever. "I'll drink with you, Amy. I'll even listen to country music with you."

The pastor's voice rose to a near shout, causing me to flinch and to tug on Steve's arm. He lowered his head, bringing his mouth close to my ear. He whispered that he loved me. I nuzzled him back, saying the same without speaking a word.

I'd never confessed to Steve that my eyes found John first that night. I wanted to save that juicy tidbit for when we were old and sitting together on a rickety porch, spouting comical jabs at one another. I always thought of us as becoming that couple—older, with gestures and soft little sounds replacing words—cherishing one another.

John was Steve's best friend. He became the brother I'd never had. I felt a warm sentiment come over me, only to have it disappear with the cold ache of the sudden loss. I had blamed John for the path Steve decided on—after all, he'd been first to suggest the police force as a career. They were inseparable, best friends, college roommates, taking the same classes. They reminded me of what Katie and I had—though I doubt Steve secretly fantasized about killing John. Over the course of one very trying weekend, Steve's plans for law school ended. His new plans? *Our* new plans? Apply for the police academy along with John. Our future had changed, but I supported him because I loved him. I was going to be the wife of a police officer. *A cop's wife*—it still sounds weird when I hear those words.

And it was through the academy and then working on patrol that Steve and John became even more like brothers, sharing an understanding that I could never be a part of. I spent many nights jealous of another man, yet I'd always felt better knowing that they were together. I thought they would be safer together than apart. They stayed tight even through the detective's exam process, when they each received their shields. And though Steve had been promoted ahead of John, that didn't matter to them. But their friendship, their brotherhood, ended when a bullet from a handgun entered John's brain one rainy Friday evening while he questioned a suspect on a small felony charge. Compared to the life of a man, the charges were insignificant. I think that is what hurt the most about John's death—the meaninglessness of it.

We entered the small circle of family and friends gathered around John's casket, which had been placed above an open grave. A flag was draped over the sadly beautiful reddish maple, sturdy and masculine, much like John. His wife, Charlotte, lifted her chin, her eyes red and puffy. She was still as strikingly beautiful as the night John had met her—we were there for that occasion. She acknowledged Steve's presence and then mine as she pulled their children closer to her. A small boy and girl just a few years older than Snacks. They swung their feet from their chairs, looking afraid and confused and not at all understanding that their father lay dead a few feet away.

Charlotte motioned to me. I left Steve's side and walked around John's casket to take her in my arms. There were no words, no glances back and forth, no trying to understand something as impossibly unfair as her husband's death. I felt the rise and fall of her chest against mine, her breathing ragged.

"Going to mess up my face again," she whispered. "Crying has got me exhausted."

"You stay strong," I told her, uncertain if that was the best I could do. "For them." I reached out, touching each of John's children, their upturned faces nearly empty, a bemused expression coming to the oldest girl.

"I will, I will," she said somberly as she sat back down. She held my fingers for a moment, giving them a squeeze before letting go. The touch was heartfelt and pained me. If I could have, I would have whisked her away from the nightmare she was living. By the time I was back and holding my husband's arm, Charlotte's posture had become rigid like a statue, unmoving. She looked as if she had been placed there like a stage prop in some horrible play. I suppose I'd shut down too if it had been Steve instead of John.

Charlotte and I had been close, on and off—in only a way a cop's wife best understands. I didn't get it at first, that is, why we'd forced some distance into our friendship. But standing on the soft grass of the cemetery, I finally understood. Other than Katie, I never had a close friend. The kind of girlfriend I'd tell everything to, say anything to, and never feel the pinch or sting of being judged by. John's wife and I almost got there, very close, in fact. But it never lasted. At times I could feel the excitement between us, like a young couple fresh and eager to explore and learn every intimate detail about each other. We'd have weeks of playdates for the kids, a girls' night out, and long conversations while drinking afternoon tea or wine. But whenever we approached that true closeness, we'd abruptly stop, the intensity fizzling like spent fireworks. The phone calls and long conversations would stop. Get-togethers went unscheduled, leaving blank spaces in our calendars and day-planners. Even the funny back-and-forth chatter about all the things that John and Steve did wrong came to an end. I always thought it was me, because I'm different like that, one to quickly shed people once I'd lost interest. But standing at her husband's grave, I knew it wasn't me. It was *us*. It was who we were.

When the circle around John's casket was complete, Steve became rigid too and his breathing deepened and sounded shaky. The sudden anguish of seeing John's casket, of seeing the open grave must have hit him. Tears pricked my eyes. I held onto him, trying to abate his pain. I loved John, but I hurt for my husband. When Steve graduated from the academy, I'd mentally begun preparing for a day like today. Priming my mind and building up a false emotional cushion to help absorb the shock of it. But when I thought of Snacks and Michael not having their father around . . .

no amount of preparation would help. I shook my head at the idea of Snacks walking down the aisle alone or of Michael leaving for college without his father to see him off.

A million sad thoughts crossed my mind, but one screamed at me: *That could've been Steve.* I searched the familiar faces. Husbands and wives that I'd talked to over the years at fun gatherings, barbecues, and birthdays. The wives and I passed wet glances, each secretly thankful that our husbands were still standing next to us. Seeing their mournful faces and teary eyes finally did me in. It was my turn to cry. I gripped Steve's arm, clutching until he pulled me closer.

"It'll be okay," he whispered into my ear. The touch of his breath sent a chill into me. I knew that he was wrong. It would never be okay—not as long as he was still on the street, working. "Love you, babe."

"Love you too," I answered, resenting who we were. I added, "I'm thinking of Snacks and Michael and what we'd do without you." He let out a long sigh and tried to hide his emotion. When I saw the wet cutting into Steve's cheek, I wiped one of the tears away but left the other alone. That one was for the kids, a reminder to him of who he'd be leaving behind if that bullet had found him instead.

The pastor began the final part of the ceremony, citing passages from the Bible and allowing those who wanted to speak at the time to say their parting words. Soon after, the flag was taken from atop the casket in a ceremony of folding and presentation to John's wife. It was also a signal the gathering was about to end. The sound of soft cries and sniffling came then, as we realized that John's time among us was really over. I shuddered. I wanted to go back to our car, but held onto Steve. For only the third time in our life together, he cried. And it wasn't an errant tear having escaped the impatient swipe of his hand.

He knelt down and pressed his hand firmly on top of the casket.

"Good-bye, John. Till next time, brother . . ." he managed to say. His voice broke when he tried to say more. I draped my hand over his back and cried with him as others came forward to do the same.

When the pastor signaled, each of us put a flower on the casket. As the crowd took leave of the gravesite, we stayed. Steve insisted, telling me that he wanted to watch them lower John's body into the ground. A few others stayed behind too, waiting for the end to come. Steve left my side to pick up a fistful of dirt when the workers began to lower John. "Ashes to ashes and dust to dust," he mumbled as he released the handful, tossing it into the grave.

The dirt clods knocked against the casket, ringing out a truth I'd tried desperately to ignore. The sound brought to me the dread and fear of having to say good-bye to my own husband forever. We sobbed and said little until we were back inside our car.

"I know what you're going to say," Steve began, trying to clear his throat of emotion. I shuddered and dabbed my eyes. "That's not going to happen to me." His words were like stings. I raised my hand to him, shutting him up before he could say any more.

"You can't say that," I told him. In my head, I saw Michael and Snacks again, which fed my fear like a dangerous wind fanning a flame. "I don't want to bury you. Don't you get that?" I wanted to say more, but felt drained. His eyes were solemn and apologetic—and every bit as beautiful as the day I'd first gazed into them.

"What do you want me to do?" he asked, shaking his head. "You know you're married to a cop. I'm good at it. I love my job."

I swiped at my nose, annoyed.

"Are you better at it than John?" I asked, knowing the words stung. He winced. "Oh, I'm sorry . . . better than John *was*?"

"Amy, please!" he shouted, shaking his head.

I desperately wanted to apologize, but couldn't. There were times when I reveled in my stubbornness. I could be a bitch when I wanted to. I hated that about myself.

"What about law school?" I said, taking his hand and feeling bad about what I'd said and how I'd said it. "When we were in college, that's what you were going to do. Remember? Become a lawyer. Go to work for the district attorney. Make a difference."

Steve looked past me, finding the grave where his best friend lay as cold as the ground he'd been lowered into. Dead.

"Can't do that. Not now," he said glumly and pitched his head down. "Too much at stake. You, the kids, the house. Can't just up and go back to school—"

"Why not?" I interrupted. "There are a lot of lawyers who started out doing something else." His hand stayed on mine, rubbing tenderly and trying to console. I yanked my arm back, realizing that he was dismissing me.

"Babe, come on."

"Just go," I demanded. "You won't even listen."

"It isn't that I don't want to. Do you even know how expensive law school is?" he asked. I resented his tone. "We don't have that kind of money."

"What if I were working?" I asked. "What if I could pay for law school? What if I could pay for more than just school?" Steve heard me. The idea of him being off the streets eased the tension. I simply had no idea how to make it work, but I knew that I had to try. My cheeks were tight from crying. Selfishly, I wanted this to be over.

"Let's talk about this later," he answered. "Oh, and the answer is no."

"No? To what?" I asked, confused.

"I wasn't better than John," Steve said, tears welling in his eyes. "He was the best cop I ever knew."

4

AS I SAT in my car and stared at my mother's house, my childhood window looked peculiar. Different. Painted in the pale shine of unfamiliar sunlight. Growing up, I always had the shade of a giant oak. My father's tree, a protector by day and guardian at night. But now my guardian was gone, amputated from our yard. And in its place I found a horrific scar in the ground the color of honey-red tinder. It bled sap and smelled sweet from the fresh-cut sawdust. The sight of it killed my spirit a little and made me feel sad, like seeing a pretty flower that had been shamelessly yanked up and then discarded.

With the tall oak gone from the yard, I'd driven by my mother's house twice before realizing it. If not for Michael calling out to say that we were there, I would have never slowed the car. I frowned when Snacks careened over the piles of sawdust and then stomped her feet on sap oozing from a woody knot.

"Pretty," she chimed, pointing at the stickiness while humming a song from a favorite cartoon.

"Come on over here," I demanded. "You'll get your shoes all sticky."

A small ache came over me as more memories about the tree came back to me—memories I hadn't thought of in years. Fond memories from a terribly difficult time. The long, slender branches first invited me in when I was fourteen. They'd scratched my window and tapped against the glass pane. I'd crept out onto my window ledge, my stomach in my throat as I spied the height, then gingerly stepped onto the outstretched bark. It was my first escape from the tyranny of my mother. During high school, when the fighting showed no hope of ending, I'd blindly make my way down to the yard. After a while, I memorized every step. But I only ran some of the time. Other times I'd climb above the line of our roof and find a set of branches that had knitted themselves tightly enough together to let me sit. With only the cloudless sky between me and the stars, I'd sometimes stay there all night.

"Shame," I said to Michael. "I really loved that tree."

"I guess I won't be climbing it today," Michael added.

"You're here!" my mom bellowed from her porch. "How was the drive?"

"We only live twenty minutes away," I answered, trying not to sound annoyed. "But it was fine, thank you."

"Only twenty minutes," she began. "Well, you'd think I'd see more of my grandkids then, wouldn't you?"

Here we go, I thought as I paused on the front step.

"Yes, Mom," I said flatly, but by then her attention had gone to Snacks and Michael.

At least she is being nice to them. Nicer than I ever remembered her being.

While our differences had rooted in my earliest years and grown wild, I was still glad my children knew her. Ours was a complex relationship—not one we could simply cut down and plant over.

An urge to check the time came over me; I forced it to pass with a thinly disguised cringe. I kept my phone tucked away in my purse, trying not to be rude. The thought of being here any longer than I had to felt like instant suffocation.

When I entered my mom's home, I saw at once that there was more missing than just my old oak tree. The inside of our house was a mere memory of what it had been. Even the smell was different—like an old person's home or a hospital—and I wondered when that had happened. My mom had stacked flattened boxes against her living room wall, waiting like soldiers ready to march. Waiting to be opened and put to use. Some of them had already been enlisted: unfolded, filled, then closed and sealed with moving tape. The dozens of pictures that usually lined our stairwell were gone, but had left shadows, their faded burn singeing the old wallpaper. The bookshelves full of my father's books and collected knickknacks were gone too. I realized that most everything that was my father's had been boxed for storage.

"What's going on, Mom?" My mother followed the children inside, offering Twinkies and other sugary persuasions—grandparents can get away with bribery. "Dad's stuff. Where's it all going?"

"That man collected everything," she said, ignoring my question with an annoyed rise in her voice. "Damned if there wasn't more than one of them, he'd collect it."

"Mom. Dad's stuff?"

"Well, it's time," she said and waved her arms around her. "I'm not getting any younger, and your father's been gone almost three years now. It's time to move on."

I never considered that my parents would live

anywhere but our house. While I didn't get along with my mother, I loved our home and the memories of growing up there. Emotion snapped at my gut. I was at a loss for words. I quickly turned away from the kids and began picking through a collection of his snow globes on the living room table.

"Do you want some help?" I offered, uncertain of what else I could say. After all, she was right. My dad was gone, and she wasn't getting any younger.

My mother briefly lowered her guard. She raised a brow. A moment later she put on a look of sarcastic surprise and answered. "Really? You're offering to help?"

"Come on, Mom. Don't start," I said, trying to coax us away from fighting.

"No. No. No. I'm not picking at anything," she said, raising her hands apologetically. "Just want to know where my place is. Don't want to take up any more of your time than I have to."

I stepped up to my mother and held her arm. "I want to help." I lied for the sake of the kids, for the sake of setting a good example and acting the part I thought I was supposed to act. "We'll get the kids to help too."

She glanced over at the kids, their upturned faces filled with half-smiles, uncertain of what we were talking about. She smiled. "I'd appreciate some help. And maybe we could talk?"

Loaded question, stay away!

She was forever trying to talk about us. About me. About how awful I was as a teenager. Truth is, I *wasn't* an awful teen. She was just a terrible mother. Katie was more her daughter than I ever was. She loved Katie, and everyone knew it. I'm not the jealous type, and my mom's affections for Katie had nothing to do with my Killing Katie designs. They're not related. They never were. In my heart, I think I am a little too much like my mother, and that is why we never get along.

"Sure," I answered with a bemused smile on my face.

"And how is Katie?"

"Mom . . . Katie mentioned she visited you last week!" I snapped. "I'm sure you already know the answer to that!"

My mother stepped back, her hand on her chest. "Was that a week ago already?" she answered coyly. "Seems so much longer than that. These days, can't tell one week from the next."

"What happened to Dad's tree?" I asked, changing the subject, changing my tone, trying to be civil.

Just be civil, I heard Steve say in my head.

He was the real reason I brought the kids to see my mother. Every four weeks or so, he'd remind me. *You should go see your mother.* My idea of a phone call instead never sufficed. He'd again give the stern suggestion: *You should go see your mother.* As if it meant more to him than to me. And maybe it did. I only needed to look at my babies to understand why. I hated to admit it, but he was right.

"You don't hate your mother," Steve often said, trying to placate me during my outbursts when I would scream and cry over something that had happened a dozen years ago. I wanted to hate her. I did. But in my heart, I knew that I loved my mother, loved the *idea* of her—I just never *liked* her.

"It was time to take that old tree down," she said, pawing at the tissue paper on the table as we began wrapping the snow globes. "God-awful thing. Ugliest damn tree in the neighborhood."

"What? She was a beautiful tree," I objected, feeling insulted, feeling a renewed loss for my dad.

"That was your father's tree. I'd been after him to cut that eyesore down for years, but he insisted on keeping it."

"Well, he kept *you*, didn't he?" I joked, pushing a bit of a dig into the sentiment. "You're an eyesore too."

"Funny girl. Aren't you?" she answered, a sly sneer on her lips that looked creepy. "You just wait until you start to fade from your husband's eye. Happens to all of us. No matter how beautiful you are."

She was trying to be hurtful. I recognized the tone, and caution signs began flashing in my brain. "Mom, it was just a joke."

"I know. I'm kidding too," she said, her voice playful yet condescending. "Thank you for bringing my grandkids over to see me. Who knows how much longer I'll have?"

I ignored her as I busied myself with another snow globe. She'd live forever. She knew it too. Not like my father. Salt-of-the-Earth tough, but a teddy bear that had more love in him than he knew what to do with. A month after retiring, a month of finally being able to wake when he wanted to, walk where he wanted to, do whatever he wanted to, he dropped dead from an aneurysm. His death broke my heart, but more than that, it put a wedge between me and my old home. Without him to act as our referee, our buffer, coming over for a visit was just too hard.

"How about some sandwiches?" Mom sung, carrying the words on a tune I'd heard since I was a little girl. Snacks was first on her feet, running into my mom's arms.

"Snack?" she asked her grandmother.

"You betcha! You can have a snack."

Watching her with my kids felt surreal, like watching a movie of someone I didn't know.

But I would've liked to have known you too, I thought briefly.

I suppose it's like that in every person's life, watching their parents act differently around their grandchildren.

Maybe it's not all bad. Maybe I should come over more. Just be civil to her, I heard in my head. I shuddered and closed my eyes.

Dad, I miss you.

5

EARLY ONE TUESDAY morning, my eyes opened. Five fifty-eight. The alarm clock's glaring red numbers said that I had another two minutes. I groaned, disappointed. Steve lay next to me, a soft flannel blanket rising and falling in a peaceful rhythm. I shut my eyes and tried to find a way back to my dreams. Random images swam into my view, telling me nothing, telling me everything. Sleep was gone—it was already too late. And no matter how much I wanted my two minutes back, I'd already lost the chance to ease into the day.

As if to confirm my annoyance, the morning news snapped on. The newsman spoke in a throaty rasp, spouting the latest stories about our small suburban town. At the top of the news, the sudden homeless problem: a vagrant exodus from the big city. The newly elected mayor could be thanked for that mess. He'd made good on a campaign promise. But the results landed on our doorsteps. Another story clicked—a woman this time—her radio voice telling of a vicious assault, a stabbing that had left a young woman in critical condition. I perked up, searching through the dim light of our room as if looking for cartoon bubbles hovering above our bed. I didn't hear the next story, or maybe I did, but the alarm had become a distant noise to ignore by then. Steve began to stir. Rolling over, he pushed his arm around my middle.

"Come on, babe," I mumbled, tapping his shoulder. "Time to get up."

"Minute," he grumbled as he pulled up closer. His warm body invited me, and I easily fell against him. We listened to the radio's morning hum while my mind moved dully through the motions of the coming day. The thought of murder abruptly interrupted. That sometimes happened. It turned on and off in my mind like a switch, mechanical and exacting.

That morning, I made a decision. Somewhere between Steve's soft snoring and the radio's drone, I'd made a decision that would change my life forever—it would change many lives. My realization was a bit like a hot wind before a storm: a subtle warning. Later, it would become a bigger part of me. As if there had never been a question. Only this storm wasn't going to pass anytime soon. The decision clicked in my mind and settled in my soul.

"It's time," I whispered sleepily. Just saying it gave me a crazy sense of relief.

"In a minute," Steve countered, not realizing what he was responding to. I wanted to laugh and cry at the same time, having never felt a sense of resolve quite as powerful as this one.

I swung my legs over the bed and gripped the carpet with my toes, squeezing the fabric while trying to remember where I'd placed my slippers. When I stood, my legs shook and felt wobbly, and my middle warmed as though a heating blanket had been wrapped around me. There were no obviously motivating factors to my decision. No revenge in mind or a need to be a martyr for some greater cause. I'd simply felt that it was time to become *me*.

Life is too short, I heard in my head. *So maybe I should do something.* A rush of adrenaline woke me up faster that morning than any coffee ever could. I nearly jumped as anticipation of what I wanted to do crashed into my thoughts. There was so much to plan. And I had no idea how to get started.

I playfully lifted the covers and sheet, egging Steve on to get up. But it was John that I saw laying on our bed—a dime-size hole in his head and a putrid smile on his face. I reeled, shocked and disturbed by the image. The smell of the cemetery was suddenly in my nose and on my skin, and the sounds of whimpering and sniffling crept into my ears, drowning the waking songbirds outside our bedroom window. I squeezed my eyes shut and waited for the image to disappear. When I opened them, I saw Steve still asleep with the bed covers wrapped tightly around his body, draping over his shoulder. The anger I'd felt at John's funeral sprang to life again and I yanked the covers back. Steve's eyes popped open in surprise and confusion. He tried covering himself, but I'd pulled the blankets back too far for him to reach.

"What gives?" he asked.

"Come on," I answered. "It's time to get up." He could read through me easily enough and shook his head.

"You're still mad," he mumbled, making his way past me. I grabbed at him, stopping him. I covered myself with his arms and began to cry. I resented my wifely tears, but I feared Steve being killed even more than being ashamed.

"I can't watch you do this . . ." I began to say. "Don't want to lose you, okay?"

"I know, babe. And I remember wanting to be a lawyer. I do."

"Would you think about it?" I asked, feeling hopeful. "Think about Snacks and Michael. Think about John's kids." His body tensed when I said that, but then relaxed as he let go.

"I will. I'll think about it," he told me, entering the bathroom. I could see him shake his head as he added, "But it's going to be about the money. Always is."

"I know," I told him.

Was there money in murder? The question came to mind and took my tears away. *What if there was a way to profit from what I wanted to do?*

The sound of the shower running came from our bathroom. I stopped what I was doing and stared through the door to watch as Steve stripped to nothing. I loved to watch him. We had a little time to spare, so I decided to join my husband. We said nothing more about death or money or law school. In fact, we said nothing at all.

From our morning shower to the first cup of coffee, I didn't question my decision. I didn't try to guess if there was money in murder. Of course there must be. A whole industry had capitalized on wanting people dead. With Snacks still in bed and Steve on his way to the office, I helped Michael get ready for school. For most of the morning, I fought the urge to scream out, celebrating the revelation that I might be able to support Steve and our household.

Too far-fetched? I asked myself a thousand times. I'd know more once I started to do the research.

Michael's small hand quieted my hazardous rush of thoughts as he reached up for his school backpack.

"Mom?" Michael's voice chirped, snapping away my attention. "I'm gonna miss the school bus."

"Right . . . right. Sorry," I stammered as my mind continued to race with an overload of a million new ideas. "Your lunch is packed, and I added a little extra for you too."

"A Twinkie?" he asked, excitedly. His voice sounded lower and I noticed a rougher quality and a break in its tone.

Was his voice changing? Puberty? Already? I realized with a stabbing sadness just how quickly my little boy was growing up.

I waved two fingers, bouncing them up and down in front of him. His eyes lit up with a hungry spark.

"You rock, Mom. Thanks."

"But only after you're done eating."

"I know," he countered, and then hitched up onto his toes for a kiss. Leaning over and planting my lips on his cheek, I realized Michael seemed taller too. I felt a mix of pride and sadness as I watched him spin around and sling a backpack over his shoulder. I followed his footsteps as he traipsed across the lawn toward the school bus stop. The nighttime chill and the autumn air had set the dewy grass to frost. My son's size fives cut into the carpet of white. Other paths cut in from all different directions—a mix of size fours and sixes and a few eights from the older kids. The paths tracked across the lawns of our small neighborhood, following a course that had been set for them.

My emotions began to mingle with my earlier revelation and the sentiments that came from watching my son. I was a mother, a wife, and a homemaker.

This is the way it is supposed to be. I'm happy, I told myself. But I was immediately struck with the fluttering reservations I'd searched for earlier. *Who am I to risk everything, anything? But Steve,* I demanded. Sure, there were jobs that didn't risk my going to prison, but my mind was set and I wasn't going to change it.

I stood on our porch and felt the cool air run across my face and through my hair. In my mind, I imagined that I was a winter butterfly, cocooned and living inside a lie. Something ticked inside me then, some deep, selfish notion that I embraced and held onto like a starving animal with food. I'd lived the life that had been scripted for me, and now it was time to hunt, it was time to eat, it was time to become *me.*

6

OUR HOME COMPUTER never looked so intimidating before. The large, blank screen stared at me, daring me, as if knowing what I was about to do, as if knowing what subtle treacheries my fingertips would search for. I quickly pushed my thumb against the power button and listened as the computer's guts whirred, coming to life.

I twisted Katie's friendship ring—a nervous habit I'd developed soon after we'd given them to each other. I had no idea where to get started. Just exactly how did one become a murderer? I doubted that I'd find a wiki page online, offering a step-by-step guide . . . or maybe there was? I simply had no idea.

But there were other things that I wanted to do too. There was so much more than just the web searches. I needed a new box, a secret box. One that would keep my designs safe. I'd kept my first one, and I often thought of it fondly. I knew that it would always be safe from curious eyes. I'd hidden my secret box beneath the floorboards of my old room. While just a beat-up, tattered cigar box from a great uncle whose face I can barely remember, I knew its every detail. When I had last opened, the faint cigar smell was as I remembered it: old tobacco, tangy but pleasant. The batting I'd lined it with had thinned and lost its cloud-fresh white, but the corners had stayed true, securing the secrets of my youth. And inside, my first Killing Katie designs were still legible—once the paper's endless curl had been straightened.

Tapping my finger atop Steve's desk, I considered my needs. The first was a new box. The screen flickered something at me, offering a list of cryptic messages about drivers.

We need a new computer, I thought as the familiar frustrations began.

We'd needed a new computer for a while. The screen rolled up, spouting message after message. Steve had mentioned that I should wait before touching the mouse and the keyboard. I stared, trying to be patient.

Maybe there was a digital box that I could use? An online version? A folder that only I could access?

I'd need to be able to get to it from anywhere and from any machine. Surely, something like that existed.

But how traceable would it be? How would it work? Would it be too risky? I wondered. *Worth the risk?* After all, my high—my need to feed the hunger—came from the planning and the designs too; half wouldn't be an option.

The computer screen blinked a flash of blue before showing a collage of last year's vacation pictures. My gut twisted at the sight of our family photos. I pressed my fingers against the cool screen, touching one of them. The photo was of the four of us sitting together on the beach, a tall ocean surf climbing behind us. A helpful stranger had taken ten minutes out of his own vacation to try and get the best angle.

"I can't do this," I mumbled, running my fingers to another photograph. Anxiety lurched inside me, telling me this wasn't right. "Not here." And not just because it felt risky, but because it felt dirty somehow, like having an affair in the bed I shared with Steve.

The computer's screen faded and then flashed another set of photos at me, but not before I saw the smudges from my fingerprint.

Gotta clean that.

I suddenly felt like an amateur and also felt equally overwhelmed, maybe even a bit stupid. I had to be smarter about what I was planning, what I was going to do. The first thing I had to do was to clean my smudgy fingerprints from the computer screen. Steve hated it when anyone touched the glass.

The screen is for looking, not touching, I could hear his voice saying in my head.

I cradled my chin, my elbows leaning on the desk as I watched more photos come to life. A holiday party, complete with a pair of horribly loud Christmas sweaters and floppy Santa hats. I think Snacks had just turned two back then. Oh, and that night. That had been a good night. I shifted in my seat, titillated by the memory. That was the night Steve and I ditched the wool sweaters and wore only our Santa hats. I wore mine in the traditional style. And Steve? Well, he wore his Santa hat somewhere else. He'd joked, asking if I'd like to visit his North Pole. The urge to laugh came to me, but I couldn't.

My eyes wandered back to the smudges.

My fingerprints. Evidence.

Steve was smart about that stuff, and the detectives in his division were *very* smart about that stuff. The excitement from earlier began to fade with the screen's photos. A stack of case folders lay there on the desk next to me; I recognized them immediately. There was a mix: some from the city, some local. The two offices often crossed since our town bordered the city, and as Steve would say,

"Criminals respect no boundaries, geographic or otherwise."

The sight of the folders spurred a memory from the year before—just after I'd made a habit of reading through them. There had been a particularly disturbing case that I'd pored over one evening. Nearly a half bottle of wine warmed my belly as I disappeared into my favorite reading chair. Yellow light from my lamp shone down—soft and familiar and in a perfect round halo. I'd opened the case file and learned more than I ever wanted to know about a dangerous pedophile. Worse yet, this man my husband was trying to put away lived fewer than five miles from our house. I'd known that last part only because Steve had openly talked about the case. I shook in disgust, recalling some of the things he'd done and the lives he'd ruined.

"I'd definitely kill the creep if given the chance," I'd mumbled, adding his name to my list. "The world wouldn't miss him."

My husband had almost lost that case, though. The conviction had hinged on a key witness who'd backed out of testifying. And to make matters worse, they'd found nothing on his computer.

"It's as empty as our case," Steve said gravely. He'd come home late, flustered and defeated and upset that the guy was going to walk. I couldn't shake his mood—no matter what I tried.

"You've got nothing else?" I'd asked, thinking through every crime scene television show we'd ever watched.

"Guys like him, they usually keep trophies," he'd said in a rant. "Thought for sure we'd find something on the computer."

And they did find something. It was a chance find. Luck, really. Dust on a bookshelf pulled the eyes of a young police officer trying to prove himself. A thin gray coat of filth covered the shelf, hinting that none of the books had been read in a long time. That is, all except one book. That book had no dust in front of it.

"Like someone had drawn an arrow and pointed to it," Steve told me. "Just needed to pull the book open." Inside, they'd found the pages had been welled out to store a portable hard drive. Thousands of images were recovered. They had their evidence. It was all they needed to convict the bastard.

But the pedophile was out already. Free these days. A year in jail, and he was sent home. The dust on the shelves had become thicker, but offered no more clues. "A courtroom fuck-up," Steve had called it. "Ten years' probation and registering as a sex offender."

"He'll be one of the first on my list," I mumbled.

With that thought, I swiped the sleeve of my shirt over the screen, erasing any traces of having used the computer. I snapped at the power button like a yapping dog, annoyed and disappointed by the lack of progress I'd made that morning.

"If I'm doing this, then I'm going to do it right!"

7

SUNLIGHT CREPT OVER Katie's shoulder, throwing the rest of her into a harsh silhouette. I covered my eyes, but not before waving her toward our table. She saw me and hurried over at once, carrying the sun behind her until she was beneath the small café's awning. It took a minute for my eyes to adjust; I blinked away the colorful sunspots.

"Outside?" she questioned as she began to pull a chair out.

"Might be our last time before the winter sets in," I answered. She sat across from me, her smile waning. Katie's eyes were puffy and glassy, as if she'd been crying. I sighed quietly so my disappointment would go unnoticed. This was going to be a *Katie* lunch, filled with *Katie* moments. Meaning something had gone wrong, and we were going to talk about whatever it was the entire time.

I shrugged to shake off my concern, realizing it was fine. I just hoped that I'd have enough patience to stomach the conversation. After all, if we were talking about Katie, we wouldn't be talking about me. And the only news I had to offer was about having decided to murder someone—not exactly the type of news one shares over a meal at a small café.

"Feels good in the sun," she said, anxiously playing around with the dishes and tableware, trying to fill the time until she could spill what was bothering her.

"Things aren't good?" I asked, feeling impatient and wanting to shortcut the filler, but making my voice sound concerned. Katie stopped fidgeting and nearly broke down, covering her mouth. She swiped at her eyes impatiently and waved off my question.

"Let's just eat and have a drink or two . . . or three," she answered. "We've got an hour before I have to get back to the office."

"Are you sure?" I asked, uncertain if I should nod or shake my head. She nodded for me, confirming. "When you're ready."

I glanced at my phone, noting the time. Michael wouldn't be home from school for at least another four hours. Steve's mother often offered to sit for Snacks—frequently hinting around that it looked like Snacks was going to be her last grandbaby. Shamelessly, I took advantage of her time every chance I could, especially on nice days like today.

"That can't be right," I mumbled. I felt giddy, realizing I'd have a small pocket of free time after our lunch.

"What? What is it?"

"Sorry, nothing." Three hours! I shook my head. Three free hours after lunch! Free time doesn't come by very often. Three hours doesn't sound like much, but to me it was a universe of time to do some more planning.

Katie had checked her phone too, but for her the phone was a tether back to her office, a virtual leash that constantly nagged and yanked on her for attention like a needy toddler. A sporadic mess of rat-a-tat-tat clicking sounds volleyed over the table as her fingernails hit against the phone's screen. And as she tapped message after message, I looked at Katie's business suit and felt a sudden, and surprising, twinge of jealousy. Katie and her husband Jerry stopped having children after their boys came into the world, which was great for my Michael. Growing up at the same time, the three boys were as close as cousins.

As best friends, though, work was where our lives went in different directions. From those first moments in the tub together, and through decades of being joined at the hip, we found ourselves separated now. Katie had gone back to working full time as a business analyst and process owner for a big nonprofit firm. She always joked that for a nonprofit, they had more money to spend than most small countries. As for me, I stayed home. I didn't get to trade in my mommy clothes for a slim-fitting pantsuit and tall, sexy heels. I didn't get to plan out morning coffees and business lunches. Another pang of jealousy leaped up to nip at me. Although I was happy with living simply, the envy I felt at seeing Katie dressed up for work took me by surprise.

I remember wanting to go back to work, however. I had planned to go back to work; Steve and I talked about it and had even set a date. But then Snacks came to us as a bit of a surprise, and I never gave work another thought. Not until now, that is. Not until the fear of losing Steve had become very real, very possible.

For now, I'd at least dressed the part, deciding at the last minute to put together an actual outfit for lunch. And seeing how Katie killed it with her gray pantsuit and heels, I felt relieved that I had taken the extra time when picking out what I wanted to wear. I decided on a shorter skirt that rode high and let my legs show a little more than usual. Adding in a new pair of open-toe heels and a champagne blouse, I felt comfortable sitting across from her. Anyone passing by could easily have mistaken us as having a business lunch.

As if she'd been reading my mind, Katie said, "Love your outfit."

"Yours too," I answered, smiling.

The conversation was starting to feel forced. That had never happened before. Our conversations had always been easy—especially when we had still been on the same playing field, sharing the same mommy and husband woes. I watched her attack the screen on her phone again. She looked triumphant as she sent off another text or email. I could text Steve's mom . . . maybe invent a reason to have her scold Snacks for me, but it just wouldn't be the same thing.

"I'm so hungry," she said. "How about you?"

"We're at Romeo's," I answered with some sarcastic charm. "What do you think?"

Romeo's Café was our place. Once or twice a month, we'd try and meet without any kids in tow, hoping to catch up. Early on, there had been playdates, at least a half dozen a month, but we could never be ourselves during them—not like we used to be.

"Work?" I asked while looking at the menu.

"Work is good," she answered, and then she lowered her menu. "But the men . . ."

"Men?" I asked, raising my brow. "Do tell."

"Oh, it's not like that . . . okay, well maybe just a little sometimes," she answered. "But the flirting is innocent. What I mean is that they are so different now, a whole generation that I don't even recognize. They . . . they seem so young."

"That's because they are," I answered without hesitating. I knew where she was going. I knew because I'd felt the same way. We weren't young anymore. I could still turn a man's head, and certainly Katie would give any man a reason to pause, but our days of getting away with thigh-high shorts and going braless had passed us by. Our bodies had changed as fast as a light switch—on and then off. Now we had to work a little harder. Prepare a little more. Men? And we'd both seen the way our husbands would sneak a peek elsewhere when they thought we weren't watching. Did it bother me? You bet! Who wouldn't want endless bounce in their tits and an ass that stayed firm forever?

Age is a fickle bitch, and there is just no staying out of its way.

A soft wind pushed a cloud out of the sun's path and warm sunlight peered under the patio's canopy. A sharp ray glinted off my knife like a jewel, hitting my eyes before bouncing across from me. I followed the bright reflection to where it landed on Katie's neck. The timing was simply eerie. It was perfect. I'm not a doctor—I had almost failed my high school biology class—but there was a pulse where the bright light washed over Katie's tender skin.

Her jugular? Was that the right term?

Blood coursed just below that spot, pumping and beating against her neckline. The sight of it was hypnotic.

A Killing Katie design flashed briefly in my head. In my design, I saw myself with the knife and running its blade over Katie's neck, opening her skin and freeing her caged heartbeat, turning the tablecloth red and throwing the powerful scent of copper and spent blood into the air.

"Amy," the wind chirped, catching my attention. "Amy! Are you all right?" I was startled, nearly jumped when Katie tugged on my shoulder. She sat back down, and the warmth of her touch quickly faded. The sun had disappeared behind another cloud, taking the strong beam of light with it.

"I'm sorry," I tried to say, but my voice was stuck in my throat. "Just distracted."

"Are you sure? Did you hear what I told you?"

I shook my head, embarrassed. "No, I'm sorry."

"I think Jerry is having an affair."

At once, my fantasy design disappeared like the sunlight. It was replaced by disappointment and empathy. Fantasy or no fantasy, I loved Katie and hated hearing that news. But at the same time, deep in my gut, a sense of disbelief sprung up. I just couldn't see her husband doing something like that. Not because he was such a nice guy and a great father—I just didn't think he was smart enough. Her husband Jerry lacked a certain something that most men had. Balls. He lacked balls. Heck, most of the time, Katie was more the man in their relationship. If anyone were having an affair, I would think it would be Katie.

I felt my face cramp as I questioned what Katie told me, and I could tell by the sudden change in her posture that she'd been offended by my reaction. I quickly moved my hand onto hers. "Are you sure? I mean, are you really sure?"

"Almost?" she answered, but in her tone I heard uncertainty. That could mean that she had found something suspicious. I wondered if it wasn't something as innocent as a business receipt for a lunch.

"Don't get me wrong," I began to say. "I love you and I adore Jerry—always have—but cheating? And on *you*? He married up, *way* up. I'm just not seeing him doing that to you and the boys."

Katie stared ahead, looking past me, her eyes wide and her lower lip trembling. There was something else. There was more, but she wasn't ready to say anything.

"You're probably right," she quickly answered,

pressing her lips together until they went white. She gingerly brushed the dampness from her cheeks and picked up the menu. "Ready to order?"

"Katie," I objected. "Wait. What else is going on?" She shook her head and put on a terrible lie of a smile.

"I'm sure you're right," she exclaimed, waving to our waiter. But I didn't believe her. There was clearly more, a lot more.

For the next hour, our conversation drifted into the familiar territories of home and family and the never-ending challenges of motherhood. Most of the back-and forth was a rehearsed banter, Katie's way of leaving behind her worries for a few minutes. But it was what she *wasn't* saying that kept me bothered. And while I remained skeptical and disbelieving of her suspicion, I had to admit to being intrigued by the idea of Jerry being so deceptive. If what Katie was saying were true, then how long had the affair been going on? How many lies had Jerry told? Just the thought of someone else in our small circle having secrets intrigued me. I wanted to know more. I wanted to learn.

Images of our home computer crept into my mind—as did my first failed attempts at spinning up a secret life. With this last thought, I stabbed a glance at my phone to check the time. I had at least another three hours.

What could I do with the afternoon? Buy a new

computer. A laptop that I could secretly keep to myself. I'll have to get cash from the bank or put it on a credit card.

My head began to spin again as I traced how every transaction showed up on our monthly bills. We shared that chore, switching off month to month, taking turns.

Was it my turn to pay the bills and balance the checkbook this month? If not, how much could I get away with spending?

Steve sometimes checked my work when it was his turn anyway, I knew.

"Can I wrap that up for you to go, ma'am?" our waiter asked. I hated being called ma'am. My mother was a ma'am, and she wasn't exactly one of my favorite people. I felt fit and sexy—did I look like a ma'am? I certainly didn't feel like one. The waiter leaned forward and repeated, "Ma'am?" I cringed at the sound.

"No, no, that's fine. I'm done," I answered primly, keeping my lips straight and tight, as if something had been wrong with his service. But then I saw his shoes—tattered, torn, and barely holding together. That pair of black walking shoes were probably older than anything I owned—except for maybe our home computer. I bit my lip, feeling the twinge of guilt. He was just doing his job and trying to be polite. It wasn't his fault I was self-conscious. I offered a smile to thank him. And as I did, my eyes fell on my next destination.

Just down the street from Romeo's Café, I saw the public library. I couldn't remember the last time I had visited the library—might have been for a school project with Michael, who had done a report on the Dewey decimal system. But I remembered seeing computers and I remembered they had access to the Internet. Its open hours would align perfectly with my schedule and when Steve's mother usually watched Snacks.

Feeling happy with my plan of where to go after lunch, I made sure to add a little extra to the tip, hoping our waiter would use the money to buy himself some new shoes.

8

THE LIBRARY SMELLED of old books and furniture polish. I wrinkled my nose, recalling its strong odors from growing up. I couldn't help but wonder briefly if I should do the same at home? I dusted, and Steve helped now and again on rainy Saturdays when the weather gave back the hours. But I'd thought the days of spraying furniture polish and wiping everything down had gone the way of the aluminum ice tray and hot-air popcorn makers.

A long counter with all the amenities stood to the right side of the entrance where a mousy-looking librarian with a nose too close to her eyes greeted me. I almost laughed when I first looked at her. There was no doubt she was the librarian. If there was ever a stereotypical picture of a librarian, it was this woman. She wore a cornflower-blue, ruffled blouse with a dark blue V-neck vest. Her hair, brushed gray by age, had been pulled back into a tight bun. It sat atop her head like a big round button. But what did it for me were her thick, squarish reading glasses perched at the end of her nose and the chains running under her ears and around her neck. She stared over the frame of her glasses with a pert smile and greeted me. I smiled back, noticing that she wore no jewelry—not even a wedding band. I wondered if there was some kind of librarian's code.

"May I help you?" she asked in a voice that sounded as old and dusty as the books on the shelves.

"Yes, thank you," I quickly answered, feeling as if I were back in high school, researching a term paper. "I'd like to use a computer?"

The librarian jutted her chin up and glanced over her shoulder. I turned in the direction she indicated to find two rows of tables, both filled with various types of computers, and all of them looking newer than the one in our home.

"No books today?" she asked. I shook my head. The librarian mumbled something under her breath about how nobody visited to check out books anymore. I supposed she was right. Sad. I couldn't remember the last time *I* actually checked out a book.

As I stepped to pass the old woman, she reached

out with her palm open. She expected something from me. I stopped, confused.

"If you want to use one of the library computers, then I'll need to hold your library card," she instructed. My throat closed, and I stepped back. The whole reason for visiting the library was to research and leave no traces of who I was. I'd never considered needing a library card.

"I forgot it," I quickly answered, trying to garner sympathy. "And I really need to use the computer today. I'm out of work and looking for a job."

Did that sound pathetic enough?

"I see," the librarian answered, but she looked suspicious. She was sizing up my outfit. "A driver's license will do. I just need to hold it until you're done."

Oh my God. Seriously?

My nerves were rattled now. A sudden sweat was making my scalp itch. The irony was that I knew when faced with committing murder, I wouldn't feel anxious or nervous at all.

"Yes. Yes, certainly." I dove into my purse, making a show of pushing everything back and forth and shooting up a flustered glance or two. My wallet was right there in my hand, but I wasn't about to turn over my license. I kept my hands hidden in my purse another minute until I saw the librarian's patience wear thin. She shifted, annoyed and uncomfortable.

She bounced her glasses back up the bridge of her nose. After another minute, she finally waved her hand to let me pass. It was good to know some of my old tricks from high school still worked.

"Oh, go ahead," she instructed, her voice sounding resigned and tired. "Nobody reads books anymore, nobody uses their cards. What does it matter? And listen, dear. You just hang in there. I do hope you have luck in finding a new job."

"I appreciate that. Thank you," I answered and rushed past her before another word could be said.

As I made my way to the computer tables, a young man caught my eye. He smiled, having watched the exchange with the librarian. He winked. Or I thought he winked. I got the sudden feeling he knew I was lying to the mousy woman.

From the look of him, I would have expected him to be in school. If he were ditching class, he'd picked an odd place to spend his time. I gave him a glance but didn't return a smile. He was all nerd. Knotty curls of black hair that hadn't been cut or combed in a while, a yellow-and-white striped shirt with sleeves that were too short for the time of year. The only thing missing were glasses and a pocket protector. I didn't like the way he looked at me, so I stared back, narrowing my eyes. Another trick from high school. I kept my stare on him until it made him uncomfortable enough to turn away. Soon he disappeared behind the computer. As I passed behind him, he dared a glance over his shoulder. I could tell that he was staring at my ass; a girl can always tell. It was an innocent reaction, and I didn't mind, preferring that he only saw that side of me, anyway.

The computers weren't just newer than the one at home, they were completely different. While our boxy tank was loud and ran an old version of Windows, the computer in front of me was a newer Apple—I'd seen these only on television commercials. It had crisp, elegant lines, and it was thin. A large black screen like onyx filled the space in front of me. I felt even more intimidated than I had with our home computer. I touched the mouse, hesitating. Without a sound, other than a melodic chime, the display lit up immediately with brilliant colors. My first thought was that Steve would love one of these. My second thought was that I had no idea how to use a Mac.

Where was the browser? How do you print? Should I print? And what about my secret box, the hidden folder I needed?

"Windows person, huh?" I heard the nerd ask. I realized then I must have been staring at the computer for a while, doing nothing, thinking everything. "Do you need access to the Internet?"

"I do," I answered cautiously. "I'm not a *Mac*

person. But not by choice. We only have an old Windows machine." I wanted to avoid eye contact, so I kept my gaze to the table between us.

"Macs usually come with the Safari browser, but the library has been good enough to install Firefox and Chrome."

"Firefox? I know Firefox. It's what I use at home," I exclaimed, thinking all wasn't lost. I looked up again, searching for the familiar foxtail icon.

"They should really put it on the desktop, but they never do." The nerd moved his seat closer to mine. I made room for him. He seemed harmless. When he was next to me, I took a closer look at him and thought he could either have been in college or just out of high school. He was a cute boy, but if he was ever going to catch the eyes of a girl, he'd desperately need a makeover. "May I?"

"Sure. Yes, thank you." For a nerd, the boy was more sociable, even likable than the geeks I'd grown up with.

He leaned in and tapped a few keys, bringing up the familiar Firefox interface I knew. "There you go. And I put a shortcut on the desktop too."

"Excellent. And I use it just like I do at home?"

"Sure thing. The Internet doesn't care about which browser you use. Just don't search for anything illegal," he laughed. At once, I took my hands off the keyboard as if the keys were on fire. My reaction gave him pause, and he stopped laughing, intrigued. "Oh. If that's your business, then you'll want to use a different browser altogether."

Five minutes into my first research session and I'd already shown my hand, already drawn suspicion. A part of me wanted to scream, to grab my things, and to run from the library.

"You know a lot about computers?" I asked. I smiled, and in a half-joking tone, added, "So you know how to search for things? I mean, how to search for things, safely?"

"You a cop?" he asked abruptly, not returning a smile. His face had gone blank, aging him a few years. "You know you have to tell me if I ask you to identify yourself."

Was I in luck? Was he also seeking the same anonymity? "I think that only works in movies. And no, I'm not a cop."

"You're not really looking for a job, are you?" he asked, motioning to the librarian.

"Nope. Not looking for a job. Just need to use a computer," I answered, and wanted to be careful about what I said. I mean, who just meets someone in a public library and then strikes up a conversation like this. *Privacy,* I thought. I'll mention privacy. "And since this is a public library, and these are public computers, I'd like my work to remain private. That's all."

"Well, then," he said and pointed toward the computer. "Privacy is a good thing. And I won't tell them you're not looking for work if you won't tell them what I'm doing."

I had no idea what he was doing on his computer, but I agreed, answering, "Deal." I extended my hand. "Call me . . . Amelia."

"Like the pilot," he said, nodding. "That way you can just disappear without a trace."

"Yeah. Something like that." It was a coincidence I'd picked that name, but I liked what he said. And more than that, I liked the way he thought.

"Call me—"

"Nerd," I answered for him. His brow narrowed, stitching together as he considered the name. Soon, a dimple appeared on his cheek.

"Sure. Nerd," he agreed. "Why not? That's a safe name. So you are here to do some research, and in need of privacy? But more important, you don't want to do it at home?"

"Uh-huh," I answered. And then repeated, "I want privacy."

"Not sure if you know, but every browser already offers a way to turn on privacy," he said, clicking the browser's menu, showing me the options for a private window. "There are other browsers too that are even better, like hide your location. But is it only privacy? Or do you need to do *deeper* research?"

"Deeper?" I asked, hearing his emphasis on the word, but unsure of what he meant.

"How much do you know about the Internet?" he asked as he flashed through a half-dozen screens.

"Same as most, I suppose."

"I mean, how do you normally use the web?"

"Well, I shop online and I check the—"

"Weather," he interrupted. "You're surfing high."

"Excuse me?" I said abruptly, uncertain of where the conversation was leading.

"You've only scratched the surface," he continued as more web pages flashed across the screen. "You're surfing in the top five percent, along with everyone else."

"So what is in the other ninety-five percent?" I asked, having heard about the darker areas of the Internet from Steve. But that didn't mean I knew how to access them. Nerd's eyes opened wide in excitement.

"Well, Amelia, let me tell you. Wait, I'll show you," he began and then opened a new browser I didn't recognize. "*That* is the Deep Web. And I think that is where you'll find whatever it is you're looking for. It's where most of us do our research. That is, when we want privacy."

"How do you know what I'm looking for?" I asked. An uneasy, urgent feeling came.

"Relax," he answered, reading my reaction. "Because that is why I am here. There's not much to gain browsing the crust, unless you're partial to Wikipedia pages."

"You spend your day in the library, surfing the Deep Web?" I asked.

"Maybe not quite like that," he laughed. "The library is quiet and safe. I write code for anyone willing to pay. And it just so happens that the best-paying customers advertise their jobs on the dark net." He glanced around, adding, "It's also an easy place to pick up tutoring jobs."

I held my purse tight, suddenly intent on leaving. I didn't know what to make of Nerd and considered that he could just be showing off. It also seemed an odd sense of luck too—my meeting him, meeting someone with his level of knowledge about the deep web. But isn't that the case with success? Call it luck or good fortune, but mostly it's just opportunity and timing crossing paths. I threw caution into the wind and decided to play out the conversation until I'd heard enough and learned what was needed to work on my own.

"You never answered my question. What am I looking for?"

"My guess . . ." he started to say, sizing me up and down. "You've got a little something-something on the side and want to keep it that way. Only, your husband is a bit too tech savvy for you to risk doing anything at home. Am I right?" His face lit up as though he'd guessed it on the first try.

"Murder," I corrected him, shaking my head. My voice sounded icy. It sounded exactly the way I'd hoped it would. I was throwing everything into the wind now and wanted to gauge his reaction. But he didn't pack up and run like I'd expected. Instead, he shrugged seemed to lose interest.

"Really?" he answered. I sensed he believed I was lying, that I was being sarcastic. And that was fine. "I'll take that as code for you're researching a new book?"

"Something like that," I answered. "Privacy is best. And that's all I want to say for now." Nerd nodded his head slowly, uncertain if I was being serious.

Sarcastic intent or not, had I said too much?

For all he knew, I could be trying to call *his* bluff.

"Not a problem. And if you're game, I can show you a few things to help you with your *research*," he answered.

"So what makes the Deep Web . . . deep?" I asked, trying to tap my immediate need and move past the current topic. "I mean, why isn't it all just one Web?"

He mulled over my question a moment and then

answered with a question. "What's the first thing you do on a computer?" he asked, moving back to the keyboard. A browser window opened, showing a familiar search box.

"I search," I answered.

"Everybody searches," he continued for me. "To make searching possible, some computer, some *server* has a list of all the other servers, and those servers have lists too, and each of them has notes about the other so they're easy to find."

"That's how the links come up in the results?" I added, questioning.

"Right. It works because of all the indexing. However, for the servers that are in the Deep Web, they aren't indexed. Actually, they are never indexed. They're there, but you have to know how to access them. And that's what I know how to do."

He brought up window upon window—all of them completely alien to me. I understood some of what he explained, but felt we'd only scratched the surface.

How vast was the Deep Web? How far would I have to go to find what I needed?

"Deep Web must be huge. An ocean."

Nerd responded with a curt nod. "You might say that. Just about every illegal activity you can think of can be found there."

"Show me," I demanded. Nerd abruptly raised his

hands from the keyboard. I felt a sudden disappointed, and confused, like I'd just been stood up.

"That kind of knowledge doesn't come cheap," he said, lowering one hand, palm facing up. I raised my brow, surprised, and a bit frustrated. But I respected how he treated this as a transaction and recalled his mentioning being a tutor. "Coding has been light and I've got to make a living. Tutoring on the side is a good filler. I'm game to all topics, including deep web navigation."

"Are you making that up?" I asked.

He half-shook his head and then nodded, "Does it matter? I have the knowledge, and I can teach you. But if it helps, I do pick up tutoring jobs here. A lot of desperate parents bring their kids to the library, hoping it'd help their kids with a failing grade or to cram for an exam."

What he said sounded reasonable. "You'll show me what I need to know? Show me how to browse and navigate securely?" I asked, negotiating. The last thing I expected when entering the library this afternoon was that I'd be taking computer lessons. It was a baby step, but it was a step.

"For the right hourly price, I'll teach you as much as you need."

Without another thought, I dug into my purse, producing a fifty-dollar bill that I'd put aside for

Michael's birthday card. The bill was fresh and crisp and smelled like ink. "Just printed," the teller at the bank had said. I hesitated a moment and then placed it in Nerd's hands. I cringed when he crumpled it into a ball and stuffed it away in his pocket.

"What's first?"

9

WHEN THE SUN had dipped low enough to reach through the library's window, I knew that I'd overstayed my time. At best there was twenty minutes of sunlight remaining in the day. I was never late. Never.

"Damn!" I blurted. "What time is it?" I didn't bother waiting for an answer. The clock on the wall peered at me as if I'd broken a vow. I focused, but I couldn't find the hour hand, and for a moment I thought the clock must have stopped. But both of the clock hands were pointing straight down, as if indicating where my heart should be. My mouth dropped. I jumped up from the table and gathered my things in a rush. I could feel Nerd staring, curious at my reaction.

Oh to be young and free, I thought with a

sentimental recall. There was just no knowing what you have until it is gone forever.

"I'm late. Really late!" I said, blurting the words.

"Library is going to close soon, anyway," he offered and began to gather his things. He didn't recognize my urgency. Why would he?

"Do we need to do anything here?" I asked, motioning to my screen. "Should I shut it down?"

"Nothing to shut down, just need to close a few things," he answered, not bothering to look up. "Don't worry about it, I'll take care of it."

He said a few other things about not needing to shut down, but I only heard mumbles as I raced to the large double doors. On my way, I offered a brief wave to the librarian. She stabbed the air with her hand, seeming to be surprised by my attention.

"I hope you find that job," she said in a breeze as I passed the counter.

"Still looking," I answered. "I'll be back in a day or two." She nodded as I punched at the door's brass handle. A second set of doors waited on the other side, leaving me momentarily in a quiet bubble to gather my thoughts and tidy my coat. With the sun nearly gone, the day had turned frigid. I put on a hat and scarf. I never liked the autumn chill, preferring the warmer side of cozy whenever I could. The bubble moment also gave me time to think up an excuse for being so late. I hit the second door and tried to clear my mind.

The outside air washed over me like a draft of cool wind. The sidewalks teemed with people hurrying around me. Car horns blared and traffic was stopped up and down Main Street. The sounds and sights were a world away from the tranquil quiet of the library and filled my head with busy congestion. It was the beginning of the evening and the ending of a workday, and everyone was in a rush to be somewhere else.

"Shit," I mumbled, looking at the rows of bumper-to-bumper cars and thinking that there'd be no point in rushing.

The air had become crisp in the fading day, and the afternoon shadows stretched long, dark fingers to touch the coming night. The sun was about to vanish, and I had no idea how I was going to explain where I'd been.

I wasn't just a little late, I was more than two hours late. I glanced at my phone and saw that I'd missed a few phone calls from Steve and a half-dozen text messages—all of them asking where I was. My heart jumped into my throat, beating hard. My skull pounded.

I glanced up at the library's pitched roof, studying the stony, curved shingles, and tried to understand why my stupid phone hadn't worked inside. The only thing I could think to do next was to go home. I quickly thumbed an apology, tapping the screen, texting as I walked to my car. My phone's screen told me that my text was delivered and that it had been read. I stood in front of my car door and peered at my reflection. A humid cloud escaped my lips, and I half-expected to see a monster suddenly emerge from the reflection. But it was just me, staring back. I looked good in the outfit I'd selected for my lunch today, and even prettier with my hat and scarf on. With only an orange glow above the hard line of the horizon, the sun vanishing before me, the extra clothes had been a good call.

I leaned into the car window until my warm breath fogged the glass, making my reflection disappear, hiding it from the world. A reservation nagged at my conscience, and I tried to ignore it. I was still innocent and without sin for the moment. The glass cleared, and I saw a fierceness in my complexion I hadn't seen before. Patient. Poised. The sight sent a chill through me. I searched for who it was that I wanted to be.

Should I ignore the reservations? Could I ignore who I'd become?

My phone buzzed and the shallow vibration made me jump. I'd stared long enough and slipped inside my car. I started the engine, willing the heat to come on as my teeth chattered. I cranked the thermostat on the dashboard until the thin white line sank into the red section. The heat would take a minute, but the idea of it being set helped a little.

Where are you? Steve texted. *Are you okay?* He didn't seem mad, but texting could be misleading as far as tone was concerned.

I'm fine, I texted back. *On my way home.*

My phone said that he read my next text message. I waited for a reply, but there was none. The dread in my gut stayed. He was relieved to know that I was fine, but he would be angry—or worse, disappointed.

The traffic was as bad as I'd expected, but that gave me time to think about what else Nerd had showed me. The Web, as I knew it to be, was nothing more than looking at a storefront. Like walking through a market and seeing what was for sale from the sidewalk. I'd only scratched the surface. Behind the doors, just a few feet from the street, there was so much more going on. In just a short time, he explained more about the Deep Web and showed me different browsers that I could use to access the Web without leaving my fingerprints all over the computer. He'd called it proxy jumping—path hopping across multiple computers, each forwarding requests without leaving a trail. It was more than making just a few simple hops; he prided himself on being able to bounce our traffic over half a dozen servers.

I understood some of what he explained, but he

could tell I was becoming lost at times. That feeling of being intimidated by technology sprang forward again, telling me that I'd need to learn as much as I could from him. I nodded like a hungry child when he offered more lessons. But at the same time, I struggled with the idea of trusting him.

Just let him show you, I told myself. *After all, who was breaking a law? A conversation is just a conversation. I could be writing a paper, doing research.*

It wasn't as if I was about to bring Nerd along or let him in on the details of my plans.

I turned onto our street. A pretty cul-de-sac with a collection of houses and manicured lawns that was impossibly suburban, impossibly familiar, and everything that Steve disliked because it wasn't the city. The bricks and lath-and-plaster, which we grew up with, had been replaced by paper shells covered in vinyl siding.

"Must've all come from the same factory," Steve had joked when our realtor brought us to the For Sale sign. "Any flavors available other than plain?" The realtor politely ignored his joking, but I remember giving him a smirk, pleading with him to behave. Our lives had been firmly rooted in the city, and we would have stayed there forever, but the city we'd once known wasn't the city that it had become. Steve still spent some of his days there, working across jurisdictions to put away the worst of the worst. After all, criminals know no boundaries. For me, home was wherever my family was. And at the time, pregnant with Michael, the best place for home meant a move out of the city.

I turned into our driveway and tried to peer through the front window to see if Steve's silhouette was there, waiting for me.

Is it too soon to say that I was shopping for the holidays? I wondered.

I could tell him that I'd lost track of time browsing in one of the newly opened boutique stores off Main Street. He knew that I wasn't much for browsing in stores, but it was the next best excuse that I could come up with. And I could also tell him how lunch with Katie had gone over on account of her news that Jerry was having an affair. I shook my head. I was never late. I never lost track of time. Some of this was my fault. On the other hand, it could be a good first step toward my other plan. I suppose that I had set a precedent and was now obligated to be on time.

That's just going to have to change, I considered. *Not that it will help me right now.*

The round handle to our front door felt as cold as the night air—it sent a chill into me. My stomach felt sour, twisting from the nerves that came with lying. I dreaded the idea of not being truthful with Steve. I held the door handle another moment but didn't turn it. During my entire drive home, I'd missed something important.

An epiphany.

Soon, there was going to come a time that I was going to *have* to lie. With murder, I was going to have to start lying to *everyone* to cover up my work.

This is practice, I told myself as I turned the knob.

As I walked through our front door, the familiar smells of home hit me. Someone had been cooking too, and with the pang of hunger, I realized that I was famished. Steve's mother was an excellent cook; the smell of tomato sauce and pasta filled our kitchen. Any minute, I was sure to see Snacks racing up to greet me, red sauce covering her front and a tangle of hair bouncing with each step. I'd laugh, loving every second of it.

Steve said nothing as he hurried around the kitchen cleaning up. A heavy blanket of silence sat between us, raising the tension to a nearly unbearable level. I put my things down, plopping them on the table loud enough to be heard, but he ignored me. Normally, I'd try to turn this around, act mad about something unrelated, but I needed the practice. I had to learn how to lie to my husband.

"I'm sorry that I'm late," I started, having rehearsed my apology multiple times now. "Katie and I had a few drinks with lunch and I needed to walk off the buzz. I just lost track of time." Not sure where that came from, but I thought it sounded good.

Steve slowed his movements over the sink, then turned the water off and faced me. He didn't look mad —that is, he didn't look at all like I imagined he would. During our marriage, I've seen Steve get angry, and the memory of those times scared me. He looked concerned instead.

"You didn't think to text and let my mom know?" Anxious guilt took a hard bite at my gut. I shrugged a shoulder and slowly shook my head. "My mom called me. You're never late. She wanted to call the hospitals. Where were you all that time?"

"The library," I answered. His expression went blank. The words were out of my mouth before I could catch them.

Did I not understand how lying even worked?

Steve said nothing. I feared that even the truth was hard for him to believe.

"The library is down the street from the café, and I just needed a place to sit until I felt okay to drive. I picked up a book and got lost in it."

"A text message?"

"The roof," I answered, adding some truth to my story. "Phone didn't work inside the library."

"I had to leave work early to come home and help," he said. The words stung like a bee. This was a slip, a bad slip, bringing up something that he knew I was already sensitive about. "My mom couldn't stay, so I came home to take care of the kids."

"Oh . . . and is that such a bad thing?" I exclaimed, raising my voice. He did work a lot of hours, and I understood the type of career he had as a police detective.

Steve stopped what he was doing, "What is that supposed to mean?"

"Would it kill you to be more involved?"

"I *am* involved," he answered, clapping a ladle against the rim of the pot. We'd had this argument before, and we both knew it wouldn't go very far. "Now tell me what's really bothering you."

My mouth had gone dry and I could taste regret. I wished I had something else to add. He stared at me until I couldn't take it. "I want to go back to work," I finally blurted. He rolled his eyes and turned back to the sink.

"How?" he asked, sounding frustrated. "I know you want me to go back to school and I appreciate that you want to help, but how can we manage the time? Please tell me that."

"First you said the problem with school was about the money," I began. "And now that I want to work for the extra money, you're saying it is about the time. So which is it?" While the argument was valid, the intent was to distract him from asking more about where I'd been. It worked, but started an argument I wasn't up to having.

Steve raised his hands, pyramiding his fingers. "You're right," he acknowledged. "Money is one thing we don't have; and time is something we have less of."

"Katie and Jerry manage to do it," was all I could think to say. I knew before I finished that I'd picked a horrible comparison. Steve knew it too and threw out a snarky laugh. I hated it when he did that.

"Oh, well, there it is. We'll follow Katie and Jerry's lead," he said. He shook his head and laughed sarcastically. "Parents of the year!"

But I did want to make time for planning. The more I thought about it, the more I realized that I needed a *lot* more time. I sensed that Steve didn't want to fight any more than I did. I stepped up to the sink to lend a hand with the dishes. A thought came into my mind; I realized how to turn this around and maybe end it.

"Are you laughing at me because I want to do more than just take care of the kids and . . . and you?" His snarky expression disappeared immediately.

"Babe . . ." he began to say, turning the water off and facing me. He took my hands into his—soapy bubbles erupted between our fingers. "I just don't know how we'd make it work with my schedule."

Now I did feel true resentment coming on. I felt the pang of jealousy toward Katie and her busy career.

"I know this is my job now, but I've got to do something else, even if it is only part time, a couple of hours a day." Steve leaned in and peppered my cheek with kisses. I could see in his eyes that he was trying to figure out how to make something work.

"We could always get one of them young foreign *au pairs*. You know, the super-model hot ones, let them live here with us and help out with Snacks," he offered, and raised his brow playfully.

"Sure," I answered. "As long as he is tall, dark, and handsome and, you know . . . very well-endowed, like I'm accustomed to!" I laughed, thumping his chest and patting his crotch.

"Or . . ." he began. "How about I ask my mother if she'd be up for the job?"

"Really?" I answered, excited by the prospect. Steve's mother would be perfect.

"Yes, really," he answered. "Dad mentioned that Mom was looking to volunteer her free time."

I hugged Steve, holding him tight. I felt his heart beating against my chest as he cradled the small of my back with his hands. "I love you."

"Love you too." He pulled back and looked at me. "So, what book were you reading at the library?"

10

PRACTICE WENT ON for another twenty minutes as Steve asked a half dozen of the same questions—albeit with a bit of trickery so that the questions sounded different each time. When at home, he was a husband and a father. He was my lover and my best friend. But he was also a cop. He was always a cop. Being a cop was in his blood, just like being a killer was in mine.

I watched as my husband spoke to me, and for a moment I didn't see a cop. I saw the man I fell in love with. I watched as his brow creased and then rose, pushing worry lines across his forehead. I watched as his mouth pursed and then relaxed. I watched as his lips parted to reveal perfectly straight teeth. I watched as his gorgeous sky-blue eyes stayed fixed on me, following me. I felt a sudden weakness and a flutter in my stomach that only came when he looked at me like that. No other man has ever made me feel the way Steve does.

As I listened to Steve's questions, keeping my answers short and never forfeiting information, some of what Nerd showed me came to mind. The idea of making real money seemed to be moving into the realm of possibility. With Nerd helping me, I could do this. I wanted to do this. From the Deep Web, I would connect with the people who wanted what I had to offer and were willing to pay for it. And they were going to pay a lot. There'd be a time when Steve wouldn't be a cop anymore . . . one could hope, anyway.

"Amy?" I heard my name and swam up through the dreamy daze of what could be if we had the money and the time, as Steve had reminded me. "Amy?"

"Sorry, are you done being a cop? I want to talk to my husband."

"Just one more."

Of course I tensed, but let him ask his last question. Steve wore his cop senses like a coat, putting them on whenever the truth seemed cold. I must have said something wrong in my short answers while thinking about how to pay for law school. It could be that he was trying to find out if I really had been shopping for the holidays—he always figured out what I got for him.

Should have used that excuse instead.

At one point, a nervous laugh found its way to the back of my throat and the fear of it spilling out became so powerful that I began to sweat.

Did he notice? Would he notice?

"And the book?" he asked, wording the question differently. "What was the book you were reading at the library?"

"A Hundred-and-One Sexual Positions for Dummies," I answered jokingly, and then motioned with my hands, pantomiming sexual intercourse until Steve began to laugh: the finger in the hole motion did the trick. "Are we done now?"

"Yeah, we're done," he said, still laughing. I'd made it through my first round of questioning and thought I should feel giddy, or feel relief, or feel something. This was a milestone for me. But instead, I felt conflicted.

Could I get used to lying to Steve?

"If you're going to be around the library, be careful. A young girl, pretty too, was attacked earlier this week."

I remembered hearing the story on the radio. It never occurred to me that Steve might be working the case. "How is she doing?" I asked, thinking what happened to her was far from what I wanted to achieve. The distinction was simple: the world would miss *her*. "Radio said that she was in critical condition?"

"She's stable. Lost a lot of blood," he answered as he motioned his hand across his neckline. Watching Steve reenact the attack put a lump in my throat, catching me off guard. I felt bad for the young woman. "The kids are downstairs. Snacks is fine, busy tearing through her toys. But Michael was worried when you didn't come home."

The kids. I got a knot in my stomach and bit down on my lip. My lies weren't just going to be to Steve. Not now. And certainly not later. It was easier when Michael was younger. Steve and I could do and say a lot more around him without his knowing the context.

A child's innocence, I thought. It was like a shield, guarding them against knowing what the adult talk was about. But Michael had become more grown-up and more curious, and we'd begun to filter what was said around him.

"Playing video games?" I asked. Steve nodded, and I leaned in to kiss him. I wrapped my arms around his middle and put my head against his chest. I stayed there like that, listening to his heart and waiting for him to put his arms around me. "I *am* sorry. I'll go talk to him." Steve cupped his hand on the lower part of my back and led me to the door.

"Love you, babe."

. . .

Snacks was on me as soon as I pressed my feet into the plush carpet of our children's playroom. I called it a playroom, preferring the warmer, cozier, more joyful name over the usual, stationary names—basement or cellar. With a heated floor and all the finishes of the rest of the house, playroom seemed more fitting. Snacks folded her arms and legs around my calf, clutching the back of my jeans while squatting on my foot and preparing for a ride. It was a good thing I'd changed into something that was more mommy than business. Heels just wouldn't have worked in this situation.

"Ride ride ride," she yelled, wanting me to walk. A smile peered at me from her upturned face. I shook my head when seeing her dark blonde hair laying tangled and out of control, strands of it pasted to her cheek with dried spaghetti sauce.

"Didn't you let Daddy clean you up?"

"Come on, Momma!"

"Hold on now," I told her as I took long sweeps of my feet across the room. I grunted as I walked and tried to sound like a monstrous machine moving an impossibly heavy load. "Time to exit."

"Aww, Momma," she complained and tugged on my pants leg until I felt the jeans slip from my backside. "Just a little more?"

"Sorry, girl, but that's all that I have for you," I said.

She let go of my leg and sought out something else to play with. "Hey, Snacks?"

She darted a hopeful look and raced back over. I grabbed her little body and squeezed until she began to squirm. Michael glanced over the couch, but then turned back to the television.

"Another ride?" she asked.

"No more rides," I answered, shaking my head. "But I think Daddy has something for you upstairs." And without another word, Snacks was off in a run. I heard the thumps of little feet clopping up the stairs and followed them with my eyes as they moved across the ceiling.

Michael kept his stare fixed on the video game, ignoring me when I sat down next to him. Now would be a good time to tell him about my work. Not the real work, of course, but that his father wouldn't be the only one working . . . so to speak.

"Got a second?" I asked, having no expectations.

"Can it wait until I'm done?"

"What are you playing?" I asked, glancing at the screen. I recognized the game, remembering lengthy discussions about whether or not a first-person shooter was appropriate. Steve objected, wanting to wait another year. I would have given him the same game three years earlier, when Michael discovered there was more to gaming than Mario and Luigi and a funny-looking princess that never needed saving.

"C.O.D.," he answered without breaking stride in a run toward his next ambush. I shivered against the chill in the playroom and snuggled up next to him. When he didn't budge, I snuggled even closer, trying to warm myself and to thaw the barrier he'd put up between us.

"I'm sorry that I was late," I began, gauging him, waiting. His fingers stopped moving, his character on the screen stood still as if surveying a war-torn landscape filled with the dead and dying. "Listen, I'm going to start working part time soon and will probably be late again. Is that okay?"

"Do you want me to take care of Snacks?" he asked, setting his game controller down to look at me. He had more questions on his face than hurt, and was completely adorable asking about his sister. I melted and forgot what I was going to say next.

"I love you," I told him, hugging him whether he wanted me to or not. "I'm sorry that you were worried about me."

"Just call next time," he said, his voice sounding muffled against my shirt. "I can take care of Snacks if you want me to."

"That's very sweet. We're going to ask your grandma to help out."

"So you're gonna get a job too?" he asked, breaking away from my hug to move his character again. The sound of the game's gunfire continued, and his attention was nearly lost to it already. I picked up the other controller and motioned to him to add me. Michael hit the center buttons in a blur of fingers, and the screen split into two, with my player on the left and Michael's on the right.

"I am," I answered. We quickly moved up to face a collection of other players. We stood back-to-back, circling and spraying bullets in a coordinated and rehearsed display, killing all that came upon us. He smiled and laughed as the other players disappeared from the screen.

"You're so much better at this than Dad."

"I know," I added with a laugh. I said little else for the next hour as we defeated team after team.

11

WITH THE SUN rising over the library's steepled building, the light shone through the high eastern-facing windows, setting afire what had been lost in deep shadows during my previous afternoon visit. If not for the thickly paneled counter and the familiar rows of bookshelves, I would have believed that I'd entered the wrong place.

As if to agree with this sentiment, a librarian working the counter caught sight of me and looked at me inquiringly. I didn't recognize her; I searched for the older woman. I stepped fully inside, shaking off the morning chill as the heavy door eased closed; a poof of air washed up behind me. The librarian offered a greeting. Tossing her head to one side, she sent folds of butter-blonde hair over her shoulder. She wore a white knitted blouse with a low neckline, revealing a bounty of cleavage that screamed "sex" to anyone interested. Sexy she was indeed, and I gave her a second look, wondering if she'd let me pass without showing any identification. The nameplate on the counter had also changed from the night before, telling me that her name was Becky. She looked more suited to one of the city's trendy stores—anything in the city other than a librarian.

"Hi," she said, fixing a broad smile while finishing with a book. "Be right there."

"Take your time," I answered as I began fishing through my purse, hoping I could get away with playing the same "forgotten library card" story.

Lean with perky boobs that pointed in the right direction—they jiggled as she made her way to greet me—I began to wonder if this young beauty might be the reason Nerd worked out of the library.

"Welcome to Mainsford Library," she said. "Can I help you find something?" Perky—that is what I decided to call her—couldn't have been more than a year or two out of college. Her skin was smooth and deliciously young, and a pang of jealousy leaped up from the pit of my gut.

"Thank you," I answered. "I'm here to use one of the computers."

"Sure thing," she snapped and motioned to the other side of the library.

"Over there, yes," I said. Then I added, "I was here the other night. I'm using the computer to look for a job." Perky turned her head. She had already begun to dig out another book from beneath the counter. I waited for a response, biting my tongue, realizing that I'd offered up more than I should have.

Don't forfeit information.

Perky barely acknowledged me. She'd heard what I'd said, but chose to check her phone after she'd finished with the book. She glanced up and quickly motioned to the computers. I took the opportunity to rush past the counter. I found Nerd's eyes peering over one of the computers. I glared back with a surprised expression. Nerd shook his head in a way that quickly made me feel like an amateur again, or as he liked to call me, a "newb."

"When Becky is on, you don't have to do, or say, anything," he said as I settled at the computer next to him. "She's barely a librarian. I mean, she has her degree and all, but she's only coasting here."

Nerd watched Perky as he spoke about her. "So you know her?"

"You might say that," he answered, breaking his stare and turning back to the computer. "Ready to get started?"

"I'm ready to learn some more," I answered as I fished out another fifty from my purse. When I handed it to him, he pinched the bill in his fingers and lifted his other hand, revealing a small flash drive. The feeling I had at that moment was like Christmas morning and opening the biggest gift under the tree. "For me?"

"Let's just say that with you, I'm feeling inspired," he answered. I ditched my smile and firmed my lips, pressing until Nerd's smile vanished. "Is something wrong?"

"So how do I know this isn't some kind of spyware?" I asked, thinking that it was the right question for a situation like this. I really had no idea how spyware worked, but the name implied caution and that was good enough for me.

"The cop question again?" he asked, stuffing the money into his pocket. "Well, what might help is if I tell you to never ever, ever, plug that flash drive into any computer except the library computer. Make sense?"

I thought about what he said and searched his face for the right response, but I was already out of my element. I didn't understand why his response was right or wrong. "Okay, tell me why."

"Aren't you more interested in what I made for you?" he asked, motioning to the flash drive. "We could talk spyware, or you could just trust that I'm in this as much as you are—actually, more than you at this point."

"Good enough," I said as I plugged the flash drive into the side of the Mac. I had no reason *not* to trust Nerd. If there was a point he was dead-on about, it was that if any laws had been broken by now, he was the one who had broken them.

A folder appeared on the desktop, cornflower blue and veiled with a picture of a skull and crossbones—only the skull had been replaced with a fat spider.

"Nice touch," I said, glancing over at Nerd after recognizing the folder was not like the others.

"Strategy," he said quietly. "A reminder to pull the flash drive out whenever you leave the computer."

"So what's on here?" I asked, clicking the folder, opening it to reveal a set of files with obscure names.

"The top applications are the proxy browsers we downloaded last time, only I've doctored them up to set up random hops so that you won't have to."

"Different every search?" I guessed, remembering how important it was to cover our Web tracks.

"Exactly," he answered, lifting his brow. "You were listening."

"So why the flash drive?" I asked, appreciating the effort, but wanting to know if there was a significance that helped protect what I wanted to do. "Why wouldn't we just download them again whenever we need to?"

His eyes grew round and huge. He raised a hand and then clicked on an icon that looked like a dead rat. "This is a program I wrote, kind of a room's view into the Deep Web. With it, you can index sites that are specific to what you are looking for." The application launched to show a list of addresses and a corresponding color bar. The colors ran from shades of green through yellow and red. A thin line hovered over the wash of colors, indicating a level that seemed vaguely familiar to me.

"So how does it work?" I asked, intrigued by the list of sites he'd already indexed.

"Well," he said. "I've started with a list of websites that can help you find just about anything illegal you can imagine."

"And the colors?" I asked. Most of the sites hovered yellow to green, but a handful were deep into the red. And with only numbers for the site names, the color was going to be my only guide.

"Those give an indication of just how illegal the site is," he answered. I felt my eyes narrow, trying to understand. "The yellow to green are mostly harmless: porn, drugs, services offered. You get my meaning."

"And the yellow to the red and the dark red?" I asked. Nerd pulled his hand from the computer and, for the first time, I saw a hint of reluctance in place of his ego and enthusiasm. "Come on, now. You know that I'm not here for porn or to pick up a date."

"How serious were you?" he asked. I saw the reluctance in his eyes deepen as he moved his chair away from the computer.

Had I found Nerd's line in the sand?

He'd given me the keys, but he wasn't going to go through the door with me.

"You were serious, and not just browsing for a fling or something?"

I paused and fixed my eyes on him, saying nothing until he began to look uncomfortable. He began to squirm, and I thought about how he'd never be able to hold up under the kind of interrogation Steve delivered.

Let's just hope it never comes to that.

But in all fairness, I was an attractive woman staring at a nerd; I was flattered by the results.

"Do I look like the type who would be interested in a *fling*?" I finally answered, but that wasn't what he wanted to hear. "As for the other day? No. That wasn't a joke. I am researching, but it might not be what you think."

"You want someone dead," he quickly answered. "That's what I'm thinking."

"How much do you know?" I asked, feeling equally

nervous that I could be a click away from my goal. How close? "Is this something you've dealt with? Indexed?"

Nerd shook his head and answered, "Not directly. Like I said yesterday, I squeak by with small hacks and some corporate spying, that sort of thing."

"The yellow ones?" I asked.

He nodded, and then added. "The ones in red, those are the ones you're looking for."

My heart began to race. I wanted to go to them immediately. I placed my hand on the mouse. Nerd followed the cursor as I moved it over one of the red links. He raised his hand, telling me to wait. "What?"

"They're not safe," he said. "I haven't perfected the filter. Some of those are traps. FBI, CIA, a bunch of other federal hoo-has. They set up mock sites for sting operations."

"I just want to see what is out there," I said. Silence fell between us and I could have sworn he heard the thundering in my chest.

"Let's talk for a minute," he pleaded. "Don't click on anything yet."

My time was short and my patience was growing even shorter. I could feel it. And it wasn't just the anxiety of wanting to act on my obsession—I wanted to establish something, *needed* to establish something soon. Otherwise, what was I doing? Nerd continued to stare with pleading eyes, his hand raised. I decided there was no more time for being vague. If Nerd was going to help, then he needed to know what he was going to help me with.

"Listen to me. I'm going to be direct about why I'm here. It's murder," I told him. He leaned forward, lowering his hand. "I don't have anyone particular in mind. Just advertising my services. Is that something you can help me set up?"

Nerd stared, slack-jawed, and said nothing. He raised himself out of his chair a little and glanced around the library.

"So you have nobody in mind?" he asked, sitting back down. I shook my head. "So you're what? Offering the *service*?"

"Yes," I answered flatly, to which he wrinkled his brow. Nerd sized me up, same as he had when we first met. Only this time, it wasn't with the intent of carnal fun. His expression turned to one of amused disbelief. I sat back in my chair, feeling defensive about what I'd shared. Crossing my arms, I asked, "What's that look? I'm not threatening enough?" I glanced over to the counter, spying a glimpse of the hot librarian. I'd judged her too.

"I'm sorry," he began, shaking his head. "I'm just not seeing it. That is about the last thing I would have expected you to say."

"Obviously," I countered. His gaze turned to confusion.

"What do you mean?"

"Think about it," I added and motioned an *aha* expression, hoping he'd see the obvious insight into my strategy. "Do you think anybody would see me coming?" Slowly, his mouth gaped open as the realization took hold.

"No, you certainly don't have to worry about looking the part," he said, moving back to the screen to circle the mouse's cursor over the yellow and red links. "So you thought that you could just hang your shingle on the door and say that you're open for business?"

"Something like that," I answered, scrambling for something better to say. But that *was* the idea, and to hear it said aloud brought the earlier sentiment back. I crossed my arms again, plodding in thought and finding nothing. "That is what brought me here . . . to the library. No traces."

It was Nerd's turn to remain quiet and for me to squirm in my seat. I glanced at the flash drive, thinking that maybe I could use it on my own to start a small online presence and go into business without his help.

Did I really need him? How hard could it be?

I moved the mouse's cursor over the first yellow/red link. My finger twitched, anticipating a shopping mall of customers looking for a killer.

"Stop!" Nerd burst out in a library whisper. "You'll get yourself caught in a sting. Not sure why yet, but I like you and want to explore this with you. I'm interested in helping you. I need the money, so it will cost a cut of the profit. I have terms too."

"Terms?" I asked, not quite understanding what he meant.

"Who."

His point was fair, and I'd already given a lot of thought to the question, "Only those the world would never miss."

Nerd pondered my answer, tapping his chin. "And it's a team decision?"

I nodded. A wave of enthusiasm warmed me when I heard him say "team."

"I can live with that."

"And the money?" I asked. His eyes regained their earlier focus as he opened a folder on the screen. A spreadsheet appeared, showing different currencies, a list of addresses, amounts. "What is that?"

"With my line of work, I don't exactly get a paycheck. Some companies pay me direct, expensing my work as a security service. That way I look legal. Even better, it's taxable. But for my other work—where there are more zeroes—I have a different kind of bank and currency. And that is also where I can help you."

"I meant, how much do you want?" I restated my

question. My eyes stayed locked on the screen's spreadsheet and numbers—his books. I hadn't even considered how to get paid. I couldn't exactly accept cash. Not safely, anyway. A paycheck was out, so what did that leave? If everything was online, was the payment online too? How would that work?

"Fifty percent," Nerd answered. Elated, I nearly jumped and grabbed Nerd, hugging him in agreement. My first business partner!

Wait, this is when you negotiate, I heard in my head. I forced myself to hide my emotion. *Agree too soon, and you'll look like an amateur.*

"Thirty percent," I countered. When he shook his head and sneered, I added, "Who's taking the risk?"

"I am," he quickly answered. "I'm setting everything up. Your entire storefront, your online profile, everything. All in advance of any actual . . . well, you know."

"And that is worth thirty percent," I said again, but it sounded like a statement instead of the question it was.

"Forty percent," Nerd offered, negotiating back. "By the time anything happens, you'll still be a bystander, but I'll be holding the bag."

I glanced at his computer screen and the spreadsheet full of numbers, then looked at the flash drive and red links—my finger itching to tickle one of them.

"And you know how to work the funds?" I asked.

"I do," he answered. "Been paying myself for over a year now."

"Agreed," I said, extending my hand.

Nervously, he took my hand and said, "You know, we've got a lot of work to do."

"So what are we waiting for?"

12

THE FAMILIAR SHOWING of sunlight through the library's western windows told me that it was time to wrap things up for the day. I never did get to click one of the yellow or red links, abiding by Nerd's request.

"Let me finish your profile first," he'd asked me, nearly pleading. I listened.

"My profile," I mumbled. An online profile, establishing me as a murderer for hire. Just the thought of progress made me feel good. It wouldn't be long now. I felt that I'd finally stoked an old fire, turned the embers, readied them for a red-hot burn. Only I didn't know who'd be the first to burn. Or how I'd do it. My mind was already filling with new Killing Katie designs.

Nerd had a good point about the risk. As of now, he

held all the risk while I had done nothing illegal. I'd merely visited a library. I'd even forgotten about the flash drive. I felt stupid and careless when he grabbed it from the computer, yanking it from the port and handing it to me. He gave me an annoyed wink and motioned to my purse, where I stuffed it away—safely pushing it down into one of the bottom liner pockets.

Was 40 percent worth the risk to him? Was he making enough? Was he safe?

This last question hit me like a bullet. If I ever suspected that his participation was a ploy or trap—a sting, as he'd called it earlier—the obvious question would have to be: could I kill him?

I stopped what I was doing and slung my coat half off my shoulder. What I saw in him was the same boyish charm that reminded me of my son. Innocence and naïveté.

Looks can be deceiving. Very deceiving.

But there was something else. I liked him. And now I wanted to work with him.

Could I kill Nerd?

"Yes, I could," I whispered, answering my own question while nodding a quick thank-you for the day's help. As a killer, I knew that I had a different makeup, a different psyche—something that made the act of murder seem trivial. I suppose I should feel disappointed, but then I wouldn't be here. I wouldn't have an opportunity to help my family and give Steve a law degree.

With Steve's mother at home and taking care of the kids, I didn't feel rushed or pressured to lie. They all thought that I was out researching what I wanted the next chapter of my life to be. Maybe they weren't thinking that deep, but a new job and a paycheck would come of my efforts. I loved my family life, but after a dozen years of staying home, something new would be a thrill. Adding murder to the job description was gravy.

I said good-bye to the librarian but she only raised her hand, too occupied with her phone to bother with anything more. I opened the set of metal outer doors, taking a step outside the library. I surveyed the traffic. Rows of headlights crawled like a fluorescent sludge—the day was ending again, and everyone wanted to be somewhere else. But tonight, I'd leave my phone in my purse and enjoy some classic rock while thinking about designs.

Nerd stayed back, wanting to finish a few things. That was fine with me. He was younger and had more energy. A glass of wine and a hot bubble bath waited for me at home. The smell of autumn mums, freshly planted along the walk, encouraged me to descend the steps. I eased down to the sidewalk as if floating. What a successful day.

"You!" I heard as I moved along the street. I stopped to look around. "You, there. Have a phone? Can you help me?" I'd already walked a few minutes, leaving the heaviest congestion behind me. I could see my car up ahead, under the dim light of a street lamp.

"Where are you?" I asked. My voice sounded thin and uncertain. I cleared my throat and searched. I twirled back around to face the library's building and watched as the traffic on Main Street spilled onto Springdale Road. Most of the traffic turned onto Springdale, which led to the interstate that ran back into the city. A few cars remained going straight, blinding me as they passed. I squinted, raising my hand to shield my eyes. The street was empty save for a few parked cars near mine. After Springdale there were a few small businesses, private offices, and Romeo's Café. I glanced over to where Katie and I had eaten the day before, but there was nobody outside. Even in the warmer night, the tables stayed empty and the chairs had been turned over, giving the patio eatery the look of a graveyard.

"Over here!" I heard a man's raspy voice say from my left, louder now. I followed it. "I'm over here. Help me, please."

"One second," I told him, shouting out in no particular direction. I took my cell phone out of my purse and turned on the screen to use as a flashlight.

Faded blue light revealed the broken sidewalk in front of me—crabgrass sprouted from between stony cracks. I followed the voice, which made a painful-sounding groan. To the left, an alley lay between the buildings—too narrow for a car, but wide enough to walk through. I peered into the darkness. Large trash bins were stacked against one building. On the other side, I found the source of the voice. Folded over like a sack, a man reached out with his hand and waved for me. And even from where I stood, I could see his legs tucked beneath him.

Was he wearing a suit?

The faint light wasn't enough for me to be sure, but I wondered if maybe he was a businessman who'd been mugged and left for dead.

I considered calling an ambulance but lost the thought as I reacted to another cry. When I knelt down to check for blood or injuries, the man's gray face peered up at me, offering a toothless grin that creased his cheeks and made his weepy eyes squint. I did see a business suit after all, or the remains of one—gray and black pinstripes, but ragged and torn and soiled with years of dirt. The man wore the too-large suit jacket like a robe. One time, long ago, he might have been a businessman, but the man staring up at me was clearly desolate.

"What's wrong?" I asked, choking from the stench

of urine and alcohol. The acrid smell was overwhelming so I leaned away from him, covering my mouth and nose and trying not to gag. From the clothes, it appeared he was homeless. Could have been eighty, but might have only been in his forties—it was hard to tell. I gagged again, finding a bottle next to him, wrapped in a twisted brown paper bag.

He grunted.

"Had yourself enough before falling down?" I asked him. He continued staring, a smile parting his lips to show me a few of his remaining teeth. "How about we get you back on your feet?"

"Aren't you a pretty one?" he said, reaching up to caress my hair.

"Yeah, I'm a pretty one," I answered politely even as I moved away from his reach. "Are you hurt? Can you stand?"

"So pretty . . ." he repeated. "Too pretty to be out at night, 'specially in the dark."

The man's tone changed, giving me a reason to pause. A sudden alarming urge came over me. A primal need to escape danger, to run. In the dim light, I never saw his other hand. My head lurched to one side, sending a painful jolt through my neck and into my skull. The homeless man grabbed my hair, yanking my head forward in a snap until my hands fell to my sides. A sharp bolt of lightning echoed through my spine, sending a tingle of pins and needles into my arms and legs. I tumbled over, unable to catch myself. The alley's stony asphalt cut into my hands and arms as I tried to regain my balance.

It's a mistake, I told myself, not realizing what was happening. *He's just drunk . . . amorous . . . trying to cop a quick feel before I slap him, that's what it is.*

The man was up on his knees, and his body positioning over mine. A cloud of his stench enveloped me. He clutched one of my breasts, squeezing violently until it hurt. When he tried wrestling me onto my back, I fought, surging upward until I was on my knees. But I didn't move after that—he made sure of it. My body went rigid when I felt a sliver of cool metal pierce my neck. I straightened then, resting on my legs, gasping.

"What are you doing?" I asked, struggling, my lungs cramping as I tried to stand. He had a fistful of my hair and jerked his arm down, forcing the blade into my neck. If he moved just a little more, I was certain the knife would cut me open.

"Now, now," he answered. "This won't take long . . . been a few days. Been storing it up, you might say." He pawed at my crotch, clutching hard enough for me to feel his fingers. I felt sick and disgusted by the thought of him inside me. But I wasn't afraid—and maybe that was also something different about me. Fear. I didn't feel it. Not like the way my friends described it or how it was portrayed in the movies, anyway. I did, however, feel utter revulsion at the thought of what was going to happen. My stomach turned and I wanted to vomit. I searched the man's creased face, looking for an opportunity. Any opportunity. Maybe I could launch myself at him, grabbing onto his face with my teeth, rip his nose off in one putrid chunk? But he'd only need to push the knife a little harder to cut me open. By now the blade had warmed and blood oozed from beneath it, running like a tear onto the collar of my blouse.

He sneered, licking his lips as his eyes wandered. I kept my head still but was able to glance at the light on Main Street. The sidewalk where I had been walking stayed empty and still, like a painting: no passing cars, no pedestrians. And we were too far from the street for anyone to see us, unless they were looking on purpose. Set back in the dark, he could cut me open before I ever had a chance to scream.

"Be careful around the library," Steve had warned.

I thought of the Road Runner cartoon and the plate of birdseed the Coyote put out as bait—a Free Bird Seed sign sitting above the trap. The only difference? The homeless man didn't paint a sign to trick me. He'd only needed to yell for help. I cringed.

How could I be so stupid as to fall for a ploy as lame as calling for help? Was this what happened to the young girl I heard about on the radio? Did she fall for the same trap? Did the homeless man know that she'd lived through his attack?

The pressure of his knife lifted. Not a lot, but enough to let me feel cool air on the small cut he'd given me. He eased away from my neck as he let go of my hair. With his hand free, he shifted to grope elsewhere and plunged it beneath my blouse. The brick wall behind him was old but strong, with sharp pieces jutting from between the mortar. When he moved the knife, I took my chance. I hit him with everything I had. He never should have let me get to my knees, get leverage. I found the strength I needed in my legs and pushed my entire body upward in one heave, smashing the back of his head against the wall. The knife cut deeper into my neck for a moment, but fell instantly. I followed the sound of the blade as it clinked onto the alley's pavement.

I felt winded, but managed to scurry for the knife and pick it up. The homeless man slumped over in a tidy squat: face down and motionless. I swiped away the cool, slippery wet that came from the cut on my neck.

Not too bad, I thought and ignored it.

"Sit up," I demanded. I knelt across from him, bringing the knife forward, pointing it like a sword. The knife's handle was a mix of tape and old clothing, wound together in a messy grip. I clutched the handle, turning the blade so that the street lamp's light glinted off the blade. It was mottled with pitted rust, but the edge was clean and sharp. Curious, I teased the blade with my thumb, running the edge over my skin to see how sharp it was. At once my skin parted, dropping blood like an errant tear.

"Bitch," he groaned. I shuffled forward, pushing the blade beneath the man's chin. I flicked it once to cut his chin. "Fucking bitch!"

"Is that what you said to the young girl the other night?" I asked. "My husband's a cop, you know, and I think he'd be interested in talking to you about what you've been doing."

"You bitches deserve it," he answered, spitting as he spoke. "You all deserve it. And don't matter. Few hours, I'll be back on the street." He shoved his hand behind his head, and I jumped back, cautious. But I wasn't afraid. Instead, I was anxious and excited. I was breathing hard and stars raced in front of me.

"The world won't miss you," I mumbled with an understanding, a realization. I was ready to begin my journey, and any thoughts of calling my husband vanished like a shadow in the sun.

"Fuck you say?"

"Did the young girl deserve it?" I demanded.

He peered up at me, grinned an ugly smile. “Yeah, she deserved it. Gave it to her good too.”

My bones became electric. My arms and hands twitched. My fingers tingled and sweat beaded on my head. I felt hot too—implacably hot, thinking I’d pass out if I didn’t calm myself.

It’s the adrenaline, I thought, realizing it was hitting me like an overdose.

I pivoted the blade over his neck, pressing harder. My heart thumped frantically and hard enough to hurt. This was my fantasy and it was coming true. His eyes were fixed on me, still cloudy and dazed from the hit, but I could see the curiosity in them as he wondered why I hadn’t called the police yet.

I didn’t hesitate. My body pulsed, encouraging me, and I lurched forward, plummeting my knee into the man’s chest. The air in his lungs rocketed out of him until there was nothing left but a dry wheeze.

“Plea—,” he tried to say. I eased up and let him take a sip of air. “I think I’m having a heart attack.” I lurched again, and his mouth fell open in a silent scream.

“The world won’t miss you,” I told him, making sure he heard me. His eyes became huge, like a full moon on the blackest of autumn nights. I slipped the blade into his neck. Just the tip at first—in and out—tentatively, reserved. My courage grew then, as did my strength. And I pushed. The man’s eyes thinned a nightmarish squint. His mouth opened and stretched wide in a soundless scream. He squirmed, arching his back, fighting to stay alive. I put all of my weight into my knee, nailing him against the wall with such force that I felt something break inside his chest.

Not so fast, I told myself.

I tried to slow down, tried to make it last. But I was ready. I'd waited long enough. I plunged the knife in until it sunk to the handle. I slowed when I saw bright red spilling over the blade and ease into a smooth rhythm.

"Fuck you," he tried to say, gargling his words as his mouth filled and spat a pink mist. When I brought the knife back out, blood sprayed with a whooshing sound. It splashed against the bricks, nearly hitting me.

"Fuck you too," I said, leaning away to avoid the bright flow. The spraying pulsed once more and then became shallow. I slipped the knife in and out again, sawing until I thought everything vital to his miserable life must have been severed. His eyes stayed fixed on me—wide and filled with the shock. The metal, wet smell was stronger than I'd expected. Hot and thick. It caused me to gasp as the power of it curled up the back of my throat. I could taste it.

I was weak and sweaty, but I felt more alive than I'd ever felt in my life. By the time I looked up, the silent screaming and the terrified eyes were gone. His head had slumped to the right and I saw the extent of how much I'd cut. The blood had stopped spraying, had stopped boiling.

The dead don't bleed, I thought as I wiped some of the sticky wet from my hands against his clothes. I stared at my first murder victim for a long time, admiring the deed. Proud. I'd rid the world of a bad man and stayed until I felt I didn't have to stay any longer.

My hands stayed sticky, his blood drying on them. I tried wiping them against the gravelly pavement, but it didn't help.

"Bottle of water or wipes would be better," I mumbled, fixing a mental reminder for when I'd do this again. As my heart eased into a normal rhythm, I finally felt what I should have felt when the man first attacked me: afraid.

A whole new sensation took over my body. From the top of my head to the tips of my toes, a frightening and overwhelming sense of being caught filled me, capturing me. My hands grew clammy and my lips trembled at the thought of being convicted and sent to prison. It wasn't just the thought of living behind bars that scared me—it was losing Snacks and Michael and the love of my life, Steve.

I gripped a handful of small stones, spitting onto them with every last drop I had in my dry mouth. I squeezed my hands around the tiny pebbles until my knuckles hurt. I cringed at the pain. I used the stones like a rough sponge, to wipe my hands clean. I threw the handful of stones down the alley. The small rocks skittered and bounced over the pavement like pattering feet—thrown far and wide, spreading and eliminating any possible collection of evidence.

When I stood up, my head felt as heavy as if I'd been drinking. A glint of light from below drew my eyes toward it. The knife lay waiting, ready to be taken from the scene and not left behind. Surely my fingerprints couldn't be dusted for—not here, and certainly not on that handful of pebbles or against the wall. I grabbed a piece of crumpled newspaper from the garbage bin behind me, wiping my hands on it some more, and wrapped the knife before stuffing it into my purse.

I gave the homeless man one last look before leaving the alley. From the sidewalk, it looked like he was sitting in the same frozen position as when he'd first called out to me, supposedly seeking help. I guess he didn't know that it was *me* he'd be helping.

13

MY CAR FELT damp and cold, as if I'd left a window open during the night. And no matter how far into the red I threw the thermostat's needle, I couldn't seem to warm up. I sighed. Tears of exhaustion pricked my eyes. I was crashing. Only this wasn't like the crashes I'd experienced drawing up the Killing Katie designs. I'd hit a new high. I'd committed murder.

I drove away from the library and the alley, keeping my purse tucked beneath my arm. My hand slipped inside, touched the blade I had used to open the man's neck. A fluttery lift came into me, giving me enough of a titillation to continue. Neshaminy Creek lay between my home and our small town. But it was a creek by name only—it was easily wide enough to be considered a river. My headlights closed in on the approach to the bridge. I slowed when reaching the apex of the span, knowing that I'd have to get rid of the knife. With no other traffic around me, I stopped my car and rolled the window down. Moist air came inside, along with the sound of rushing water. I held my prize, the evidence, another minute. The knife was my first trophy and I didn't want to let it go.

My rearview mirror stayed empty, and the road ahead showed only a possum or raccoon crossing the blacktop. Beady eyes flashed in my car's headlights before scurrying off the road. The newspaper was soaked through with blood and had already begun to dry. I quickly unpacked the knife, then held it in front of me for longer than I should have. I turned it over, finding it to be as miserable-looking as the one who'd brandished it. But it was my first weapon, so I brought it up to my lips, feathering it with a kiss before throwing it over the bridge. I held my breath and waited until I heard a splash—just a subtle sound, like my toes dipping into a warm bath. I was ready to go home. The newspaper followed the knife's trajectory until I saw the wind catch it, taking it beneath the bridge, where I'm sure it disappeared forever.

Steve welcomed me home, excitement in his tone, asking how I'd made out in town. He wanted to know if

I'd found what it was that I wanted to do. But when I entered the kitchen, his face emptied and his color paled.

"What happened to you?" he asked, rushing around the counter. "Amy?"

"What? Just fell is all," I said, shaking my head. "Why are you making such a fuss?"

"Babe, your neck. And your clothes," he answered, lowering his voice, trying not to scare the kids. "What happened?"

"I fell," I repeated, my words solemn as I quickly glanced down at my blouse. I had avoided the blood's main spray, but had I avoided all of it?

"Mom, take the kids downstairs," Steve instructed. There was a quaver in his voice as he spoke. And from the corner of my eye, I saw Steve's mother pick up Snacks and lead Michael out of the kitchen.

I shook my head, raising my hands. "I'm fine. I tripped leaving the library and fell down the steps."

"Looks like you caught something on the way," he said, leaning in to look at my neck. "Have you seen this?" I stepped around the counter to face the oven door and lifted my chin in order to see my reflection in the glass. The blade had run around the front of my throat.

Had the homeless man really held me long enough to do that?

In my mind, the attack seemed to begin and end in a moment. A blink, a struggle, and then he was dead.

Maybe I'd let him hold me, cut me, leading him to think that he'd had control over me. Had I set a trap?

I glanced above my head, looking for the imaginary Wile E. Coyote sign that read Free Bird Seed, and then began to laugh uncontrollably. Only my laughing sounded like hysteria. The fatigue was beginning to surface like lava from a volcano.

"What's wrong with mommy?" Snacks cried. "Is mommy okay?"

"Mom," Steve said again. "Please!"

I must've appeared frightful to my baby girl—an out-of-control crazy she-monster. But I couldn't help myself. I laughed harder. "I'm so sorry," I said, but I knew it didn't sound sincere. "It was such a nasty spill. I feel so foolish about it." Steve's arms were suddenly upon me, carefully easing me around to face him. He kept his hands just above my clothes, the tips of his fingers barely brushing over me. He gently touched my clothes and inspected my skinned knees. I realized that he must have suspected that I'd been raped. I searched for the kids and his mother, but she'd already led them away.

"I think you might need a doctor," he said, sounding grave. "Babe, I think you might need a hospital."

"Don't be ridiculous," I told him. I wasn't laughing anymore. I knew I had to be careful. He continued to look me over, recreating in his mind a scene of what he believed had happened. "Let me save you the time," I said. "I was alone, coming out of the library, and I fell."

"You're sure?" he asked. I nodded as he put his hand inside my jacket and began to feel my ribs. His fingers tickled and I jumped at the touch of them.

"Hey there, mister," I said, pulling his hands in front of me. "Not without a few drinks first." I winked, but he didn't smile. Instead he dove into my jacket with his other hand, checking my side.

"Show me your eyes," he told me. "Let me check and see if you hit your head."

"Seriously?" I demanded, growing annoyed. "I'm fine, okay?" He stood without any expression, waiting. I obliged and looked up into his face, opening my eyes until he was satisfied.

"What's this?" I heard him say. He took some of my hair into his fingers. I let out a short cry when he tugged it: my scalp hurt terribly from where my hair had been yanked. "Sorry about that, babe."

"What is it?" I asked. A sense of dread washed over me when I saw the brown smear on his fingertips. Dried blood, flaking and smudgy. It wasn't mine, but I'd have to make it sound like it was mine. I had to convince Steve that it *was* mine. Where could it have come from, though?

"Gross. Must have gotten some blood in my hair," I answered, taking his hand in mine and quickly wiping them until the brown flecks were gone. "Scratch on my neck must have bled a little. Not a lot, but enough."

"And your blouse?" he asked, pointing down.

"What about my blouse?" I followed his eyes, knowing that I'd checked it over when I had first gotten in my car.

Or had I?

Again, I felt the pressure in my lungs. I expected to see more blood—a large stain of crimson brown, clotting and drying stiff, smelling rank. But I didn't find anything alarming. What I found was my blouse, creamy white and without a single spot of red. It wasn't the homeless man's profuse bleeding that I'd carried into my home, it was the evidence of his hand pawing at my breast. Two buttons were missing from the middle of the blouse, and a small tear along the hem left the satiny material hanging like a short necktie.

How did I miss that?

"Oh, that," I answered, sounding as though it was nothing. "This is an easy fix. I'll take it to the tailor this week." Steve remained concerned, but then gave me a hug and said he was sorry that I'd been hurt. The gesture was sweet and unexpected and warming.

While I told him thank you, my mind was already upstairs, imagining my legs dipping into the bubbly wet of a hot bath. I wanted a glass of wine. I wanted to rest. I *needed* to rest. As I broke away from the hug and made my way to the stairs, Steve added, "You'll still be able to go in a half hour?" I stopped at the bottom of the staircase and leaned over the rail, disappointment souring my plans. Steve turned to finish making dinner for the kids, but stopped when I didn't answer him.

"I can be ready," I answered, but had no recollection of our having made any plans.

"I'm sorry," he said. "I'm being selfish. If you're not up for it, that's fine. It's just Romeo's for a few drinks and dinner. My boss will understand."

Lightbulbs flashed—a thousand watts—blinding and searing. I'd completely forgotten about the dinner with his boss. Charlie Dawson and his wife were at least two decades older than we were, and as Steve's boss, he was finally moving on to a new role: less detective work and more house work. Retirement. Charlie had just one name on his list of who it should be to fill his shoes. Steve. Tonight was the traditional couple's dinner—a pastime at their station for nearly a century.

"What, and miss your big dinner with Charlie?" I answered, trying to sound enthusiastic. He shot an *"Are you sure?"* look at me, and then waited. I went to him, pulling him close. "I'm so proud of you. Do you know that?" His expression immediately changed to one of boyish pride. Adorable.

"Thanks, babe," he answered as he patted my ass. "I'm glad you're okay and that you're up to going."

"I might be up for even more later," I quickly added, winking and hoping a hot shower in place of my planned bath would magically revitalize me.

I made my way to our room and then the shower, doing so in a daze and emptying my mind. The steamy water rained over me, washing away any leftovers from the homeless man and what I'd done to him. I stayed in the shower for as long as I could, enjoying the run of hot water as it pelted against my chest and neck and back. At one point, I could have laid down right there and gone to sleep.

"Fifteen minutes!" Steve called out, rapping his hand against the door. By the time I met him in our foyer, nobody would be the wiser to what I'd gone through earlier in the evening.

When I came down, Steve's gaped-mouth told me that I looked as stunning as I thought. He gave me a whistle and put his hand above my head, encouraging me to spin around for him. I did so, kicking up my high heels so that my skirt rode up my thigh.

"You look amazing."

"Delicious enough to eat?" I teased, licking my lips.

Steve said nothing, smacking his lips instead, before motioning behind me. The kids and Steve's mom saw us off, but not before I made sure they knew that I was fine.

14

I HADN'T CONSIDERED the drive back to Romeo's. I hadn't considered the bridge over Neshaminy Creek and the knife I'd thrown into the water, hiding what I'd done. The threat of being caught caused a fresh ripple of nerves. My teeth chattered. I tried to control my emotion, but shivered whenever I clenched to stop the noise. Gooseflesh rose on my arms too, and my nipples became firm, the outlines showing prominently through the front of my dress.

"Charlie is really going to be happy when he sees you," Steve joked, taking my hand and lifting a finger to touch the front of my dress. "Cold?"

"These aren't for him," I answered. Then I added, "I'll be fine." I'd brought a shawl, knowing the evening would be chilly, and threw it over my shoulders.

When we drove to the peak of the bridge's deck, I

peered over. My body stiffened, and I clutched my seat when I saw the glint of the knife.

But that's impossible, I told myself. *It's too dark and we're up too high.*

My nerves were playing with me. More flashes of light came then—the moon's reflection breaking on the water. I sighed and distantly wondered if the creek's water would wash away the blood, wash away my sin.

As we entered into the center of town, I saw the first indication that the murder had been discovered. Soft flashes of red and blue blanketed the trees and cut harsh wedges into the road. The car's headlights washed the colors away for a moment, but then more light came from behind us. Police cars drove around us and pulled Steve's attention like a scurrying mouse before a cat.

"I wonder what's going on over there?" Steve asked as we pulled up to Romeo's.

"Where?" I answered, playing along as though unaware of what lay in the dark alley.

"Across the street, a block or so down," he answered. "Didn't you see the patrols?"

I had. The patrol cars straddled the road and sidewalk, blocking the entrance to the alley. A tornado began to swirl in my mind, throwing visions of the homeless man's body on a gurney and handcuffs around my wrists and being guided into the backseat of a squad car.

Play it cool, I told myself, trying to calm my nerves. *You're not practicing anymore.*

"Sure did," I answered in a flat tone, remaining unemotional. I leaned toward Steve, distracting him by pointing to Romeo's. "Look. A parking spot in front of the restaurant. See if you can grab it."

"I should probably stop over there and see what's going on," Steve said, turning the steering wheel around. I chewed on my lip and tried to ignore the fluttering in my belly. The car rolled into the parking space.

"Nice fit too," he said. "Good eyes."

"Want to go inside first?" I asked. "We can get our table, then meet up with Charlie and Vickie, maybe order some drinks?" But Steve's eyes were locked on the waves of blue and red lights circling atop the patrol cars. A parade of uniformed officers made their way in and out of the alley. Some came out empty-handed. Others did not.

Even in the faint light of the street lamps, I could see the library door open. Nerd stepped out. My heart seized and I stopped breathing. Nerd shrugged his shoulders, shifting his denim jacket up against the chilly air. Instinctively, I slowly lowered myself, sliding down in my seat until my eyes were just above the headrest.

"Looks like Charlie beat me to it," Steve said, opening his car door. "Vickie is still in their car. Why don't you two go inside and get started without us?" I heard Steve, but couldn't stop watching Nerd. When he saw the activity around the alley, he stayed on the street, clearly choosing to avoid the police.

"How long will you be?" I asked, setting a tone in my voice to make sure he knew that I was annoyed as well as concerned.

"Long?" Steve waved to Charlie, who'd already motioned to him. He leaned back into the car so I could see him roll his eyes. Then he fixed his features in an apologetic expression that was familiar. It was his way of saying he had no idea how long they'd be. I knew it would be a very long night. Over the years, I'd come to loathe that look.

"It looks like they've got something already," he began as he slipped on a pair of latex gloves with a rehearsed snap. I hadn't realized he kept the gloves in the car, but the idea of them being available was interesting to note. "We might be a while. You know what I like. Could you order it for me?"

"So you won't be long?" I said, needling. Over his shoulder, I could see another officer walk out of the alley. The chills returned and my teeth chattered. I lifted the front of my dress.

The buttons! I realized with a startle.

I flattened myself against the car seat, trying desperately to think of where the buttons from my blouse had gone.

Had the homeless man been clutching the front of my blouse when I killed him?

I imagined them wrapped up in his death grip. A portly officer stepped into the thin light—an evidence bag hung from his grubby hands. Did I see buttons in there? I could have died. "Can you get a ride home?" I forced myself to ask.

Steve stepped back, shaking his head, "Babe, we might not be that long. Are you sure you don't want to wait?"

"No, no, that's okay," I interrupted. "I'll fix myself something at home. See you after you're done here." As I finished talking, I heard Charlie call out Steve's name. I watched as his wife drove away. She flashed me a quick look that said, "Oh well, that's what you get when you marry a cop." She put her hand out of the window and gave us a quick wave.

Steve waved and turned around, his loafers crushing a stone with a loud noise. "I guess that answers that," he said with a heavy sigh.

"What do you mean?"

"Charlie is sending Vickie home. They must have found something significant." For a moment, all I could see were the empty screams—the homeless man's mouth hanging open and his eyes staring wide and looking like two creamy, white buttons that had once been sewn to my blouse.

"I'll see you at home, then?" I managed to get out just as Nerd crossed the street in front of the library. Go the other way, I wanted to yell.

Had he seen me?

He didn't know Steve or the car we drove, but he'd recognize me in a minute if I stayed where I was. I jumped over the center console and moved the driver's seat up so that I could reach the car pedals. Steve cleared me by a foot, so I came only up to his shoulders; that worked out great most of the time, but not so much at other times. Case in point: our car.

"Love you, babe," I said and closed the car door, forcing Steve to jump out of the way.

"Well, okay," he said, a hurt in his eyes from having read my urgency as being directed at him. "You understand, don't you?"

"Oh, I'm fine," I answered, pushing up through the car's window to reach him. "Kisses."

Steve dipped his broad shoulders below the window and set his lips onto mine. He tried to be a little romantic, touching my face, turning his head sensually. I appreciated it, but I was in a rush to get out of there. I peered into the side mirror, behind the car, to try and find Nerd. I couldn't see him, which eased my nerves.

We finished our sloppy kiss and I moved back in front of the steering wheel. As I backed up to pull out of the parking spot, Nerd appeared in the side mirror. He saw me. Nerd stopped at his car—keys frozen in his hand. He didn't move, didn't motion toward me. He did nothing. We locked eyes in the mirror. Then I heard Steve's voice.

"Hey. You!" he called to Nerd. I slipped out of the parking space, squealing the tires. I headed back toward the bridge. I watched through the rearview mirror as Steve urged Nerd to come over to him. He wanted to question him. While that was a standard practice, Nerd would certainly find out that my husband was a police detective.

I put everything out of my mind and entered our home as if everything were normal. I told Steve's mom about the dinner being canceled on account of something happening across from Romeo's.

"Could be another attack," she said, shaking her head as she spoke—a gesture that I'd seen in Steve too. "I sure hope they catch that fucker!"

"Mom!" I said, taken aback by her language. She was a churchgoing woman, and we rarely heard her cuss. "Yeah, I think they'll catch the fucker." She giggled, sounding grandmotherly again, and then helped me gather up Snacks to put her down for the evening.

Our house became eerily quiet after Steve's mother left. With Snacks in bed and Michael playing on his computer, I tucked myself under the flannel blankets on our bed and closed my eyes. In the darkness I saw a veil of red, as though the sun were bleeding through my eyelids. I began to fall asleep when the smell of blood flared up in my nostrils again. There were no blue flashing lights, no police, no evidence bags—just me and the knife and the man I killed. I had plunged the knife into his neck but failed to control his hands. I grabbed my chest and felt for the buttons I knew were gone.

Before I went to bed, I'd taken the possible evidence and hidden it in the garage. Finding an old box—a temporary secret box—I stuffed my blouse away, inspecting the broken threads where the buttons had been. Tomorrow I'd take the blouse out into a field at first light and burn it under the rising sun. If there was an evidence bag containing my buttons, they'd never be able to match them up to my blouse then.

Steve eventually crawled under the blankets and cozied up next to me. How many hours had I slept? I had never heard him come home, never heard a car pull up or the sound of our front door opening. He eased his hand onto my stomach, then slid it down between my legs.

He said not a word about what they had found in the alley or what evidence had been collected. Nothing. I didn't find that alarming, since Steve often said little when it was early on in a new case.

"Where were we?" he asked, propping himself above me.

"Right here," I answered, wrapping my legs around him. I was looking at Steve then, staring into his eyes, I thrust my hips upward, inviting him. We groaned together when he entered me.

"Wait a second," I said. I quickly moved around so that I was on top, clutching the sheets and driving up and down.

"Hey babe, slow down," he said through choked grunts. But I ignored him and drove our bodies together again and again. Desire rose in me like a fever, heavy and fast, thrusting and leading us toward orgasm. "I can't—"

"I'm almost there too," I interrupted, coming with him. A shiver ran through my body and I collapsed on top of him. We stayed like that, panting, connected. I could still feel him inside me while we feathered one another with the simple kisses that meant everything to me.

"That's a nice turn," he said, planting his lips on my neck.

"What is?"

"I'm usually the one that can't hold back."

Our bodies bumped up and down in the type of quiet laugh shared between lovers. We said nothing more. I felt him slip out of me. We drifted to our designated sides of the bed, quickly falling asleep. I guessed we would have very different dreams.

15

A WOMAN'S LIPS, red and glistening. A white glow captured them in the moonlight. The image was surreal, electric, and sensual. I saw nothing else, only her parted lips against the ghostly white light. In the darkness, upholstery and thinning carpet rubbed against my legs. I tried to move, hating the feel of the shag on my bare skin.

The air was summertime humid—hot and thick—and a thin sheen of sweat covered my body. It was the time of year when crickets chirped and tree frogs sang. Only I didn't hear them tonight. I'd been sitting in the darkness a long time, huddled down behind the backseat of our car, waiting. My knees had cramped and my backside had been numb for a while. A crack above me let just enough moonlight in to touch my arm. Goose bumps rose on my skin. They had come when I heard the man's voice, when I realized that the night would end the same as before.

There were other smells too. There were always other smells. I raised my chin so that my face was closer to the window. I was being careful not to be seen beneath the jungle of metal skyscrapers towering over our car. I sniffed at the air, taking in the smell of cigarettes and oil and the heavy scent of spent rubber—the kind of rubber that comes from truck tires. And the smell of fuel was strong too. Not gasoline, but truck fuel. Diesel.

"The only kind of fuel used to drive a big rig," the man with the drinking breath had said before opening the car door.

It wouldn't be long now.

I heard a bell, the kind that rings when a car drives over a snaking black hose strewn across concrete. I heard teasing laughter too, intimate and wet with slippery kisses. I heard them moaning then, their sex sounds becoming louder.

The red lips came into view again. Eclipsed with tiny beads of sweat, her lips were pursed and readied for a kiss, but she didn't want a kiss. Not now. Instead, she placed her finger in front of her lips, resting it on the dimple at their center.

Shush, she motioned while rising up and down. I understood what she was asking me to do. I'd been as quiet as a church mouse—invisible to the men who'd come to visit, always invisible. She had another one with her now and she wanted me to come out of hiding. It was time.

My eyes snapped open, fluttering. My mind raced as confusion replaced the dream-filled images that had already begun to leave me. I never dream, but tonight I had seen something. And it wasn't the randomness of the day's sights jumbled together into a senseless story. It was something I'd seen before; it was familiar. A memory?

My skin felt wet, sweaty wet, as though Steve and I had just finished from the night before. I propped myself up onto my elbows to see over his shoulder. The alarm clock only read five fifteen. I had forty-five minutes. Steve rolled onto his back, still asleep. I closed my eyes, hoping to go back to that place where the dream might be lingering, waiting for my return. I wanted to see more, to know more.

Was I the little girl?

A snore jolted me. Another followed, and I sat up. Steve hadn't been able to sleep on his back without snoring for years now.

"Snoring," I muttered, sounding frustrated. I

nudged his shoulder until he rolled over in the other direction. I tried to find that place one more time by closing my eyes, slipping back into the gray light of early morning.

16

THERE'D BE NO more dreams for me that morning—only the broken torture of waking up and falling back to sleep, again and again. The torment lasted another hour before I had to start my day along with the rest of the house. Steve said nothing about the alley or what was found there. And to my surprise, the news broadcaster's raspy voice made no mention of it either. Somehow the police had been able to keep the crime—keep what *I'd* done—out of the news. But our small town had a voracious appetite for gossip, and it wouldn't be long before there was talk of another attack. Within a few days, I'd surely wake to the radio broadcaster reporting on it.

I parked my car just around the corner from Romeo's and watched the alley across the street. A throb came to me, a yearning for more.

Could I be hungry already? Was that how this was going to work? Are murderers like vampires, taking a sip, gulping a drink, killing whenever the need set fire to my gut? Maybe killing the homeless man turned me last night.

I'd certainly lost my innocence, my virginity. I was becoming who I was meant to be. A monster.

I exhaled, spilling a puff of white air like a smoky drag off a joint. I smirked, an evocative sense of nostalgia hitting me. Back in my college days, I'd experimented more than most—and regretted none of it. I tried to puff out a smoke ring, forcing a short breath. Disappointingly, it just disappeared into a white mist. Oh well, I'd made my share of smoke rings. It was in college that I'd learned to smoke weed, roll a tight joint, blow a man, and make a woman come. Yes, I'd learned a thing or two in college.

Money well spent. I shook my head, thinking back to how reckless I'd been while searching and trying to find the person I wanted to be. Steve found me before I found myself. It had only been a matter of time before I caught up, though, falling in love with him. With *us*. And now I'd jeopardized all that.

"What if he gets assigned the case?" I muttered, then realized it might be for the better. Images from his case folders flashed through my mind. "I'd have access to those. All of them."

A knock rapped on my car window and startled

me, popping my contemplative bubble. I nearly screamed. Nerd stood outside my car, his skin gray and his eyes glaring. He rapped his gloved hand on the glass again and pointed toward the library. He didn't say a word or wait for me, choosing instead to walk ahead. The memory of the previous night's red and blue colors flashing around the car came back to me. It was better that we had no contact outside of the library.

I gathered my things together and got out of the car, crossing the street toward the library. I kept my head down and stayed to the right. The sidewalk was crumpled and old, with large, stony blocks pushed up by the roots of huge sycamores lining the curb. I didn't remember seeing any of that the night before. I watched my step, jumping over the thick cracks and avoiding the sprouting weeds that had already begun to brown in the colder temperatures. I paused just long enough to face the alley and scan the ground. I saw nothing resembling the buttons from my blouse. A gusty breeze caused a knot of tree branches to clack together, telling me I'd already overstayed. As far as I could tell, my buttons weren't there.

Anxious nerves dampened my upper lip. I heaved a disappointed sigh and watched as a heavy cloud rushed out of me. "Could've gotten a ring from that one," I joked to myself, swiping at the irritation beneath my nose. At once, I smelled charred fabric on my fingers. While the buttons might have been found by the police, my favorite blouse had disappeared earlier that morning in a quick spark followed by a vapid blue flame.

But what else could be found on my buttons? A fingerprint?

I plunged my hand into my purse and dug out a small bottle of sanitizer, squeezing out an extra-large glob to help mask the cindery odor.

The steps leading to the library doors seemed steeper and longer than they had the day before. They played tricks on my mind as I climbed them. My legs and arms ached, hurting as though I'd stayed too long my first day back in the gym. I was exhausted and scared and nervous all at once, and wondered if I should have stayed home, stayed away from the crime scene. I felt a cool pinch in my lungs, and clung to the round metal handrail. The older librarian suddenly appeared through the door's small rectangular window. She saw me standing there and gave me a quick wave.

"Shit," I muttered, trying to find the energy and the confidence to lie my way past her.

Before I knew it, I was standing in front of her, telling her how much I admired her black, squarish glasses.

"Really?" she said, adjusting them, straightening them. On some level, I appreciated that. I couldn't stand when a person paid no mind to their glasses—leaving them to sit crooked on their nose. "Just a pair from the Sears optical department. But they're a lifesaver, you know. And how is the job search going?"

"Oh, it's going. Taking some time, but you know how it can be," I answered as I watched her eyes fall to my purse as if expecting me to pull out my identification. I glanced over and saw Nerd at his computer. I made a mental note to ask him about what identification he'd been using. "By the way, any chance that the library is looking to hire anyone? Maybe something part time?" The librarian quickly stepped back and made herself busy. I watched as her expression changed. I'd somehow made her uncomfortable, almost surprised—as if I'd just asked how old she was when she lost her virginity.

"Well, I don't know," she began. Then she hurried a stack of books into her hands, ensuring her eyes didn't meet mine. "You see, we just hired a new librarian. Still learning and working toward her degree. But she fills the hours needed and does a decent job . . . some nights. Good luck in your searches today. Hope you find something." And just as quick as I'd asked, the old librarian moved on and let me move on too.

"We have to talk, Amelia," Nerd blurted as soon as I

circled around the computer table. "Or should I say Mrs. Sholes, wife of Detective Steve Sholes? Please tell me that wasn't your husband questioning me last night."

I gulped at the air, speechless. The truth was, my mind had been so occupied with what I'd done and the loss of my buttons, I'd completely forgotten that Steve had talked to Nerd. I said nothing as I settled my things and sat down in front of the computer. When I turned back to answer, I saw the large gray pouches he was carrying under his eyes, his half-tucked shirt, and the dread in his expression. Even his shoes were a mess—he was wearing one Nike and one Chuck Taylor.

"What's going on?" I asked.

"Really? That's what you're going to start with? How about: I have no idea who that police detective was!" He was trying to sound comical, but his inflections remained nerdy.

"So what if he's my husband?" I answered snidely. Immediately, I regretted my tone. Nerd went green. I mean, the boy actually turned green and slumped over to puke. "Listen, it doesn't matter. I don't understand what the problem is. If anything, it will help."

Nerd bolted up, and a part of me was glad to see color come back into his cheeks. "The problem?" he exclaimed, shaking his head back and forth. "The *problem* is that your husband is a cop and I've already given you enough to have me put away. What if he finds my flash drive?"

"He barely uses the computer at home," I said jokingly, stretching the truth a bit. "Listen to me. Steve isn't interested in your flash drive or whatever you're doing in this library."

"So what happens when—"

"Our business begins?" I finished for him. He nodded, listening, breathing easier, the color in his face continuing to return. "Simple. We don't get caught."

"Yeah. Simple," he countered. And again, he tried to sound snarky and comical, but only came off as sounding nerdy. "We weren't exactly going to advertise our business anyway, but you're sleeping with the enemy."

I didn't like to think of Steve as the enemy, but I could see how it must look from Nerd's perspective, so I let it pass. "And isn't it better to be close? Close enough to listen to him, to read his case notes, to keep my finger on the pulse of the investigations?"

Nerd sat back. I'd given him a lot to consider. "I suppose," he answered, deciding I was right. "I never thought about it that way. So you've got all this figured out?" Nerd managed to squash my enthusiasm with a single question. I sighed, wishing that I had, but shrugged my shoulders. "Not all of it, but some. Enough for us to get started."

"Speaking of which, before we can get started," he said, "I need to feel like we're making some progress."

"First tell me what the questioning was about?"

Nerd glanced over, a brief glimpse of surprise in his expression. "You mean you don't know? What about your finger and the pulse thing?"

I shook my head, "Doesn't work quite like that. I'm sure I'll find out later today anyway; I'm just curious about what he said last night."

"Some old geezer bought it," he began. "The cops—your husband included—passed me around, asking questions for an hour. What annoyed me, though, was how they asked the same freaking questions, over and over. Had I seen anything? What time did I arrive? Was I alone? Blah, blah, and blah."

"Old geezer?" I asked, wanting to hear more. A touch of heat rose up from beneath my collar. I gently grazed at the side of my neck with my fingers. "Dead?"

"Best they can tell, it was a fight over booze. You know, with all the homeless around. Two of 'em fought it out, one killed the other and took off with a bottle and whatever money he had."

"Sounds simple enough," I said. My throat felt scratchy and dry. I opened my water bottle and chugged a mouthful to settle the itch.

"But I overheard two of the officers talking. I wasn't supposed to hear anything, but they mentioned that the geezer was holding onto something. Had a death grip on it, one of them joked."

"Is that so?" I said, but my voice had thinned and fell to a shuddering whimper.

"Probably nothing," he finished. But then he turned and looked at me, and there was concern in his eyes. Panic had suddenly struck me. It stole my ability to think or speak or breathe. All I could see in front of me were buttons. Two creamy, white buttons.

17

WHEN MURDER FOR hire is summarized in a list of forum posts, perspectives change. They change a lot. I could have been reading a hot news story, breaking news about a Hollywood star, juicy drunk and hanging sloppy in the front. But instead, murder had suddenly been conveyed in a simple set of links—characters and lines of text, a deadly proposition merely a click away. Was murder really that simple? *Should* it be that simple? I brushed my hands over the keyboard, feathering the alphabet, tempting the power it gave. Death from a handgun comes with the pull of a trigger. My trigger? A keyboard and a mouse.

"That's right," Nerd said, motioning to one of the red links. "Go ahead."

"Just click?" I asked, trying to contain the

excitement in my voice. My finger twitched on the mouse as a hollow flutter thumped in my gut. "And then what?"

"Nothing," he answered. I hesitated, still feeling new to the online shopping, so to speak. I glanced at the flash drive to make sure it was seated correctly and wouldn't fall out. After that, I moved the window on the screen, making room to the right of it for whatever might pop up. I was stalling. "Go ahead, already. You'll know you're there when you see it."

"All right!" I said, blowing out any hesitations. "Let's see what this one is." A click and the link opened up a new window listing hundreds of posted messages. The left column had a different set of icons—none of which I recognized, but the remaining columns were easy enough to figure out. Subjects, number of views, and replies. I quickly figured out which posts were the most popular and looked at them.

"Seems kind of open to the world, doesn't it?" I wouldn't have expected the level of detail. I felt enough paranoia to cover my screen. "Is this safe?"

Nerd fixed me with an amused look. And it wasn't the usual eye-rolling "nerd teaching girl how to format a spreadsheet" look; there was some surprise in it. "You're catching on. Caution is best," he said. "But these are safe. Otherwise, I wouldn't have them."

"You're sure?" I repeated, concern in my tone.

"I'm sure," he said. This time I got Nerd's condescending and slightly irritated look. "Don't forget, none of what you see there is indexed. Your average user won't just accidentally come upon any of these links. I did some extra work so my program would filter what I think you're looking for. 'Curate' sounds even better."

"But the level of detail?" I added. I was beyond impressed but eager to get started.

"I guess criminals want to know what they're buying too," he laughed. "How about that one? I saw it last night before leaving. And it's local." I moved the cursor down to Nerd's finger and clicked on the post.

Ax to grind—Want to finish the job?

"Looks like this one was posted last week," I said, having no idea what constituted an old post in this criminal world. "Only one person interested?"

"The original post is real enough," he replied, seeming not to take undue notice as he busied himself on his own screen.

"Ax to grind . . ." I mumbled. "But maybe I'll keep shopping. Sounds too messy." I scrolled down the page, tiring quickly of seeing the same type of announcements: *Some like it dead. Kill my boss. Got a beef?*

"That one is new," Nerd said, glancing at the

screen. I stopped scrolling and highlighted a post titled: *A little bit of justice.*

"And sounds like it might fit with our company's mission statement," he said, winking.

The details of the post offered a contract on one Todd Wilts. Price: five figures, exact amount to be negotiated. Seems that Todd Wilts had been the fortunate benefactor of a court system fuck-up and had been released on a technicality.

"Given a twenty-year sentence, released after serving less than a year. That doesn't sound right."

"No, that doesn't sound right," Nerd said, repeating my sentiment. "That sounds fucked up."

I thought of the pedophile who had been released on a technicality Steve had told me about. I could still hear Steve's voice in my head: "I can only imagine what that fat bastard is doing. Laughing at us, for one thing." I thought for a moment the post was for the same pedophile, but the name didn't ring a bell. Technicality or not, same name or not, I licked my lips, hungry. I stared at the post, unwrapping it with my eyes like it was a gift. Something leaped up inside me then—a dark sense of caution. I yanked my hand back involuntarily, as if the mouse were buzzing with dangerous radiation.

"I don't want to sound stupid, but how do we know the police aren't looking at this too?" I thought back to what I had seen in Steve's case files and desperately searched my memory for anything similar to what was on my screen. Empty. I found nothing. But that didn't mean there wasn't a division that spent its days doing exactly what we were doing now.

"Part of the risk, I suppose," Nerd replied with uncertainty and lifted his shoulders, shrugging. "I'll be honest, this is outside of my realm. These aren't the type of jobs that I pick up. I guess that is why the prices are so high."

I pushed my concerns away, deciding I'd try to find out more from Steve—indirectly, of course. He'd mentioned a recent move to a "new system." He hated the week of training that came with it, saying he could have done more in that one week than months with the new system. All I could think of while he talked was having access to all those cases, in one place. The old and new. The solved and unsolved. Goose bumps sprang up on my legs and arms.

What if Nerd had access? I wondered. *Buttons? Could he find out if the police had my buttons?*

"Amelia?" I heard Nerd say. "Amelia?" I looked at him curiously, but then remembered Amelia was the name I'd told him to use.

"Can we find out more?" I asked. "You know . . ."

"Will the world miss him?" Nerd answered for me. "Give me a minute."

The possibility of what might come of this sparked the familiar anticipation that grew into a small flame. The possibility of taking on my first "case" was suddenly real, and I wanted to know more. I opened a browser and began to type a search in for Todd Wilts.

"Whoa!" Nerd said, pulling the keyboard from beneath my fingers. "Listen, don't forget where you are. Or what browser you're searching with." He closed the window and fixed me with a firm look, rocking his head back and forth. Embarrassment rushed through me.

"Oh my God. How stupid," I said, grimacing. My cheeks flushed. "I'm sorry."

"Wasn't fatal," he answered glumly. "Not this time, anyway. You can search, but use the tools on the flash drive. No traces."

I nodded, understanding, but I still felt rattled by the stupidity of my mistake. "Did you find anything?" I asked, deciding to leave the deeper searches to Nerd.

"In fact, I did," he answered as he turned his monitor in my direction. "What we've got here in Todd Wilts is a rapist who prefers the younger teenage girls. Convicted on multiple charges of assault and raping a fifteen-year-old. He claimed it was consensual on account of having met her in a bar, but the DA made a case and got the conviction."

"And the young girl?" I asked, but immediately

wished I hadn't. This wasn't about her. It was about him, and that was who I needed to focus on.

Nerd fidgeted a little in his chair, having become restless with the questions. He cleared his throat and scrolled down the page. "Okay, so the young victim was found across from where the attack took place. She was naked, viciously beaten, raped, and—"

"Never mind," I said, cutting him off, regretting that I'd asked. "We don't need to know any more."

"A young girl like that, I'm surprised that he survived in prison even that long. I thought they would have eaten him up."

"Is the job search going well?" I heard from behind the computers. There was the librarian, lights glinting off her glasses like a cat's eye shine. She was craning her neck, trying to glance at our screens.

"It's going wonderfully," I answered, offering an enthusiastic smile.

"That's great to hear," she answered, retreating and moving on. "Won't be long, now. You'll see."

"That was close," I told Nerd.

"Nah," Nerd said, waving a hand toward her. "Wouldn't know what she was looking at, anyway."

"Who's the post from?" I asked, letting the thrill finally reach my voice. Todd Wilts could be our first mark, our first paying gig. "Wait, wait—that was a stupid question. Never mind about who. Just tell me what to do if we want to make a move on this one."

"We won't know who. We should *never* know. That's the beauty of it," he added. Nerd leaned against his chair and ran his fingers through a thatched mess of black hair. "Protects all parties."

"I understand," I said, agreeing. "I'm voting we take the job."

He turned his monitor back around and rapidly tapped on the keyboard, popping up screen after screen—all of them were unfamiliar to me. "So we're going to do this? I mean, we're actually going to take this one?"

I fingered the screen, "Is that me?" Nerd had brought up a reply cursor; he was waiting for me to narrate a response. But what I noticed was my profile picture: a faceless, gray-filled, and oval-round, unisex being with the name Candy Cane beneath it. I cringed. "Candy Cane?"

"Seemed a festive name," Nerd said and snorted a short laugh. "I mean, given the time of year we're coming into. Don't worry, these profile names never stay around for more than a few weeks."

"I hate that name," I told him, "A few weeks is all?"

"We're not looking to make friends, you know," he said in a sharp tone. "Just business. And we'll never meet anyone. That'd be the beginning of the end of this if we did."

"Except for . . . well, you know . . . the mark," I added. "So, what do we say?"

Nerd turned back and tapped the keyboard with one finger. He spelled one word: *Interested.*

"Done," he answered. "And now we wait."

"That's it?" The rush I'd experienced quickly dissipated, like a sudden bedroom interruption. "Seems a bit casual, a bit platonic. Don't you think?"

"Yeah, well, that's it," he repeated. "I don't know about platonic, but there's nothing *casual* about it. If I had to guess, we've just broken a dozen laws, maybe more. And at least a few of them are enough to put us away for a while. Orange jumpsuits and all. Do you like orange?"

I shook my head and assured him, "We're careful." The words felt right, but the enormity of the risk made my face flush like with a fever. "How long do you think?" I asked, staring at our reply. It was there alone, listed as one of one, and showed just beneath the original posting.

Would there be competition? Was that how this worked? A bidding war?

"Shouldn't be long. Gives us some time to get things started."

"Time to get started?" I asked impatiently. I stared

at the post, expecting to see an immediate response. After all, we'd put ourselves out there. We'd stuck our necks on the line. I'd never felt more vulnerable. I hadn't realized it at first, but I was getting off on the risk. I was high, running on a rush. Just the idea of the police barging through the library's heavy doors at any moment left me squirming in my chair.

"Time for you to figure out *how*," Nerd answered, and it came to me then that I'd only just crossed the bridge into an entirely new world. "Just don't forget to use the tools."

"Oh, I won't," I answered, tilting my head back and winking at him. "I think I'm going to be here awhile."

"You search on the how, and I'll work on the where and when."

"The logistics," I added.

"The logistics," Nerd repeated.

18

WHILE WE WAITED for a reply—Nerd had given no estimated time beyond "not long"—it was my turn to figure out the how. And the answer was hidden somewhere behind one of those yellow links. An open market was the only way to describe what I saw on the screen. According to Nerd, everything and anything illegal was up for grabs. I only needed to make a decision and click a button to buy my "wares." As to how we would pay for my first murder weapon? Well, that detail I left up to Nerd. I suspected these sites wouldn't have the kind of digital shopping cart I was used to.

Nerd fed me specifics about our potential mark. I took mental notes, repeating what he said in a whisper, all the while wishing I could draw up a Killing Katie–type design. I needed something to help me think it through. Within moments, I was lost in the computer's equivalent of pencil and paper, listing a few notable items to help spur a plan.

The first link I clicked was all about metal: pure metal. From guns to knives to metal-forged weaponry I didn't recognize or have the first idea how to use.

"Too complicated," I said, closing the window. I wasn't planning on going to war, and had no interest in anything messy. I'd had enough of messy already.

Another window brought me to a list of bomb-making instructions and kitchen recipes, showing me how to mix up a batch of what looked like a doughy gray block of Play-Doh.

"Too loud," I complained. "Wouldn't use *that* with the Play-Doh Fun Factory!" While the idea of a car bomb intrigued me enough to make me glance over the designs, the thought of the explosion and destruction felt obnoxious. "Not for me."

What I wanted had to be quiet, had to be sexy, sneaky—the kind of attack that my mark would never see coming. And better yet, that would make sure nobody ever knew I had been there. I raised my chin, searching the library's ceiling for an idea. When my gaze settled on some intricate designs in the plaster, I had an epiphany. I needed a quiet killer, a cancer. No smell or touch, but 100 percent effective.

"That's it!" I chirped, jumping high enough in my

seat to turn Nerd's head. I'd found our strategy. Our market differentiator—to coin one of those terms I'd learned in college.

"Did you find something?"

"Not quite," I answered. "But I found the approach. In fact, I found the strategy we'll use for *all* of them." In the entire history of assassins, I'm sure the idea of a quiet approach wasn't exactly new or profound. But it was new to me and was how I'd go about my Killing Katie design for Todd Wilts.

"Whatever you're cooking up, it's gotta be big," Nerd added.

"Big?" I asked, confused. "Why? What have you found?" I settled back into my seat and looked at his monitor to see what he was concerned about.

"The man is enormous!" he exclaimed.

His words fell silent then as we both stared at the image he had found—my mouth gaped open as I considered how I was going to kill a monster. My thoughts then went to the fifteen-year-old he'd attacked. What monsters did *she* still see at night?

"You're going to need a canon for a gun."

"Might be that my new strategy is the best way to do this," I muttered.

"Stealth?" Nerd replied, sniggering.

"Poison," I said solemnly, stiffening my voice.

"Poison . . ." Nerd considered.

"The yellows," I began. "Do you know how to buy from the links?" Nerd lifted his head and sneered as though I'd just insulted him.

"Of course I do. I've got enough Bitcoin to buy just about anything in the yellow!" he exclaimed. I was confused by some of his jargon, but trusted that Nerd could deliver. He shifted in his seat, his head wobbling. "Maybe not *anything*, but plenty that's out there. Tell me what to get. I can have it in a few days."

"A few days?" I asked, trying not to show my surprise. "I've just got one item in mind."

Nerd's eyebrows stitched together, listening. "Just one?" he asked.

"We need a poison that is fast acting—and, considering his size, it has to be strong in a small dose. Got that?"

"Could use strychnine," he offered, rushing his words. "It's available—seen a vial of it recently, but it's not cheap. And you'd have to inject it."

"That means getting real close," I said grimly. "Injectable only?"

"Might be available in other forms," Nerd shrugged, unsure. "But that's what I've seen recently. Just one dose."

"Is it fast?" I asked, thinking of how I could get close to my mark.

"Let's find out," Nerd said as he opened a browser

window, proxy jumping his search over eight different servers, maybe more. He had an answer in seconds. "Oh yeah, stuff is fast. Not just fast, but soon after it hits him, he'll convulse like a fish out of water."

I gave him a crisp nod, satisfied. "And I think I'll be able to pick up a syringe at a pharmacy," I added, hoping that I was right. I really had no idea, however.

Nerd tapped on his keyboard and swished his mouse around. A click later and he brought up a picture of a young, pretty girl.

"What are you doing?" I asked, narrowing my eyes. I knew where he was going, and it pissed me off. I began to collect my things to leave. "This isn't about her. You have to focus on the mark, not the victim."

"Just wait," he pleaded. "I want to show you."

I slumped my bag onto my lap and frowned. Nerd's expression was filled with pity, so I reluctantly decided to give him a minute.

"Fine," I said and followed his gaze back to the screen. I saw a school photo of a young, beautiful girl. It could have been Snacks in ten years. She had long walnut hair, a touch of sunlight highlighting what had been carefully woven into braided pigtails. She wore a plaid skirt, cut just above the knees, with a maroon knitted top—a school logo was embroidered in gold on the front. "She's a beautiful girl. But what does that matter?"

"She'll never have children," Nerd said, gazing at me and then back at the monitor. I could hear the emotion in his voice. "She was in a coma the day that she turned fifteen. I'm thinking that maybe it shouldn't be quick. Don't you agree?"

"No," I said, shaking my head. I jabbed at my screen, tapping on the rows of links until he followed my hand with the cursor. "We're not in the pain business. I'm sure there are plenty of leg-breakers for that." Nerd winced, but said nothing. He needed to know that I was in the elimination game only. An exterminator, controlling life and death.

"Doesn't seem right, though. Just doesn't—" Nerd began to say.

"Are you up for this?" I asked, interrupting. I fixed him with a firm look, showing no emotion. I'd begun to have some doubts about him. I felt bad—horrible—for the girl, but this was about the mark. "You know, we're bound to see worse. Much worse."

"I'm good," he said, closing the photograph of the girl.

"Sure?"

"Yeah," he assured me. "How are you going to get close enough?"

It was my turn to shoot him a sneery look as though he'd insulted *me*. He raised his hands, backing off jokingly, which helped lift the tension.

"Got an address?" I asked, an idea coming to mind that called for a road trip.

"Address," he repeated, searching through what I assumed were the police reports on his screen. "Not a house address. A bar, I think. White Bear. He's a bear all right. Why the address?"

"I'm going to see if he's moved on or if he's decided to stick around," I answered and glanced at my phone to check the date. Steve worked some nights, but tonight he would be home. I decided to tell him that I had a dinner date planned with Katie. My gut cramped at the thought of the small lie, but the distraction was subtle, easier. There'd be more lies, and they'd get easier too.

"Like I mentioned, he's local. Here's the address. Might be a coincidence, but that's the only address I see for him. A room above the bar maybe?"

I tapped the address into my phone. "Bring up his photo again?" I asked, then grabbed his mug shot with my phone's camera. Though I didn't think I'd soon forget the face. He *was* a monster, and if I had to guess, he'd probably only gotten bigger while in prison.

"You're going *today*?" Nerd asked, sounding concerned.

"Just want to get close enough to take a look. This is a part of it. It's the type of homework we'll have to do."

What I didn't share with Nerd was that I wanted

things to move fast. Putting together a Killing Katie–type design would help me prepare mentally, but what I hadn't expected was to feel fear, trepidation. When I looked at Todd's photo on the phone, I stared past it, trying to think of how I'd get the courage. I wasn't just afraid of him, I was terrified of getting caught. My heart thumped hard, beating in my chest and head, and my stomach went rigid with knots; I felt dizzy. But there was another feeling too—an intensity. A hunter's instinct before a kill. If I could pull this off then I could pull anything off.

19

THE TAVERN'S BRICK facade slumped sadly. Loose mortar stuck out in messy clumps, barely holding jutting bricks in what looked like a gapped-toothed smile. A tall and narrow building with peeling paint hanging off it in stringy vines, the original colors faded by countless passing sunsets. The White Bear stood alone on the narrow city street. The nearby buildings had been abandoned and left to die—a sign of how run-down the neighborhood had become.

Sad, I thought, distracted by the urban blight. The second floor of the White Bear held two black windows that stared down on those coming and going. *Was this the bar where Todd Wilts had met her? How was it that a fifteen-year-old wound up inside a place like this?* I shuddered at the question. In my mind I saw Snacks as a young woman, wandering inside the White Bear like a lamb to slaughter. *How would I react if she were attacked?*

"I'd kill anyone who touched her," I muttered. My breath fogged the car windows, and I turned the heat on, fanning the air to clear the humid mist from the glass. There was no telling if Todd Wilts might show up. I needed a clear view. The street remained empty, though. A thin mist hovered above the blacktop. The scene was eerie, haunting. The White Bear could have been a house of horrors, complete with special effects.

I circled the block again and slowed long enough for another good look. I imagined what was inside—a cherry-wood bar surrounded by stout tables, each of them filled with dangerous bikers. They smelled like the earth and sat squatly with shoulders hunched, their eyes like white beads set deep in their browned skin, aged by years of sun and wind. They covered themselves in leather and drank sloppily, celebrating an overdue break from the road. And their women clung to their thick, tattooed arms, wearing torn jeans and carrying wildly dyed hair that draped over naked shoulders. Local women were there too, some dancing, some kneeling, some feeding men shots from the hollow between their breasts—too naïve to know any better.

I imagined that the air was choked with smoke and filled with the scent of beer and piss and a funky musk.

I imagined the bathrooms' sticky floors and doorless stalls that wore heavy coats of black, chipped paint. I imagined a grab-and-go machine hung crooked on the bathroom wall, vending tampons and tropical-flavored condoms for a quarter. I imagined all these things. At once, I knew that I wanted to go inside.

As if to confirm what I saw in my mind, the toothy grin of an old biker caught my eye as he approached the tavern. Long, rangy legs, thin to the point of looking emaciated, his high cheekbones dagger sharp, his face coming to a point on his chin. Bald in the front, graying hairs sticking out in the back beneath a blue-and-white kerchief. He had lively, bright eyes that happily gazed around without a care in the world. A silvery metal chain swung from around his hip, connecting to his back pocket. It glinted in the gray autumn light when he turned away from my car and headed toward the door. He took the steps in sets of two, spry and light-footed for his age, his boots clopping against the slanted concrete.

Just then, a younger man came from around the corner and called out his name, giving the biker a curt wave. He was younger by a few dozen years and dressed in a preppy college fashion. He wore catalog clothes—from his fall-semester jacket to dark denim jeans and black shoes that were at once casual and formal. His hair was sandy brown and moppy, hanging down to his neck. Broad-shouldered and fit.

An athlete, I thought. *Rugby, maybe.*

The biker stopped at the top of the steps and they exchanged a few words. The younger man gave a laugh. Clearly, they knew each other.

"What is going on here?" I muttered, trying to understand the dynamics of the White Bear. Then I saw the school logo on the younger man's shirt.

"The university! Of course," I said, nearly jumping. Just a short walk from the tavern, a popular university —the oldest in the city—housed thousands of campus students. How many of them must have had their first experience of college boozing at the White Bear. The sad state of the building, of the neighborhood, told me all I needed to know.

Might have been a biker bar once, but the college kids are keeping it open now.

Another group of students appeared from around the corner, waving at the two men. Moments later, they all disappeared inside. I tried to understand what might have happened to the girl. Had she been with a group of the college students? While in high school, I hung out a few times with college kids—but never as a sophomore, never at fifteen. But that was me. And where did Todd Wilts fit in at the White Bear? Renting the room above the bar, like Nerd suggested? Or was he a biker or maybe even a student—no expiration date on that these days. I'd guess the former, and that the room above the bar was just an address all the bikers shared. After all, the road was their real home.

I turned my car off, committing to my first field trip. The engine rumbled before shutting down and spouted some motor ticks while it cooled. I gave myself a look in the rearview mirror, hoping that I could blend in. This was my homework. I needed a mental map of the place—though I suspected I wasn't about to find anything overly complex. If I could get away with it, I'd try to snap a few pictures with my phone. And delete them later, of course.

I guessed I could pass as a college kid's parent. I smoothed some lip gloss on my mouth and pushed my hair up and over—I wanted to create an older version of myself. Rocking my head from one side to the next, I grew wary of what the mirror showed and questioned if I could pull off the look. Another push, farther back this time. I added a hair clip, and the college mom came into view. I'd have to do a lot more work to prep myself for the visit to kill Todd Wilts, but for now, the college mom would do. In my gut, I wished I could try and get away with being an older college student—a grad student, maybe.

The road was damp and puddly. I walked over crushed cigarettes and avoided broken bottles littered around. I stepped onto the sidewalk and then onto the first of the bar's crooked steps, listening to the crunch of an errant piece of glass beneath my heel. When I walked through the door, the cozy smell of the tavern swept over me like a warm blanket. But the mysterious and dangerous biker bar that I'd expected died in my imagination.

The interior of the White Bear was bathed in a honey-golden light. It immediately gave off a warm appeal, like a cozy ski lodge with a massive fire at the center. The single room centered around a large bar surrounded by high-backed seats. The old biker I'd seen earlier lifted the point of his narrow chin from behind the bar and fixed me with a short look before pouring a drink for an elderly woman with harsh red lipstick that glowed garishly against her ghostly skin. She picked it up quickly and set her lips to the glass. She found my silhouette, squinting against the outside light, and tried to focus. Her curiosity lasted for less time than it took her to take a puff on her cigarette, though, and she went back to the freshly poured drink in her hand.

The familiar sounds of rowdy college students came from a far corner. I followed the noise and found a group of young men huddled together in a large booth, two pitchers of beer at the center of their attention. They raised their sloshy mugs and sounded off sporadic clinks, toasting the end of their semester and the beginning of winter break.

"Congrats again," the bartender called out, holding up a shot glass. He slugged it back in one smooth motion. "You guys deserve the break, but keep your celebrating down to a low roar."

The boys laughed and raised their mugs again. "To Sam and keeping it down!" they shouted, tapping their glasses. "Two more pitchers, Sam."

"Nope, nope," Sam countered. "Not till you finish what you've got—and no fucking puking in my booth either. Tired of that shit."

"To puking!" they toasted.

I wanted to laugh at the banter. Memories flooded back as I made my way over to the bar's curvy run of finished wood. I took one of the seats and placed my hands on the smooth wooden top.

Sam waved another shot glass in the air toward the boys and gulped it down.

"What can I get for you?" Sam asked me. I didn't know what to order. The shelves beneath the bar were lined with bottles of every color, shape, and style.

"Whiskey," I blurted, and then shrank back, surprised at myself. It was the first thing that came to my mind; and it didn't seem to faze Sam. He threw his arms beneath the bar to grab a glass. He pulled a bottle off the shelf behind him, and then stopped.

"Neat?" he asked. I nodded. He skipped the ice and water and placed a thick-bottomed glass in front of me. "Something to warm you?"

"You might say that," I answered. Having never had whiskey, I expected the drink to be unpleasant, like cough medicine or something only burly men with gravelly voices would drink. But I forced a sip and let the taste sit in my mouth until the toffee flavor numbed my tongue. Sam watched for my reaction. I squirmed, uncertain of how I should act. I wasn't used to a bartender waiting around.

"Good, isn't it?" he asked, encouraging me to agree. "Distilled right here."

"Delicious," I managed to answer, wanting to be polite. Steve would have been better at this. "You make your own?"

"We have a label. Small one," he answered, pouring me another. He held up a pretty round bottle, a creamy white label showing a picture of the building. The name White Bear was emblazoned across the top. "Free one for you. Pass the name around."

"Sure thing," I answered. "Would be glad to." Sam dipped below the bar for a moment and then resurfaced, producing some cards. He handed them to me. Then he moved away again, easing back to the other side of the bar to pour another pitcher for the boys.

The door opened and the outline of a man appeared in it. Harsh light cut a path across the bar, piercing it with a narrow swath of light that caught the shimmer of dust. He grunted once and stomped a foot before entering, announcing himself in the kind of way I'd expect.

It was Todd Wilts. Even with his face in shadow, I could tell that it was him. My mouth went dry.

I took a big sip of the whiskey and swallowed. My belly warmed immediately from the spirit. I kept my head down but followed my first mark out of the corner of my eye as he made his way to the bar. Sam greeted him and lined up two shot glasses. They chased their shots with one more before Sam placed a set of keys on the bar.

"Delivery truck is out back," he told him. "Full tank, filled it this afternoon. And the delivery is Delaware."

"Got this," Todd answered in a low baritone voice. "Back by eleven."

"Watch the state line," Sam hinted with a wink.

"One more?" Todd asked, lifting his shot glass.

Sam shook his head. "Long drive," he said and then tapped his head. "Keep your head clear, got it? You can have all you want when you get back."

"Line 'em up for me at eleven," Todd instructed. "Got that?"

"How could I forget?" Sam answered with a joking frown. "Don't I every night? Listen. There's gonna be other jobs. Delivery is what I got for now."

"Whatever," Todd scowled. "Be back by eleven." He scraped the keys off the bar and said nothing more.

I'd finished my whiskey by the time Todd passed me again. I dared a broader, riskier, look then, turning enough to face him. But he didn't notice me. He didn't even see me. My stomach hardened. I was disappointed. My plan was only going to work if I could offer him something he wanted to see.

"You've got some work to do," I mumbled to myself, glancing down at my outfit. "A lot of work." But I had gathered a lot more information than I thought I would have gotten. He worked for Sam, delivery or something, and returned to the White Bear in the evenings around eleven. I celebrated with another shot of White Bear whiskey, and even bought the bartender a shot. He appreciated the gesture but told me it wasn't necessary since he was the owner. He drank the shot with me anyway, talking up how it was the best whiskey this side of the Mississippi and maybe the best in the entire country.

I realized something else when I eventually made my way back to my mom-mobile. I liked the taste of whiskey. White Bear Whiskey.

20

THE GRAY POUCHES were back. It had been a few days since we'd last met so, selfishly, I'd expected to find a fresher face. It was still fleshy, puffy, and carrying Nerd's bloodshot eyes. His hair was messier too—something I didn't think was possible—a scraggly knot of misplaced locks, torpedoing in different directions. A new pair of heavy creases cut across his forehead, aging him a decade. I began to wonder if a decade's worth of troubles had suddenly found their way onto my new partner's lap. What was going on that could put him in such as state? Or was this normal for the younger generation? What was it they were called? Millennials, Gen-X'r? I didn't know one from the other.

The look of him told me something had him worried. It couldn't be anything we were doing, surely.

We'd only just started. At first glance, I thought he'd maybe tied one on, but he didn't come off as the type to drink anything stronger than Mountain Dew. Or maybe he'd just picked up a nasty flu bug.

"You okay?" I asked. My question was met with a plea in his eyes that I hadn't seen before. He wanted to talk. Rather, he needed to talk. But selfishly, I only wanted to work on our planning. I just had two hours and didn't want to waste a minute of it. "One too many last night?"

"Nah," he answered and raised his flash drive.

I quickly brought out mine, raising it with a touch against his in a mock-ceremonial cheer, hoping he'd laugh, but his face remained unchanged. I sank my flash drive into the computer's port. The screen came alive, mounting the drive and then popping up the collage of green, yellow, and red links. Immediately, my soul filled with an empty hunger that urged me to grab the mouse and begin clicking at random.

"Just some personal stuff—" he said.

"I don't have to know," I said, interrupting in an annoyed tone. "And probably best that I don't know. And that you don't know about me."

"Less is better," he agreed, but his eyes looked hurt. He shrugged the sentiment off and returned to the work in front of him. I must have a look about me that invites people to open up. I thought I only had that effect on Katie, but had begun to wonder over the years. If they only knew how much I'd like to kill them rather than listen to them.

What an ironic twist.

"So," Nerd began. "What did you learn on the field trip?"

"I saw him," I said, trying to contain myself. "He *is* big. The pictures online didn't show us just *how* big. I can do this, but will need to get close."

"You saw him?" Nerd asked. "Did he see you?"

I shook my head. "I stayed for a drink, watched him talk to the bartender, and then I went home."

"What's he doing there?" Nerd chirped, his cheeks turning red. "Is the apartment his?"

"One at a time," I answered, raising my hand to calm him down. "I don't think anyone lives upstairs. According to the bartender, also the owner, most of the building is used as a distillery for White Bear Whiskey. He even gave me a card." I fished one out from my purse and handed it to him.

"This is good," Nerd said, speaking more to himself than to me. He flicked the card with his fingers and added, "They're legal, so there will be plenty to find online that I can check out."

"Why?" I asked, and then shook my head. "Never mind that. Our mark works for the distillery. He drinks there too, but delivers in the afternoons. If I can get his attention, get a few drinks in him . . ."

"How?" Nerd asked. "I mean, no offense, but you're not exactly his type."

"What do you mean, not his type?" I asked, frowning. Till now, I'd always thought of myself as being *any* man's type. "And how would you know his type?"

"What I mean is that he likes them young, really young. Makes sense, right? Think about what he did, why he got locked up in the first place."

"Yeah," I answered, remembering the pretty girl with the sunny highlights. I suddenly felt old and passed over. I tossed my hair to one side and added, "But you haven't seen me. *Really* seen me." Nerd shrugged with a laugh and then brought his backpack around, resting it between us, perched like some grand prize waiting to be shared.

"You're sure?"

"Yes . . ." I answered, uncertain to what he was referring.

"Say the word and I can toss what's in my backpack away. Never to be seen again. Otherwise, there is no turning back for either of us."

I felt my neck stiffen, realizing the line I was about to cross meant some of the risk was on my shoulders too. I moved to the edge of my seat, eager to see what he'd brought. "Show me," I insisted.

"Committed!" Nerd said flatly as his hands disappeared inside the backpack. A moment later, he held up a clear plastic sandwich baggie with a syringe and a stout glass vial inside: brown, slender, a metal hat on top with a dim blue-rubber cap. And inside the vial, a liquid that could have been any color and made up of anything. I knew it was the strychnine. "This is it. I even managed to swipe a syringe from my dog's vet . . . well, you don't need to know that part."

"How did you get it so fast?" I asked, feeling inspired by Nerd's efficiency. "Wait, I don't want to know. That's another area we'll keep to ourselves. Safer that way and—"

"Less incriminating," he finished for me.

"May I?" I asked. My fingers clutched at the sandwich baggy like a jeweler would a rare gem. "How much?"

"Three grand," he said, and at once my eyes bulged. I winced. "That's not a bad price, considering the form."

"Considering the *form*?" I asked. I had assumed the cost would be a few hundred. Nerd turned the bag over to show the label on the brown bottle. It was in a foreign language, but I'd seen the writing enough on television to recognize it. "Is that Russian?"

"It is," Nerd answered excitedly, his voice pitched high. "Liquid. Potent. A good call, don't you think?"

"And that's why it is more?" I asked, still not understanding.

"Look at this. We're not talking about crappy, powdery stuff that's been cooked up in some schmo's kitchen," he explained. "This is *manufactured*. A high-potency injectable. One shot of this and Wilts is down in under ten minutes."

The syringe's needle seemed sturdy enough, but I was still going to have to get close. The image in my mind of Todd Wilts suddenly made me nervous. Not so much a fear of *him*, but the dangerous possibility of the hit going terribly wrong. I touched the syringe through the clear plastic and tried to see the needle through its cover. If it was too thin, there was the risk of it breaking before I got to use it. But if it was thick enough, I'd be able to plunge it, sink it like a knife, and deliver the poison.

But then I saw the problem and let out an impatient huff.

"What? What's wrong?" Nerd asked as he began to inspect the bottle.

"How are we supposed to get the poison into the syringe safely?" I asked, answering his question with a question. "I don't think we want to chance that rubber cap. Do you?"

Nerd raised one brow, then winked. The expression didn't seem natural for him, but I understood the sentiment. He held up a finger, telling me to wait. Then he produced the biggest sandwich baggie I'd ever seen. Identical to the smaller one, but the size of it was comical.

"We'll use this," he said. "Probably overkill, but that's the point. We want to be safe."

"What are we supposed to do with that?"

"Observe," he instructed, placing the vial and syringe into the larger bag and zipping it closed. "With a five-gallon bag, you can fill the syringe, put the caps back on, and reseal, all through the plastic. No need to touch anything directly or risk getting some of it on you."

As Nerd spoke, I could see that whatever was bothering him was steadily moving on, clearing from his mind like a passing fog. His mannerisms had become more animated, more normal, more of what I'd grown accustomed to seeing. And that made me more comfortable too.

"Or . . ." I began, then dug into my purse to show him one of my own tricks. "We could use *these*." I flashed him a pair of latex gloves that I'd swiped from Steve's car.

"Yeah, that'd work too," he grinned, peering down at the bag in his lap. "Not sure how old this is. Might be best to use both." Nerd handed me the bag—then the corners of his mouth turned down as though he'd just stepped into a pile of dog shit.

"So, you'll add the three grand to the forty percent?" I asked, hoping the job paid more. "You know, we took a bit of a risk buying inventory before knowing if we got the job."

Nerd shook his head. "We got it!"

"We did?" I yelled, clapping my hand over my mouth. I tipped my head back and quietly stomped my feet with excitement. "How much?"

His face soured, and I felt a twinge of disappointment. "Only eighteen."

"Eighteen hundred?" I asked, dropping my shoulders and foolishly wondering if there was a return policy on the strychnine.

Who was I kidding? My first job and I'd already put us in the red.

"Eighteen *grand*," he announced and then pitched his eyes up, moving his lips without saying a word. "So that makes my cut a little over ten and yours a little under eight."

"That's doable," I said, realizing how much money we'd earn for a few hours' work.

Eight thousand to me. What kind of dent in law school tuition would that make? Was that how much a life was worth? I shook off that last question. *After all, the mark meant nothing. The act meant nothing. This is work. No emotional connection. A paycheck going to a greater cause.*

"You thought it should have been more?"

"If I'm right," he began as he pointed toward the red links. "We'll find marks for thirty grand, maybe even some for fifty grand." The numbers sounded staggering.

Why so high? How much was there to gain by someone else's death? And then I thought of all the murder-conspiracy and thriller novels I'd read over the years.

A sense of relief came over me. If fiction was based on real life, then our potential market was huge.

"I guess fiction is real, and fairytales *can* come true."

"Huh?" he asked.

"Never mind," I answered, waving off what I said.

"When?"

I took a deep breath and answered, "Tonight."

21

TONIGHT WAS THE first night of the rest of my life—that is, a life after Todd Wilts. But Steve had other plans for me. We'd just finished dinner when somehow the conversation wrapped back around to a mention of my blouse and the night of the homeless man's death. That is the way Steve put it, "the man's death." He didn't call it what it was: murder. I rushed to clean the dishes, hiding in the invisibility of being busy—a cue he usually took as my being on the fringe of caring. Like I said, I could be a bitch sometimes. And always when it worked in my favor. I needed it to work in my favor now.

I watched the clock, knowing the hours Todd Wilts would likely be at the tavern. He'd told the bartender that he wanted to get shit-faced drunk after he was done for the night. I wanted to be at the tavern before eleven. Late for a Thursday evening, but still early from a college student's perspective. They'd be filling the White Bear, cooking up the start of a long weekend by then.

My plan was to dress up to look like a grad student, seducing my mark and getting close enough to lead him somewhere private, alone. The clock showed nine. I anxiously scratched at my arms. I slipped away for a few minutes to rehearse how to fill the syringe, holding the brown bottle of strychnine in one hand and the syringe in the other.

"Did you drop it off?" I heard Steve ask, but my mind was elsewhere. "Babe?"

"What, Steve?" I asked, hurrying my hands over a plate before dumping it on the dish rack. "Sorry. Little rushed."

"Rushed for what?"

"I'm supposed to meet with Katie later for a couple of drinks. I told you last week. Remember?" I asked. That was lie number one for the evening. Katie's involvement was purely fictional. Steve looked uncertain as he tried to focus on a memory that wasn't there. I rolled my eyes immediately and added, "You forgot, didn't you? She was supposed to catch me up on what's going on with her and Jerry?"

Steve gave me a quick nod as if he remembered. He always preferred agreeing rather than admitting he'd forgotten. Now who was lying? I tried not to laugh.

"Your blouse?" he asked, quickly changing the subject.

"Which blouse?" I answered, playing dumb to what he'd said earlier.

"The one you were wearing the night you fell at the library," he said. He touched my shoulder, drawing my attention away from the sink. Lie number two for the night was coming. I could feel it. "I picked up the laundry from the dry cleaner, only they didn't have your blouse. Said that you never brought one in."

"The torn-up one?" I asked, traipsing my hand over the front of the shirt I was wearing and then wishing I had avoided touching the buttons. "Tossed it." Steve's face emptied, becoming blank as if all his thoughts were lost. I turned back to the sink, keeping the conversation insignificant. But inside, I was nervous and scared. I squirmed at the sting of sweat beneath my arms.

"Wait, what do you mean you tossed it?" he asked, raising his voice. I thumped my hand on the faucet, shutting off the water, doing my best to look annoyed.

"It was ruined. Cheaper to buy a new one," I answered, lifting my brow as though his tone surprised me. "It was an old blouse. I've got a dozen more. And since when do you care at all about my clothes?"

There was moisture on his upper lip, and the sight of it kept me from turning back to face the sink. His lip twitched too, but he tried to hide it. His warm hands were on my arms then, his eyes locking with mine, searching for a truth that I had to keep hidden.

"What happened after you left the library?" he asked. I shrank away when I heard a strange tone in his voice. It wasn't harsh like he'd use in an interrogation, but soft, a near whisper. It cut right through me. He was afraid for me. "Please, Amy. Please try to remember."

"I . . . I told you," I repeated, stammering. My voice cracked against the sudden dryness in my throat. "Tripped and fell. Hit the railing." I tried to bring my hand up to my head, but Steve closed his hands tighter, gripping my arms as though he would try and shake the truth out of me.

"Do you still have the blouse?" he pleaded now. I shook my head as images raced through my mind. I saw charred remains of the fabric, black snowflakes being picked up and whisked into the breeze, carried by the dying heat of the small fire.

"I don't," I said flatly. "What is it? Why do you need it?" He pushed off then, nearly shoving me away as he leaned against the kitchen counter and drove his face into his palms.

"Do you remember that night?" he half asked and

half stated. "The night we skipped dinner because of the crime scene outside of Romeo's?"

"Yeah, sure," I answered. "But what's that got to do with my blouse?" I kept my voice level, thin, and directed, but my insides tumbled out of control. I braced against the counter, clutching it until my knuckles hurt.

"We found something at the scene, and God help us, I think it's from your blouse."

"What?" I nearly shouted, doing my best to sound surprised and oblivious. Steve only shook his head, waving his hands at the air. "What was it?"

"Best you don't know. Not yet." I touched him then, rubbing my hand against his arm, trying to soothe what troubled him. He shook his head. "If only you still had the blouse."

And I realized then that his hope was in finding that the evidence collected that day *couldn't* be connected to my blouse. With the blouse destroyed, that was already the case—he just didn't know it, yet.

"If there is anything I can do to help . . ." I began to say, but he only gave me a brief glance before leaving the kitchen. I reached through the tension, hoping Steve would take my hand, but he ignored me.

"Enjoy your drinks out with Katie," he said, his voice rigid and trailing down the hallway as he made his way into his office. If he'd brought home the case files, a glass of wine might be in order. Who knew? One of the case files could be about my homeless man.

It was clear to me now that the homeless man had grabbed my buttons, holding onto them as I'd taken his life. Steve thought he recognized them but wasn't able to marry them up to my being there—not without the blouse. There were a hundred other scenarios Steve would consider before considering the one that put his wife at the scene of a murder.

What if the homeless man had simply walked by the library, finding two creamy moons staring up at him from the sidewalk? Would he believe that?

And then there was the obvious choice—telling Steve the truth.

This last option had never crossed my mind. I had been attacked by the homeless man. That part was true. The man's intentions were to rape me and then slice me open, like he'd done to another girl. And then it occurred to me that the homeless man was just like *me*. He was a hunter, a prowler, and he would have continued doing what he'd been doing if I hadn't ended him. If it had to happen, if I had to offer a story, it would be the truth. All of it. From the blade held to my neck to the hit I'd planted against his head and then taking the knife from him. It would be a terrific story of self-defense. And to better the story, I'd add how I was filled with shame and embarrassment that kept me from coming forward. Isn't that always the case?

I could get away with this, I thought.

The only thing I'd have to leave out of my story was just how much I enjoyed murdering the man.

22

I ASKED MYSELF a thousand times whether I could look the part. *Could I pull this off?* Skinny jeans *were* what the college girls wore. I had confirmed it when driving around the local campus after my first field trip. I had made other mental notes too: shirts, hairstyles, and shoes to name a few. A grad student could get away with looking older, but I wanted Todd Wilts to see me, and I needed Todd Wilts to want me.

The only suitable pair of jeans I had were already too small—Levis from my college days. I tried them on, pulling on the denim, feeling the tightness wrap around my thighs like a stocking. They were uncomfortable, but to pass as skinny jeans at the White Bear, they were perfect.

And in the same bin of old college clothes I found a sultry black top, a V-neck, extra low in the front, with bare shoulders. The top would offer plenty of distraction, giving my mark something else to look at when I was close to him. I changed my hair a half-dozen times, and then my shoes three or four more. Todd was a big boy and, at best, I came up to his shoulders. I would need leverage to plunge in the syringe. At the back of my closet, I found a pair of black pumps—a bit high in the heels. I'd have to lean on my toes when the time called for it. They were dusty and hadn't been on my feet in years. I winced when squeezing my toes into them. They would hurt, but I'd make them work.

I glanced in the mirror hanging on our bedroom's closet door, keeping the lights low, careful to try not to stir Steve from his sleep. I blinked when I looked at my reflection and shook my head. I'd done it. I thrust my front out and arched my back, pushing myself into a sexy curve. I looked damn good—hot.

"Let's just hope Mr. Todd Wilts thinks so too," I said under my breath.

Seeing isn't feeling, though, and I hoped some of that confidence I saw in my bedroom mirror stayed with me. I stopped at one point, on the bridge over Neshaminy Creek, ready to turn my car around and call it off, my nerves getting the better of me.

There's no way he'll think I am a college student.

But the need to feed came—the hunger pangs

more physically present than I ever could have imagined. It wasn't about the money. I wanted to do this, needed to do this. Vampires *were* real—I believed that now.

I rolled my car window down, letting the late-autumn air tumble inside and caress my bare shoulders like a trainer relaxing an athlete. A crescent moon hung in the star-filled blackness—a glowing sickle threatening to cut open the sky. It was all I needed to see to urge me on.

Todd Wilts kept to his schedule, ending his delivery late in the evening and showing up at the White Bear. By the time I'd arrived, he was already leaning against his bar stool, gripping a longneck and dropping shots of the tavern's own brand of whiskey.

"Gonna make a fortune on that stuff," he exclaimed, his lips brimming sloppily. Sam gave him a curt nod, agreeing, but didn't return the smile. He hesitated filling the shot glass with another pour.

"No trouble tonight. Okay?" Sam asked with caution in his tone. Todd leaned over the bar, tapping the barkeep's shoulder comfortingly. Sam shrugged off Todd's hand and added, "I'll kick you right out of here. You know I will."

"No trouble, Sammy boy," Todd answered. I could see his shoulders rocking up and down as he laughed.

The night scene at the White Bear was a surprise. It

had me thinking this would work out better than expected. Music moved through my body, pumping and pulsing, making me want to dance. It was a thumping funk-filled rave music meant to cater to the college crowd. The pleasant honey-colored light from my earlier afternoon visit had disappeared. Now flashes of electric light bounced from every surface, reflecting disco colors.

"It's perfect," I decided. A dark corner, or maybe a booth, or even a bathroom stall—any of them would do. I only needed to figure out how to lure him. I'd found a small table, round, perfect for two, and scraped a chair's stiletto-thin legs back and sat down. I waited. The seat was just ten feet from the bar, ten feet from my first mark. I waited for him to see me.

I felt the outline of the syringe in my pocket, hoping that its shape didn't show through my jeans.

They wear them so tight now!

And as I'd hoped to see—counted on seeing—the tavern was filled with college students. They lined the walls and filled every table and every booth. They leaned in and out of the shadowy corners, dancing and loving. They filled every inch of the White Bear.

Todd saw me!

Distracted by the crowd, I'd almost missed his gaze. I remained composed, though, and raised my leg just enough to hang my pump from the end of my toes, dipping the heel. I was fishing and wanted to see if he'd bite. His gaze wandered, up and down, staying on me. I had him. I pretended not to notice, but saw him move his stare from my shoes to my thighs and the low-cut reveal of my breasts. When he was finished, his gaze moved up and met mine with a leer. He was an enormous man, muscle upon muscle. I saw the appetite in his eyes, and the idea of tempting him excited me. But when I remembered the monster he was and what he'd done to that poor girl, any alluring element evaporated. I was sickened.

"World isn't going to miss you . . ." I muttered.

"What's that?" he asked, cupping his hand behind his ear. Thinking I'd said something to him, he waved me over.

I took my time standing, giving him more to ogle. When I was ready, I walked into a razor beam of electric-blue light and popped my chest, hoping the extra lift erased a few years from his view. Sam fixed me a look as I approached, seeming to recognize me from the other day. A moment later someone called out his name, and he disappeared from behind the bar before he could make the connection. I made my way over to Todd—sauntered over might be a better way to describe it. When I reached him, I tucked myself between him and the bar, purposely bracing his knee to lean in and say hello over the hard thumping coming from the speakers. His response was quick and steady. He moved his hand to the curve of my waist, holding me.

I wrapped my fingers around his longneck beer and tugged. He tilted his chin, his eyes never leaving mine, and offered permission without my asking. I playfully drank back a sip, showing just enough tongue to set the tone and to leave nothing to question.

"My name is Ginger," I quickly said, cringing inside at the name. I needed to do better and eased close enough for him to look down the front of my top and to catch my smell.

"Of course it is," he answered, smiling. I could feel his hand on my side, cradling, acting like a gentleman, but all the while teasing with his fingers as they ran along the curve of my breast, barely touching.

Catch this monster, I reminded myself as I straightened to face him.

"Want to drink?" I asked, dropping a twenty-dollar bill on the bar.

"Sam! Some shots?" he shouted over the music. I sipped his beer and turned away from the bar while Sam set up the shots of whiskey. "And then what?"

This was too easy. Did I have him already?

"I like my shots big and fast," I told him as I drank one down. Todd drank two, dropping them one after the other. We repeated the one for two, drinking more shots. By the third, I could feel my head swimming. I held back. I needed to focus. I could see from the hard outline in his pants that Todd was ready to go anytime I told him.

I felt for the syringe but found his hand on my pocket instead. I stopped.

Had he figured out why I was here? Impossible.

He brought his lips over to my ear, laying his hand on the side of my breast, and mentioned another room. When his thumb brushed over my nipple, my stomach churned sickeningly, but by now, I was all business. I'd set the trap and had my prey. And now it was time to go in for the kill. Anything else would just be toying with him like a cat with a mouse.

We stepped away from the bar, my hand in his. My fingers looked like a child's in his meaty grip and there came a moment when fear slowed my step. I could still run away. But I didn't. Instead, I followed, treading softly behind him, colors skipping into my eyes and washing over his shoulders, turning his shirt into a hypnotic mural.

He could kill me with little effort, I thought even as I pushed the concern out of my head. *I have him,* I told myself again.

There was a room beneath the stairs—a small room—hidden in the dark and nearly invisible from the rest of the tavern. I followed him inside as I took a peek around one last time.

I never heard the door shut. Todd spun me around and shoved me into the wall, pinning my head against the plaster. I saw a flash of light as my brain registered the hit. There'd be a bruise for sure.

"Easy," I said, but he ignored me as he palmed my breast, squeezing hard, grunting with enjoyment. I winced but slipped out a moan to mask the pain. He groped with both hands then and began to grind against me. I freed myself enough to look around the small room. Shards of silvery light leaked through the back side of the staircase—I saw a shiver of dust afloat like muted fireflies. And I found a ray streaking inside from beneath the door. Shadows approached, paused, and shuffled back and forth before disappearing again.

His body swallowed me whole, covering me like a blanket. I couldn't move, and the feeling of being suffocated suddenly became real.

Was this what happened? Did he bring her into this room?

I heard the sound of his pants coming undone, and I squirmed, trying desperately to turn around. Then his hand was gone from my breast and he spun me back around to face him. The smell of liquor, of his hot breath was sickeningly strong. "Choke it!" he said in a gruff voice and shoved my hand onto his cock. "You got me so fucking hot. Finish it!"

At once, my hand warmed as if holding a tall coffee. The touch of him in my palm put me in control. I had my chance. I moved around to his side. I squeezed until he grunted, distracting him. I kept one hand in the front, stroking in response to his groans, but put my other hand behind him. He pumped his hips, encouraging me to grip him harder. There was no romance, no pleasantry shared caressingly with another—he was brutish, primal, and all about reaching a climax.

"Feel good?" I asked, rolling my eyes in the stark darkness while I fished out the syringe with my free hand.

"Oh yeah," he replied. "Needed this. Harder. Choke it harder." My gentle pumping wasn't enough, and he clutched at my hand, shoving it harshly.

"I got it," I said with the end of the syringe in my teeth. I gripped the needle's cover between them, yanking the safety cap off. His hand went to my shoulder and pushed down, telling me to finish with my mouth. I stayed on my feet and wrapped my fingers around him as tight as I could and rocked my hand faster. He grunted, pleased by the change in rhythm. A moment later I could feel the first pulse, almost in time with the lights pumping to the music. I stabbed the fleshy part of his ass, or at least I hoped I had.

Mental note: driving sharp objects into people in the dark is not recommended.

"Oh yeah!" He grunted as he thrust his hips. "Fucking yeah!"

I squeezed the plunger, pushing the strychnine into his body as he spilled onto my arm. I shuddered, disgusted, and quickly pointed him away from me. I collapsed the plunger until all the poison went into his body. He shook as a chill came over him, gooseflesh rising. The act was done. I had finished nearly the same time he did.

"How was that?" I asked, quickly removing the syringe as he pulsed and jerked a few more times.

"Fuck yeah!" he panted, sounding winded and on the verge of passing out. "Felt that one in my ass!" His arms went up, and he hammered his fists against the underside of the staircase, cheering.

"Glad to oblige," I said flatly. There was nothing else to be said. That was my cue to leave. I listened to him work his pants up while I hid in the darker corner, recapping the syringe before carefully tucking it back into my pocket. I put my hand on the doorknob, wrapping the metal with a bar napkin from the floor nearby. I hesitated. My feet should have been moving, but I couldn't help waiting. My eyes adjusted to the dim light. I wanted to see what was going happen to my first real mark. He came into a fuzzy view as he tucked himself away. I needed to know if the strychnine did the job. But more than that, I wanted to make sure the little brown bottle from Russia hadn't been filled with plain water instead of hope.

"What are you waiting for?" he asked. "Appreciate the tug, but don't expect nothing in return. I'm not one to reciprocate." I didn't expect him to say anything else. But then I saw his hand come up and cradle the back of his neck, cocking his head to the side as if a sudden stiffness had settled deep. He drove a truck all day, delivering White Bear Whiskey. A little stiffness would not tell me much of anything, but I held onto the hope.

Was it working already?

I'd used every drop I could fit into the syringe and shoved it into his body.

"That *was* a big needle," I muttered to myself and then gasped silently. Nerd had mentioned lifting it from a veterinarian's office—but what size *was* it? "Doesn't matter." After all, it seemed fitting to take down an animal with a veterinary syringe. And he was an animal. My mind went back to the girl he raped and maimed.

What life would she have now? What memories would haunt her?

When my mark fell to his knees, clutching at his

neck, I knew it was time. I turned the handle and opened the door. Disco lights bled over me, beaming abstract neons from long tubes of black light. The ultraviolet revealed a coin-size stain on my arm. I stopped and tried to recognize what I was looking at.

How stupid, I thought, remembering he'd come on me.

It left a glowing, flat pearl: bright and impossible to miss. I wiped it away, cleaning my arm with the bar napkin. I felt a thump on the floor and saw that my mark had fallen over—his hand clutching the air, seeking my help.

"I won't reciprocate," I mumbled as he crawled forward, scratching at a sliver of light creeping into his tiny love hut beneath the stairs. His face turned into a contorted mess—convulsions twisted and tortured and wrestled with the demons that made him who he was.

"Help me," he mouthed with a breathy gasp.

"World's will not miss you!" I yelled over the music as I kicked the door shut. My body was a giant electrified pulse, aware of everything, feeling everything. I felt impossibly indestructible, like I could take on anything. I found the exit sign and headed in that direction, floating across the floor, floating past the college students and the bar. A fresh-faced bartender gave me a quick glance before moving on to serve a pair of redheads. Glimpses of their hair touched the side of my view, and I dipped my head, careful to limit any eye contact.

"That was almost too easy," I mumbled as I focused on reaching the door handle just in the front of the tavern.

That's when I saw Jerry.

My body was suddenly drained of all electricity as if it just shorted out. I gasped, but forced myself to continue toward the door. Katie's husband sat in a corner, alone, and my first thought was that Katie had been right, that he *was* having an affair. The City Hall office where he worked for the mayor was only a few miles away. An easy walking distance or a stopover on the way home. He could have picked up a young college student for himself, promising her the world amid flirty kisses she would mistake for love.

He didn't see me. For Katie's sake—and my own selfish interest—I found a safe, dark corner and stopped long enough to watch the booth and to see who he was with. I thought of Steve and the skank with the three hearts. I never wanted to know her name, never wanted to see her face. But I thought, for Katie, just knowing the truth might help set her free. Jerry's arms were draped over the curve of the booth, a smug look of comfort on his round face. He'd even combed his hair differently, slicking it into a style I hadn't seen before.

Is he trying to look younger too?

I glanced down at myself and wanted to laugh. We had taken the same measure for different motives. But he didn't have the face of a man hiding an affair, taking cautions in where he was or who he'd been seen with. He gazed out onto the tavern without fear, exuding a confidence I didn't recognize.

"Jerry, what are you up to?" I mumbled to myself as I slipped closer to the door. Sam came out from behind the bar just then and made his way over to Jerry. He plopped down next to him, without a greeting. Straight to business. He produced a white envelope and handed it to Katie's husband. Neither of them gave a second look at who was around them—not like they do in the movies. They didn't care who was watching. Jerry stuffed the fat envelope into his jacket and nearly touched the bottom of his nose with a brandy snifter.

When I heard the first scream, it sounded faint. It could almost have been a part of the music. But then a second came, drawing Sam's attention away from Jerry. When he stood, Jerry shuffled his things together. He was leaving. In my mind, I ran for the doors. In reality, I struggled to hold myself in check, to walk as fast as I could toward the exit sign and get out of there without drawing attention to myself. As I passed a small pocket of college students, another scream erupted over the music. Shoulders and faces turned like dominoes.

Jerry stood. He saw me! I was tempted to acknowledge him, instincts taking over, but pushed through the doors. The smell of early winter filled my nose and mouth.

Did he recognize me?

I raced to my car, scrambling to start it and drive away.

The raw excitement vanished—it had been replaced by the terror of Katie's husband seeing me. Red and blue colors spiraled into the night sky, painting the trees and pavement while the sound of sirens warbled and echoed in the distance, ringing with a Doppler effect as my car sped away from the bar. I couldn't control my breathing. The street in front of me was doused in foggy blackness, and starry lights crept into my view.

"Don't you pass out," I screamed. "He didn't see you!"

But my words rang hollow, even to me. I had no idea if Jerry had actually recognized me. I had a realization then. Satisfying. Golden. Katie's husband worked for the mayor. What was he doing at the White Bear, accepting a stuffed envelope from Sam the bartender? Katie's concerns about an affair were misplaced. There was corruption in the mayor's office, and Jerry's hands were dirty. Even if he had recognized me, he'd never come forward. For the sake of Katie and their boys, he'd never risk going to jail. I could count on him for that. No balls.

I stopped the car at the top of the bridge again and opened the door. Neshaminy Creek greeted me with the familiar trickle of rushing water. I needed the air. I needed to calm down. I needed to ditch the syringe and the brown bottle with the Russian label. I blindly aimed for the larger rocks at the center of the creek, hoping to shatter the glass so that the water could carry the pieces away. The syringe went in with one gulp, but I heard the bottle explode on top of a rock, the remains clinking off a stony surface before plopping into the creek.

My first job was done.

23

IT WAS NEARLY one thirty in the morning by the time I set foot in our bedroom. My shoes were off and I stretched my toes, digging into the carpet, rooting to let the evening fall out of me. My feet ached from the tight shoes, but wearing them had been worth the pain. Steve rolled over onto his back, breathing heavily. A rattle from inside him erupted into a shallow cough. I was glad my first job was over, that my first mark was dead. I was glad to be home. But I was still flying high, filled with an energy that I couldn't turn off. And if I'm honest—at least with myself—I didn't want to turn it off. I felt alive in a way I'd never experienced before.

I eased the bathroom door closed, flipping on the light, and stared at the woman in the mirror. Disheveled, straying hairs that were stiff with spray and jutting out awkwardly greeted me. My lipstick had smeared and given me the appearance of having a fat lip. I quickly brushed the excess away. A bruise rose from the scrape on my forehead, pale red with veins of purple and a touch of shine in the light.

"Where did you come from?" I asked. And then I recalled how Todd had pushed me into the wall. "I was buzzed, but didn't black out. Or did I?" I shrugged off the question. With the bump just above my brow, a bruise might spill around my eye and turn it black and blue. A shiner? Concern ticked inside me. I'd cover it with a dab of concealer tomorrow. Steve was definitely going to notice. It was only a matter of time. I could hide it for a short while, but this wasn't like a new hairstyle. He'd notice. Maybe nobody else would, though. But in a day, maybe two, I was bound to get a coy stare from the woman at the market or while volunteering at my daughter's school. The markings would be ripe enough for speculation and gossip—plenty for a gathering of housewives to chew on over tea and cucumber sandwiches. I hated cucumber sandwiches.

I did look hot, though. Minus the wear and tear that came with murdering someone. My tits looked firm and bouncy—I'd used some tape underneath for lift, a push-up trick I'd seen in *Cosmo*—and the old pair of jeans gave my legs a shapelier tone. A snore came from our bed, and the remains of an ache stirred in me. I wished Steve were still awake. Maybe it would break some of the earlier tension. A saunter, a swing, maybe a sway of my goods, teasing him until he had to have me. I had my peanut butter and wanted the chocolate.

When I saw a rough outline of drip marks on my shirt, I froze. Todd had hit more than just my arm. Four, maybe five spots had dried and become stiff, leaving behind a scabby stain that couldn't be wiped away.

"What have you done?" I mumbled, disappointed in myself. I had just inadvertently brought my target's DNA into our home—forever connecting this house with Todd Wilts. Shaking my head, disgusted, I tore the shirt off in a single motion. I rolled it into a ball and then used the tape from beneath my breasts to cinch the cloth ball tight, carefully wrapping the stain in the center.

"Loved that shirt," I whispered as I stuffed the evidence under the sink. I made sure to hide it deep inside, behind the toiletries and cleaners and my lady things that Steve always managed to knock over. Nobody would see the shirt, let alone understand what it was if they did.

"Two down. Burn that one tomorrow."

I had to get better at this. I'd watched the forensic

shows on television enough to know that I'd broken a dozen rules.

How much of my his DNA had transferred to me when I'd touched him? And how much transferred to my body and then the inside of my car and our home?

But none of that mattered. None of it should ever matter. It only mattered if I were to become a suspect. As long as I remained unsuspected, I was safe.

The excited charge waned in me after a cool shower and a glass of wine. I'd found the endless pool of energy did have a bottom, but there was enough in reserve to carry me through the night. I'd take a small nap before Steve and the kids were up and then send them off into their day before finally laying down to sleep longer. Nerd would be waiting for me in the early afternoon. We'd completed our first contract and earned our first commission. It was time to pick up the next job.

I cleaned up, poured some wine and went snooping in our home's office. From the looks of Steve's desk, he'd spent the evening in and out of the office too, leafing through one particular case. Papers and photographs were strewn across the top, shoved around like a deck of cards. In my heart, I feared that it was the case about the homeless man. They had the buttons, that was something, and Steve seemed convinced that he needed my blouse.

I pinched the corner of a photograph and slipped it out from beneath a short stack of court documents. As the crime scene photo came into view, I nearly spilled my wine. The photograph showed me John's beautiful face—a bullet hole above his eye, his perfect skin blown apart and caving into a black chasm. His eyes were open, which surprised me. Just half slits, but enough to see them staring up at me. There was no color in them anymore. The piercing sea-green that captured every girl's attention had turned pale, almost gray or white beneath a dull film. A lump of hair and skull and brain matter spilled out of the top of his head where the bullet had exited, showing the small eruption of gore that had killed him.

I gasped and turned away, hating to see my friend like that. I put my mouth to the lip of my wine glass, spilling the fruity taste onto my tongue.

"Why are you doing this to yourself, Steve?" I mumbled, trying to understand what it was my husband was searching for.

"Maybe this was John's fate," someone had said at the funeral. I'd wanted to turn around and smack that person in the mouth. Steve had held my arm, coaxing me to remain calm, and soothing me. A cop's wife never wanted to hear those words. And it wasn't just me; the moist eyes of those around the casket had stared sharply, fixing hurtful, witching looks on the asshole behind me.

"It's fate, I'm telling you," he'd continued. I had begun to spin around again, but stopped short when Steve spoke up.

"Maybe you need to shut up," Steve had whispered harshly over his shoulder. I hated that there was some truth in what was being said. But sometimes the truth was best left unspoken. I shook my head, hearing and feeling the echo of the man's sentiment.

Fate could be cruel. A minute more, a minute less, and John would still be alive.

Fate is cruel, I thought. *A moment, a flash, a pull of a trigger, and lives changed forever.*

John's family was in my mind, and the sting of a tear came to my eye. Maybe John's death had given Steve the idea, a small miracle, that he should take charge of his own fate.

"Is that why you're looking at these?" I slurped down what remained, chasing the earlier whiskey buzz, and swiped at my eyes before pouring enough wine to fill the round glass again.

A yellow legal pad cradled another pile of case files. A pen sat atop, perched and threatening to roll. All the markings on the page were in Steve's familiar scratchy handwriting. I peered over my wine glass, gulping faster, pouring more, beginning to feel a little drunk. Fleshy blue lines had been scrawled across the yellow page. The curvy scratches connected circles with other circles and dates held inside penned boxes, along with names.

Names? What names? I wondered, thinking John's case had been open-and-shut.

At the center, I saw one name that Steve had firmly traced over and over again, circling it until he'd nearly torn through the paper: Todd Wilts.

24

WHEN I FINALLY laid my head on my pillow, I was drunk from the wine. I pushed what Steve had written on the legal pad to the back of my mind. I stared up at our ceiling and imagined beaming lights of vibrant colors jutting across our bedroom. My body thumped to a bass tone that wasn't there but that rattled our bed, humming through me in a steady rhythm.

I was in the tavern again, surrounded by college students and drinking shots with Todd. He gave me a starved look that said "I want to fuck you," and then placed a shot glass in front of me. A woman's moan sounded from far away. I threw the shot of White Bear Whiskey to the back of my throat, choking down the fire in one gulp, and heard the moaning cries come again.

The smell of diesel fuel and the sound of gas station bells forced my eyes open. I'd dozed. She hated it whenever I fell asleep. "After all," she'd said, "I'm doing this for you too." The moaning became loud—a man's voice whispered sex-filled words I'd heard before, but his voice was new. The air was moist with humidity, steamy. I sat up and peered through the car window. Semi-trucks were parked around us, but behind them I saw the woods and heard the chirp of tree frogs singing while fireflies danced, blinking on and off like strings of holiday lights.

The man was almost done, and the woman was close behind. By now, I'd learned the sounds and recognized the changes in their breathing and the whispery chatter that went back and forth, leading, urging, and encouraging. When I looked over the seat, her lips were in full view, her finger poised and pressing against them.

Shush, she motioned. I moved forward, climbing from the trunk of our station wagon to the middle seats—my skin was sweaty-wet and slipped against the vinyl. When I made my way to the floor behind the front seats, I found the belt she'd placed there. I picked it up and traced the wings on the buckle, running my finger over the raised metal.

"Make a loop," I whispered, remembering what she'd showed me, pinching the belt's hole over the metal stud. "Backward and inside out so the buckle faces me." Then I wound the tail around and fished it through the hinged ring. The noose was ready. I grabbed the loose end and glared above as the sounds of their sexual peaks rained over me. She eased his head back with a practiced proficiency, her fingers in and out of his mouth, perching his neck over the edge of the seat. He made sucking noises and his panting became heavy, filling the car with the smell of liquor. And when he began to grunt, I raised the belt loop and did what I was told, throwing it over his head. The leather stretched immediately, creaking as it cinched tight against his neck. I hung on, my body bouncing up and down while he choked and tried to free himself. Her moaning was all I could hear then, like an explosion of thunder after a lightning strike. She held on too, riding him, her hands clutching his neck. She climaxed then—her screams heightened by the sudden death of her lover. There were no sounds after that. Only quiet satisfaction.

My eyes opened wide with a start, my stomach flipping and groaning harshly. A dull throb ached in my balloon head. I had seen more of the dream this time. I remembered more of it too. And it scared me that I knew who the little girl was: it was me. I wanted to cry.

I rushed into the bathroom, the urge to vomit

making my mouth water. All that came up were gassy burps. I managed to hold it in, making it to the sink where I hung on to the stone lip and rushed water over my face. I'm not sure how long I stayed like that; I might even have dozed in that position. Until I heard Steve getting out of bed.

Waking in a haze, bloated, bleary-eyed, and seeing doubled images—all the bad that comes with a gut-wrenching hangover—marked my morning. The front of my head weighed me down like a stone. The drinking didn't help, and though I can be a lush at times, I think the hit against the wall made the morning worse. The mark above my eye had swollen horribly, turning into a juicy bruise full of color. That would definitely turn some heads. I should have put an ice pack on it instead of cracking open a bottle of wine. I scooped a finger-full of concealer and creamed it over the egg, wincing when I neared the center.

Another look in the mirror gave me the urge to vomit again. That last part was all wine. I was sure of it. I still felt drunk. No wonder, since I had finished the entire bottle while pouring over every case file on Steve's desk. I had stayed up until I heard the first of the early morning traffic, searching for connections that related to my first mark.

Steve entered the bathroom and lifted his nose as he passed me. I wouldn't have time for a shower. I headed for the kitchen to get the day started. Our bed called to me, urging me to climb in, and every part of me wanted to wrap myself up in a blanket and stay there until the storm in my body passed.

Maybe later, I promised myself as the sound of the shower came on.

The rest of the morning came and went like the dream I'd had—my body in motion but my mind a vaguely detached observer. I wasn't entirely there, yet I'd managed to make my way to the kitchen and go through the motions of getting the kids breakfast and sending Michael off to school. Steve barely said a word. No amount of alcohol was going to rinse away the tension from the night before. While he didn't mention my missing blouse, his frustration and suspicions, and maybe even mistrust, lay on me like an itchy blanket. There was only so much of it that I could take.

"He's a cop," I told myself. "You're only fooling yourself if you think that this is going to pass."

I caught him glancing at the empty bottle of wine in the sink, tilting it as if reading the label.

"We're doing this now?" he asked, his voice sarcastic and uncaring. But what hurt more was the purposeful distance he put between us. He never made eye contact, not once, and even seemed to go out of his way to avoid me. We'd had tense times in our marriage before, but nothing like this. It was taking us to the edge. I could feel us getting closer. It wouldn't take much more before falling into that place that was so impossibly hard to climb out of.

"Just had a few glasses," I said, but I heard the slur in my words and stopped talking out of embarrassment. I caught his stare, brow raised and wondering if I was still drunk. I tried to make it sound better than it was, adding, "Had some drinks with Katie too." I began to clean the kitchen, trying to look busy. My hands jittered as I picked up and put down flatware and plates for no reason other than to burn nervous energy. I'd lied. I'd been lying. I felt guilty. And that was what Steve was picking up on, he just didn't know it.

But nothing I could say or do would help. Steve didn't care about the drinking. We'd been drunk around each other a thousand times—played drinking games, nursed each other's hangovers. He did care about the truth. The air between us was only going to get thicker as long as the truth about what happened with the homeless man stayed hidden from him.

25

WHAT I'D LEARNED from Steve's notes was that Todd Wilts had been a known acquaintance of one Luis Garcia, the man who'd shot and killed John. Steve wasn't just browsing through John's case file to feed some morbid act of mourning—he was investigating. He'd found a clue that had connected Luis to Todd. Picking up and reviewing all known acquaintances was any detective's usual procedure. But, in this case, Todd happened to be my first job. By now my first contract was completed and my hit, my mark, was lying on a steel table, growing colder and awaiting an autopsy.

What did that mean for me? For Nerd?

There was one other name on the notepad. I could almost see the hesitation in Steve's handwriting: Jerry. And below his name, Steve had added the word "license." Katie's husband wasn't having an affair—he'd gotten himself involved with the folks at the tavern. I just didn't know with what exactly, and maybe it was better that I didn't. College kids might like the tavern for the dancing and the booze, but it was business when it came to the liquor that Sam had told me about.

Was there more? Why would Sam pay Jerry?

For most of the morning, I remained puzzled by what Steve had written on his notepad. Jerry? Even as Katie waved to me at Romeo's—our weekly lunch had come around again—I couldn't stop wondering what connection her husband had to Todd Wilts. I waved back to her and opened the door to the café. This would be a short lunch; Katie said that she wouldn't be able to stay, and I was eager to meet with Nerd and discuss what I'd found anyway. While the flash drive he'd given me was great for browsing the Deep Web, I thought—hoped, really—that he'd know of a way to find out how Jerry was involved with the White Bear.

"What happened to you?" Katie asked, but I hardly heard her words. For the first time in our lives, I was concerned for my friend. She wasn't dressing the business part today. Jeans and a shaggy mop of hair, with a shirt and jacket that had clearly just been thrown on. She gazed at my head. "Did Steve . . ?"

"No. Nothing like that," I answered, interrupting

with a wave of my hand. I led us to a table by the tall windows and ordered wine spritzers. It was hair of the dog for me. I hoped a drink would smooth the rough edges. I just wasn't sure a wine spritzer would be enough. Given how Katie looked, though, I thought she might need much more than a spritzer.

"What's going on?" I asked. "Don't take this the wrong way, but you look terrible. Are you sick?"

"Well, fuck you too," she said with a giggle. Then she added, "Thank you very much."

"Talk to me, Katie."

She perched her elbows on the table and stared outside for what seemed the longest time. Yellow daylight shined on her face, and I could see the toll her worries had taken on her. I'd never seen the creases above her brow or the ones creeping away from her eyes. And though she continued to laugh quietly at what I'd said, I could see that she'd been crying, which added to the redness and swelling. She drank the wine spritzer in a single gulp and asked for another.

"Actually, can you make that a Scotch? A double?" she corrected. I tried to remember the last time I'd seen Katie drink anything stronger than wine. Jello shots at a college frat house, maybe? And even then, she couldn't stomach more than two. Katie was a lightweight when it came to booze. Or at least she used to be. The waiter delivered the whiskey. My stomach dipped just looking at it, but I knew a drink might settle me. I motioned with my hand, saying nothing, and he disappeared to get another. Sunlight sank into the glass, glinting from atop the whiskey, bouncing as Katie raised it to her mouth. She stopped and peered through the glass at me.

"What? I'm not driving."

"I'll drive you," I told her. If the need were there, she could have my drink. I slid my hand over the table, taking hers. Icy and rough and scathed from tiny cuts, she wore three bandages on her fingers: two of them blood-soaked, her fingernails beneath in question. "What did you do to your hand?"

She shook her head. Her other hand had faired the same; it too was roughed up and scratched, bandages covering the worst of the damage. I fixed her with a curious look that quickly turned to annoyance. By then, she was ready to start talking.

"Packing," she finally said. "In a hurry too. Ripped the shit out of my hands on those fucking boxes and crap luggage. But we're not taking everything. Just a few things."

"Packing?" I asked. "What do you mean, packing? To go where?"

"You can't tell anyone," she said, her glassy eyes huge as she shook her head and searched around us. "Jerry's got us packing. Told me that we have to run."

"What?" I nearly laughed, thinking her story had to be a joke.

"It wasn't an affair. There wasn't another woman. But Jerry . . . he fell in with some people. Bad people," she continued.

The tickle inside—the urge to laugh—went away then. My stomach soured and ached. Whatever was going on had to do with my seeing Jerry at the White Bear.

"He's gotten himself involved with this group—these bikers—and he did something, but won't tell me what it is, only that we . . . we have to run. Hide. Like fucking animals."

This wasn't the Katie that I knew, and that began to scare me. This wasn't a joke. As much as I wanted it to be, I could sense real danger.

Todd, I thought.

But the timing wasn't right. Not yet, anyway. Poison wouldn't show up until the autopsy. Or better yet, the toxicity screening. I'd done my research. So if it wasn't a connection between Todd and Jerry, then it had to be about the money, the envelope.

But what would Jerry have to do with bikers?

Sam was the only biker I'd seen at the Bear.

"Bikers?" I asked. "Katie, you're not making any sense." She was crying heavily and swiped at her tears impatiently. I pushed my glass over, sliding it in front of her. She only sipped the whiskey this time as the last drink rose into her mouth. She caught it, pressing her lips, and held it in.

"All I know is that a year ago, these bikers wanted to start a distillery or something like that, and so Jerry helped them."

"Do you know the name?" I asked, sounding abrupt, sitting on the edge of my seat. I knew the answer, but had to hear Katie say it.

"I've only overheard Jerry say the name Sam."

"Which you thought was the name Samantha?"

Katie nodded, daring another sip. "He's the owner, but a whole group of them is involved. Not just here, but all over the East Coast."

"Money?" I asked, wondering if Jerry had tried his hand at extortion. Corruption in the mayor's office was the norm, but the current mayor had remained untouched by it through his first term and well into his second term. Jerry might not have had an affair, but he surprised me with the balls he'd shown in taking a taste from the White Bear. "Was it Jerry, or was it his boss?"

Katie began to cry again. "I don't know," she managed to say. "Amy, I've got to go."

At that moment, watching Katie finish her drink and collect her things, I realized that I didn't know when I'd see her again. "Wait!" I pleaded, feeling dread slow me down.

"It's too late," she answered as she wrapped her arms around me. Her body shook against mine with a soft whimper. "You're my sister, Amy. Always will be—don't forget that."

Her words sent a shiver through me. I fought the emotion, but choked up. I gathered my bag, paid for the drinks, and tried to catch up to Katie. But she'd always been leaner and taller, and her long legs carried her faster. By the time I reached the front door of Romeo's, she'd disappeared into the back seat of a black town car.

The car must've been waiting.

I clopped over the sidewalk, raising my hand at the car window, unable to see anything except my oddly stretched reflection as the car passed me and drove away. My friend was gone.

A thousand fluttering wings suddenly sounded in a feathered breeze, and a black rain fell from the highest trees behind Romeo's. The sky turned dark with the flight of blackbirds diving, twisting, and circling around me in an orchestrated cadence that seemed like magic. I watched the car drive away, wondering if Jerry was driving. The sputter of white exhaust puffed harshly as the sound of winged flight grew.

I glanced up, finding a mix of summer iridescence

and speckled winter gray in the wave of tiny blackbirds. The birds dove, then rose straight up, and then funneled sharply, turning together like one amoebic body, whispering secrets as to which direction they were going to go next.

What was Katie's secret? Which direction would they be going?

The large flock suddenly exploded above me, creating a daylight spectacle—a pale rusty sky filled with black stars—an impossible wonder that stole my voice. I wanted to scream out to Katie, but didn't need to. The sedan turned at the furthest corner, disappearing onto Springdale, driving toward the interstate and into the city.

Why was she going into the city?

When the blackbirds reformed, they jetted across the street, disappearing into the alley. *My alley*, I'd begun to call it. The birds became noisy once they landed, and I wondered how much they'd witnessed the night the homeless man had called to me. Did birds even fly at night? Had they been huddled together in a feathery brood—their marble-black eyes open wide, watching me?

My body shook then, but it wasn't from the late autumn air or from being sick with a hangover. I was afraid of what might happen to Katie and her boys. I could go to Steve, tell him what Katie told me, hope that he could do something. I decided to skip the visit with Nerd, leaving that to the next day. I'd find Steve and tell him what was going on.

By the time I was home, my eyes were damp. Steve listened to me, seeming to have forgotten about the buttons and my missing blouse. His arms went around me when the fact of Katie running overtook me. At his suggestion, I'd tried calling her phone. All I heard was a recorded message that the line had been disconnected. He made a few phone calls too, but didn't share the details. He said only that he was going to put some eyes on Jerry and Katie and make sure they were safe.

Later that night, hours after I told Steve about Katie and Jerry—leaving out the details about the White Bear—a soft knock came at our front door. I peered into the gray darkness, then fell back to sleep. Another knock came at the door, stronger and rapid, thumping louder. The abrupt sound woke me, stirring me enough to make me sit up and focus. Steve sat up too, and swung his legs over the bed.

"It's two in the morning," I said, grabbing his arm as he lifted the remains of our warm covers. "You don't know who it is."

"That's why I'm going downstairs," he answered, his face blank and half-asleep. "It could be a patrol.

They might have some news. I don't know, won't know till I answer the door."

The knock came again—they didn't ring the doorbell, as if they knew not to wake the kids. Katie came to mind. She could be outside with the boys, coming to us for help, for Steve's help.

"Wait then, I'm coming with you."

We hurried on some clothes and covered ourselves enough to go to the door. Winter had found our home, and it threw a frozen wall of air at us when we opened the door. Standing there, alone, his hair uncombed, his eyes bulging huge and bloodshot with a face stained from crying, Jerry looked to Steve and then to me, shaking his head.

"What?" I shouted, knowing immediately that he had something terrible to tell us. "What's happened, Jerry!?"

"Katie is dead," he managed to say as anguish stole his words. He tried to say more, but that was all he could manage to get out before collapsing.

26

I DIDN'T JUMP when the tea kettle whistled, urgently hissing and spitting hot droplets. I heard it, but ignored it. Hot steam spewed from the spout's small hole, escaping the water's violent rage. As much as I wanted a release of my own in that moment, I had none; my rage had to remain inside. I could feel myself boiling, blood coursing, rolling, heartbeats in my ears, sweat on my brow. I wanted to hurt Jerry for having started whatever it was that ended with Katie being dead. By now, Steve had heard back from the station, confirming that Katie had indeed been killed. There was a hole in my heart, and a part of me wished my world would be sucked into it and disappear.

They had been packing, just as Katie had described. Jerry confessed everything to Katie about what he'd been doing at the White Bear. He told her the trouble he'd gotten into with the bikers. He told her how he'd been taking money from the owner, taking money from a lot of bikers.

"And the twins?" I'd asked. They were apparently safe, sent to his sister's place to get picked up later.

"I told Katie how I'd been doing favors, but I didn't have anything to do with what happened at the Bear last night," Jerry went on to say. "When Sam went nuts, when he threatened me, I told Katie we had to run, hide for a while. I even had a driver from my office take her to meet with you."

Spittle hung from Jerry's lip and touched his chin, glinting with the light from above. He swiped at his mouth impatiently and blubbered again, sucking in as he tried to tell us more.

"There was a knock," he'd said. A knock at their front door, the kind of sound that you hear but don't hear. "I was boxing what we needed when I heard Katie's footsteps come down the hall. I'd heard the door, but never gave it a second thought. Until she opened it."

He told us there had been no words, no screams, just a pop and the sound of a wet splash before he heard Katie's body crumple in their doorway. A motorcycle, maybe two—the kind with the deep throaty sound—sped away as he held her, but he didn't see anything else—he didn't have to. Sam Wilts wanted retribution for his son's death, and he was going after anyone he suspected of being involved.

I swallowed hard, my heart stuck in my throat. He was talking about my hit on Todd Wilts.

Oh my God, did I do this? I leaned against the counter, my legs wobbly.

"And you think it was this Sam person?" I struggled to say, seeing the bartender's toothy grin and straggly hair in my mind. My words sunk into a whimper as I spoke, like a dying breath.

I killed Katie.

"Babe!" Steve whispered harshly. He lifted the kettle from the stove's burner, placed it on the stony, flat counter to cool. "Careful."

"Uh-huh," I muttered.

"How are you doing?" he asked, rubbing my back, seeming to ignore my question. I leaned against his warm hand a moment before continuing.

"Hanging in there," I answered, deciding to listen.

That's safest, Amy. Just listen.

"Do you have to do this here?" Whatever Jerry had going on with the bikers had to be beyond anything that I'd done. What stuck in my gut like a hot stone was believing that I might have hastened their actions against Jerry.

But he opened that door. That's what I told myself; then the stone turned.

Steve glanced at his phone, his lips moving as he read a text message. "Won't have Charlie there for another hour," he said. "Prefer the station, but need to get what's fresh."

I poured myself a cup of tea, eager to feel the herbal burn chase down the acid rising in my throat. Steve decided on a glass of water. Jerry wanted a stiffer drink.

Whiskey, perhaps? I wanted to ask bitterly.

Steve insisted that he stick to drinking water or coffee.

"Coffee, thank you," he answered. I dumped the bitter-smelling contents of an old instant coffee packet and watched the dank, freeze-dried pebbles dissolve at the bottom of the wet cup. I prepared the coffee without effort, keeping it steamy black. I placed it in front of him. This was Steve's area of expertise. I wasn't even sure I should be in the same room.

"Listen, Jerry. We should really do any questioning at the station—"

"I don't care where we talk," he interrupted. "Why . . . why the station?"

"Because your wife was murdered, Jerry. Much of what you told us I'm going to have to ask you to repeat. I've had the station on the phone the last fifteen minutes. Your wife was found in the doorway of your home with a gunshot wound—that part corroborates with your story. I've got forensics there now, probably be there most of the day."

Jerry winced. "I know how she died," he said, angrily. "I was there." He reached for his coffee, his hands shaking, but he managed to set his fingers on the cup's handle and take a sip. He gestured appreciatively in my direction. I glanced at his face, then quickly turned away and tried to make myself busy.

Steve revealed his detective's badge then, pulling it out from his back pocket—his shield, he liked to call it. He'd also changed his clothes after we let Jerry inside, putting on what he'd usually wear at the station. With its thick and heavy leather backing, his gold shield looked like a fallen star that he had managed to catch in the palm of his hand; as if he held some kind of mystical power. And maybe he did—after all, just the sight of his gold shield gave most people reason for pause. Steve placed his badge on the table, sliding it to the middle so that Jerry could see it, so that Jerry knew that he was officially talking to a cop. If Jerry had come to our house because of my friendship with Katie alone, he had come to the wrong house. But I suspected that he had come here because Steve *was* a cop, because he felt Steve *could* protect him and the twins.

"So that there is no mistake, and for your protection and mine, I'm going to record this conversation," Steve explained as he placed his slender phone on the table. He touched the screen, opening the voice recorder application. The digital needle began jumping with each spoken word. "Is that okay with you, Jerry?"

"Yes," he answered gravely. He moved closer to the table, uncertainty in his posture. "Yes, that's fine."

"This is Detective Steve Sholes interviewing Jerry Dawson with regards to the death of Katie Dawson. Relationship: spouse." Steve announced to the voice recorder. "Who showed up, Jerry?" Steve asked.

"Can't be sure of exactly who, but they were bikers. Bikers that work out of the White Bear. It's the—"

"Yeah, yeah, I know about the White Bear. It's been under investigation for a while now," Steve finished for him. "They've got biker gangs up and down the coast doing business out of there. But maybe you already know all of that?"

"I did a favor for the owner, Sam Wilts. Big supporter of the mayor. Lots of donations."

"And the favor?"

"About a year ago, during the reelection, Sam—the owner—donated to the campaign. Big enough amount to get noticed, big enough for a meet-and-greet with the mayor. Afterward, Sam took me aside and asked if I could help him out with a distillery license."

"Distillery license?" Steve asked.

Sam's face popped into my mind, proud and smiling as he'd placed the White Bear Whiskey card in front of me. "Tell a friend about us," he'd said, or something like that.

"They already had a liquor license, but he said they had an old moonshine recipe they wanted to bottle and sell legit. Only problem is that a distillery license is issued at the state level."

"What did you do?" I asked. Steve spun around in his seat, raising his hand. I hushed, embarrassed, realizing that I wasn't supposed to say anything. I raised my shoulders defensively, playing ignorant. Steve stopped the recording, rewound over my interruption, and then resumed.

"What did you do then?" he asked.

Jerry straightened his shoulders so that he could see me past Steve. "I knew someone who worked out of the governor's office. I made a call. One call led to two to three and, for some cash in hand, we made it happen."

"You extorted them," Steve said flatly.

Jerry squirmed and gulped his coffee. "We called it

a campaign donation," he countered. "That's politics. Everything is bought. The *extortion*? That came later."

Steve sat up in his chair, pushing a case file over the table. He slowly slipped one photograph out from the folder, and then another. I recognized the faces from the other night. I tried to shake out the tingling in my hands. My palms were clammy, knowing what he would show Jerry next.

"Do you know this man?" Steve asked, pointing to a picture of the man who killed John.

"Seen him at the Bear," Jerry answered, nodding. "Luis something?"

"And him?" Steve continued, but this time he pointed to a picture of Todd Wilts. My stomach cramped.

"That is Sam's son. They found him dead last night," Jerry answered as more spittle found his chin. "What do you think started all of this? It's why I came to you." Jerry slapped his hand against Steve's badge.

"What do you mean, dead?" Steve asked. "Todd Wilts has been under investigation. We have reason to believe that he was an accomplice of Luis's in the murder of a police detective."

"You mean your friend John? I don't know anything about that," Jerry answered, shaking his head. "Sam's boy died at the Bear. Looked like he stroked out—all twisted up—maybe too many drugs, too many steroids or something. But Sam freaked out, blamed me, said I was in cahoots with a rival or some crazy shit. He declared war. The guy is fucking nuts."

"Why, though? Help me understand this. You're a nobody. Why would he blame you?"

Jerry began to weep. A pitiful cry, sloppy and wet. For a brief moment, he had the face of a twelve-year-old boy who'd just skinned his knee. I wanted to hate him, but he wasn't all to blame.

"The extortion. There were others. I played them all like I was some kind of big deal. I kept demanding more money." He swiped at his nose, where more snot hung. I grabbed a box of tissues and handed it to him. "I got greedy. I knew what was going on at the Bear, what was coming in and going out. I tried to muscle them, telling them they had to keep paying for the license, or they'd lose it. Worse, I threatened to have his son's rape case reopened. Guy was an animal. Did you see what he did to that girl? But it was an empty threat—double jeopardy and all that. Just greed."

"Wait," Steve said, confused. "What do you mean that you knew what was coming in and going out?"

"Pennies, man," Jerry said. "My monthly taste was nothing. White Bear Whiskey was just a front. And I legalized it, can you believe that?"

"You mean the . . . the cash in hand?"

"Uh-huh," Jerry answered. "I got a taste once a

month from Sam. I paid that up to my contact, but we went for more. The bikers have the real money, spread up and down the coast, on two-wheel hogs going sixty on the interstate. I was taking money from anyone I was in contact with."

Steve brought his chair around the table, scraping it over the floor tiles with a screech. He sat across from Jerry so that their faces were awkwardly close. I couldn't help but wonder if this was a normal interrogation tactic.

"Listen," Steve began and snapped his fingers until Jerry's eyes went round, focusing. "Pay attention to me. I want you to clear your head and concentrate. What was it you found *exactly*?"

Jerry sat back, his shoulders slumped. He hesitated as if he didn't seem to know what to tell Steve. "I'm rethinking how much I should say," Jerry answered, scratching the thick patch of whiskers on his chin. I hated that sound. "I gotta think of the boys now."

"Whatever you have on them is what I think John may have stumbled onto, and it got him killed. It got Katie killed too. Let's get ahead of them, before they get to anyone else. So what *is it*?"

Jerry teared up and reached down to his side. With an instinctive reaction, Steve also reached to his side—for a gun that wasn't there. Jerry stopped and then slowly raised his hands. He held a photograph in one of them.

"You can't be serious? I just want to look at my family before I say anything else," he said. His words sounded thin and sheepish. "It's the count. What I've got on them, what I tried to muscle them with. The count. What's coming in isn't what's going out."

"Count?" Steve said, repeating the words. "What does that mean?"

"There's too much raw stock—corn, sugar, you know, for the distillery—for the amount of whiskey they are selling. The White Bear tavern is a front to serve the college locals, a small operation that even has a boutique whiskey label. But the Bear is really a hub, a manufacturing hub, serving whiskey from Florida to Maine. Might even go as far west as the Mississippi."

"But I thought they had a license?" Steve interrupted. Jerry glanced up, surprised. "I mean, you helped get the license issued. They're legal, right?"

"That's just for our state. Distillery licenses are like gold. Issuing them is like printing money, but only for the state they're issued in," Jerry countered. "The Bear has bikers picking up to distribute, to sell, and to bring the cash back from as far away as their tanks will carry them. The Bear is a moonshining machine and the bikers are the bootleggers."

"That's all you have?" Steve asked. I heard the

disappointment in his voice. "You're talking about a few bottles of whiskey hidden in bikers' saddlebags that may or may not have crossed the state line?"

Jerry shook his head. "No, no, no!" he exclaimed, raising his voice. "Not just a couple of bottles. What would you think if I said a million dollars? And that's tax-free too."

"A million a year . . ." Steve repeated, sitting up and browsing his notes.

Jerry shook his head again, a bemused smile on his face.

"A *week*. That's a million a *week*. Who do you think would be interested in protecting an operation like that?"

27

I STAYED IN bed nearly all of the next day, suffering in a way that made me feel like I'd never feel right again. I held onto Katie's friendship ring, twisting it with a wistful touch. Sadness. For the first time in my life, I felt a pain that numbed my mind to all reason. It left behind a hurtful sense of abandon and desolation that could only come from having lost someone. And for all of my stupid Killing Katie designs, the only thing I wanted now was to hear her voice, to hold her, to tell her how much I needed her.

I found comfort in hiding beneath layers of flannel sheets and a down blanket, my face warm and drowning in plush throw pillows. Katie and I used to do the same when we were kids. Sleepovers were our thing—weekends and days off from school. We'd bring our favorite stuffed animals, mine a purple striped zebra with yellow ears and hers a pillowy pink elephant that was missing one eye. We'd eat ourselves silly, filling our souls with sleepover foods like salty chips and ice cream and chocolate syrup. We'd tempt our bellies afterward, running back and forth in the hallway, sliding across the wood floor, our feet padded with our footie pajamas. Later, we'd huddle up close together beneath the bedcovers, shining pocket flashlights beneath our chins and telling spooky stories until we thought we'd bust open in screams. Our last sleepover was special. It had snowed that night, and we woke together, kneeling at my bedroom window, our noses touching the frosty glass while staring at a world that looked like it had been covered in white icing. That had been our last sleepover. We'd never have another now.

"I'm so sorry, Katie," I whispered, visiting the memories while stifling a cry as I curled up into a tight ball. "This is my fault." My body shuddered. I was broken inside.

I sank deeper beneath blankets, closing out the world over my head. I disappeared into the darkness. I imagined Katie telling me a story the way she used to. I could hear her recounting one of her favorite anecdotes, and I moved my lips along with hers—I was her best friend, so I knew the story by heart. And in my grief, I'd come to understand what it meant to have lost someone who would be missed.

"The world will miss you, Katie," I whispered softly into my pillow. At times I'd fall asleep. I called it sleep, but with my eyes half-closed, lying still, listening to the world go on around me, I was really only taking a break from grieving.

The kids came in a few times, checking on me. Steve stood in the doorway, peering in, mouthing words to ask if he could get me anything. I'd shake my head, showing just enough of my face to be able to see the light creeping through the open door.

Michael—so sweet with worry—told me how sad it was that his Aunt Katie had died. He didn't pry as I'd expected him to. He was surely curious to know the details, but he didn't ask how or why. I wouldn't have known how to answer him. And Snacks, well . . . with mommy in bed in the middle of the afternoon, that was just another excuse to play. She had no idea what was going on. She jumped up and down, thinking the tall stack of blankets was a sign that I was having fun without her.

"You want to come inside with Mommy?" I asked. She nodded eagerly, crawling under to join me beneath the blankets. "Comfy?"

"Comfy," she answered as she lay next to me. "Smells kinda funny." I let myself laugh, but the overwhelming guilt doused the joy. Snacks cuddled up, and I wrapped myself around her body. I could feel her tiny heartbeat pattering against my chest. The intimate moment with her lasted only a minute, but was powerful enough to stay with me forever.

“Love you, Snacks,” I whispered to her.

“Uh-huh too. But Mommy, it’s too hot,” she answered, popping open my comforter sanctuary and tumbling out to the floor. She flipped her hand behind her, waving as she ran to the door, leaving the room empty. I listened to her feet race down the hall and then to the top of the stairs, which she stuttered down in a set of shuffled steps, her legs short but careful. “One foot. Two feet. Step,” I’d taught her, and that is what I heard.

Maybe, when I felt better, I’d invite Snacks to have a sleepover in our bed and show her how to use a flashlight when telling stories from beneath the covers. I’d bring a stuffed animal and tell her to bring her favorite stuffed animal. It’d be fun and something she could show her best friend.

I lost track of the day after that. I didn’t know what part of the morning or afternoon it was in or if the evening was already upon us. Grieving steals time. It crowded out everything else and forced me to think about what I’d done. The hardest part of lying there was the constant mind-fuck. I puzzled over what had happened. There had been no way for me to know that Sam Wilts was the father of my first mark. If Jerry was playing hard-ass and Sam believed others were involved, then I'd probably sparked a war when I killed Todd Wilts. And Katie was the first casualty.

"I killed her," I said into my pillow. "I killed you, Katie."

"What was that?" I heard Steve ask. I tugged the comforter up over my head to hide in my bubble. My face warmed again in the total darkness. His hand pressed against my back. The mattress leaned under his weight. "Babe, you can't think like that. Katie had just told you what was going on. Even if I had more time, there might have been no stopping it. We're talking about a bad bunch. Killing to them is like ordering breakfast."

"Could have done more, done something sooner," I answered sleepily. He'd never know just how much at fault I really was. He'd never know that *I* was the one who'd ordered breakfast. "I'm sorry. I need more time."

Steve lifted the lip of the comforter, slipping his hand inside my tiny protective world. I shivered at the early winter air that crept in uninvited and felt gooseflesh rise on my arms.

"Come on, babe," he began to say as he pushed the comforter back.

"What are you doing?" I scolded, angry that he'd broken my cocoon.

"Let me help you," he said, but I stayed confused and uncertain about what he meant.

His hands were beneath me then—fingers crawling, scrunching, fishing from front to back, one arm beneath my shoulders and the other beneath my legs.

"No, babe," I objected. "That's not what I want to do." But there was no flirting in his touch, only tenderness and care, the kind I'd seen shared between old couples, the kind I'd always imagined us becoming. He lifted me without hesitation or strain, and I felt my body rise into the air.

"Don't worry," he answered. "That isn't what I have in mind."

Instinctively, I wrapped my arms around his neck and laid my head on his shoulder. It had been years since he had picked me up like that, but my body fell into his arms, remembering. His smell woke me up too. I nuzzled against him and tightened my grip on him, wanting to stay like that, wanting to tell him everything.

What if I told him the truth about the buttons and the homeless man? What if he knew that it was my fault that Katie was dead? Would he stay?

In my heart, I always thought he'd be there no

matter what. But the mother of two boys—Michael's closest friends—was dead.

Steve carried me to the bathroom. The sound of running water rushed around me. He eased me down, leaning me against the wall. He took my hands in his. I opened my eyes, finding the room bathed in golden light from a dozen burning candles. The walls and mirror were sweaty from the heat of the drawn bath, water still running, a layer of bubbles wading atop the surface. A tall glass of wine was perched on one side of the tub, a carafe next to it on a small plate of cheese and fruit.

"Lift," he said, taking my hands in his and urging me to raise my arms. I did as he asked and he pulled my bedtime T-shirt over my head. He disappeared then, crouching, and slid my underpants down my legs. The instructions came again, "Lift."

"Why are you doing this?"

"What?" he asked, standing to face me, looking hurt by my question.

I didn't want him to help me through this. I deserved to feel bad. The tears came then, powerful, painful, zapping what little strength I had.

"She was my best friend," I managed to say, feeling my legs turn to jelly as I fell to my knees. I cried harder than I'd cried all day. "I feel like I can't even breathe without her."

Steve knelt in front of me, tears wet on his cheeks. "I know this is hard," he began. "But it does get better. Come on." I put my arm around my husband and let him help me. I was drained, exhausted, too tired and filled with shame to do anything.

I dipped myself into the hot water, sinking up to my chin, disappearing into the cloud of soapy bubbles as they raced to the edges of the tub. Steve rolled up his sleeves and dropped his hand beneath the water, pulling my arm up. He began to sponge my skin. My sobs had settled into rattles that I chased with a gulp of wine. I tried choking back another wave of sobs, finishing my glass and refilling it, but could only shake my head and let them happen.

"Now tell me everything," Steve said, pushing the sponge around my back and across my neck. He gently rubbed my side next, brushing against me in a way that was soothing and intimate and loving. But his words put me on guard, leaving me to wonder if he knew something. I shook my head, confused. "Tell me everything about Katie. All of your fondest memories."

"Oh," I answered, leaning over to kiss his arm. I tried to smile, but nothing came.

"Just start with one," he encouraged me. "A small story."

Both of Steve's hands were in the tub with me, massaging the soap, causing a small wake that lapped against my bare skin. When the bubbles separated enough to show my nipples, I shivered in the cold.

"Need more bubbles," I said, suggesting without asking. I turned the knob on the hot water faucet with my toes while he emptied the bottle of the remaining bubble bath into the running water.

"All out—" he began to say.

"There's more under the sink," I finished for him. And, as I should have expected, the sound of hollow thumps came when his clumsy hands knocked over my personals.

The shirt! I suddenly remembered.

I hastily added, "Or maybe not!"

Steve jumped at my voice. I'd forgotten about the shirt. Balled up and stained with Todd Wilts' semen.

"Hold on, I think I have it," he said, his arm lost up to his shoulder under the cupboard, but I could tell he was moving around. "What's this?"

I shook my head. "Please. Don't worry about it, babe."

"Got it," he said, producing the bottle. Hot water crept over my legs, rising to my middle and then hugged my belly and breasts while Steve stirred in the bubble bath.

"And how did you do that, anyway?" he asked, moving my hair away from my forehead. "I saw it earlier, covered up with makeup, but didn't want to ask in front of Jerry." Steve's hand drifted from above my eye and down to my cheek. I cupped his hand in mine, kissing his palm.

"Snacks," I answered shamelessly. "Caught one of her toys in a tantrum."

"I think you need to go see your mother," he said abruptly, sneaking in the suggestion when I would have least expected it.

The idea of visiting my mother hit me like a stone and made me groan. I dropped his hand and shut off the hot water, kicking the faucet's knob with a thump. The valve snapped shut, and he gave me a look that asked me to take it easy. Sensitive plumbing. Sensitive subject. The *last* thing I wanted to do was visit my mother.

"Why?" I asked, sounding distracted while I worked the sponge over my neck and shoulders. There was a long silence between us, filled with thousands of foamy bubbles erupting, popping with each squeeze of my hand. Steve took the sponge from my hands and wrung it out. He washed my front but kept his touch innocent. I stared long and hard into his eyes, watching my reflection. Finally, he answered.

"Your mom should hear about Katie, but not on the radio. The news—as hard as it is—should come from you," he explained. "She shouldn't hear about it on the news." I supposed he was right. I laid against the back of the tub, making a swell of water rise against the sides and douse his rolled sleeves. He didn't flinch. If my mother was going to hear about Katie, she *should* hear it from me. Katie was the daughter my mom always wanted; I was the best friend that parents dreaded their daughter bringing home.

28

THE DOORBELL RANG, a sharp noise that caused my skin to crawl. I clutched my shoulder, shielding myself from the interruption. I felt awkwardly sensitive and tried ignoring the distraction, but remained still in a restless stance.

"I wish they would go away, leave our house alone," I muttered. "It's better to be alone, anyway."

Since Katie's death, I hadn't seen anyone other than Steve—even the kids had been scooped up and hauled away to give me some grieving space.

Alone time, as Steve's mother had put it. *Amy just needs some alone time.*

She offered to take them before leaving for her annual trip to Florida. I nodded, hesitant, but half agreed. Michael fixed me a puppy-dog look that made me want to cry, but he listened to his father and grandmother, taking to the backseat of her old sedan with a brief wave. And Snacks blindly followed her older brother, nary a question about where they were going. Another bell came from the door, followed by a rap against the glass. I cursed under my breath and thought about going upstairs and hiding beneath the folds of flannel sheets and the down comforter. But when I peered through the door's smoky glass and saw the outline of a man shuffling back and forth, my heart warmed. I recognized the figure at once, and welcomed the sight.

The dinner ritual, the one where Steve's boss, Charlie, hands down the keys to his new job, had never taken place. My work in the alley with the homeless man had had a play in that hand. But it was a necessary tradition at the station, and Charlie wasn't going to retire officially until after all formalities had been properly concluded. That's what he told his wife, but I tend to think he was hanging on for as long as possible just to piss her off. She wasn't shy about complaining to anyone who'd listen: "Charlie should have retired five years ago. I waited thirty years. It's my turn to have him." And so, on the second day after Katie's death, Charlie decided to visit our home and to make things official.

I opened our door, greeting him. He wrung his

arms together, batting a chill, and motioned to come in without asking.

"Yes, of course. Please," I told him. Steve joined me as Charlie blotted out the light from outside while he shuffled his feet on the foyer's throw rug. The cold had made his nose run while a soft wind had teared up his eyes. He snatched a knitted cap from atop his head, revealing a poof of cloudy white curls that matched his wiry brows. His smile warmed me with grandfatherly affection; it showed fat dimples on his rosy cheeks. Although it was almost midday, the winter cold seeped in from the north, leaving the recent warm spell to become an abandoned memory.

"Winter's coming fast, I think," he said, clapping his hands against his arms. "That, or my thermostat is turned to Florida weather." He laughed at his own joke, which got me and Steve chuckling. Charlie brought a warm vibe into our home. Without the kids around, the air had become heavy with sadness, so much so that it had begun to feel normal. I think I needed a jolt from my sulky brooding, like a good stretch after staying in one position for too long.

"I think you're right," I added. "Colder than it's been."

"That it is, darling," he agreed. His face turned serious then, almost grim, and he cupped my arms in his thick hands. "And how are you holding up?"

Angst nipped at me, just a bite—a tiny razor bite—but it was enough to cause my lip to twitch and tremble. I said nothing, but swallowed hard and blinked away the sudden emotion.

"She's strong," Steve said for me, rubbing my back.

"There, there," Charlie said, his arms circling around me in a hug. He was a bear of a man, and I disappeared from the world for a moment while he finished his condolences. "It's so tough when we lose a close friend. Hang in there, kiddo."

"I will," I was able to squeak out.

"Me and the missus are very sorry for your loss."

"Thank you," I told him as we made our way into the kitchen. "And I am sorry we never got to reschedule our dinner."

Charlie swung a large white bag up from behind him then, "Romeo's" dressing the side in a bright-red cursive script. "I took the liberty of ordering the most popular items. Thought we could make this a bit of a working lunch too, if that's okay? Put this tradition to bed once and for all."

"I'm fine with that," Steve said, but then motioned to me. "Is that okay?"

"Oh yeah," I answered, appreciating that Steve had asked. "You two would have talked shop no matter what, anyway. Am I right?"

Charlie laughed, a hearty chortle that sounded unfamiliar in our house. "She's got us pegged."

The three of us set the table and got out the take-out containers. I couldn't remember the last time I had eaten—then I thought back to the lunch with Katie. But we never ate, we just drank.

Has it been days, I wondered?

My stomach grumbled, agreeing with that estimate when the smell of the food wafted up from the pasta and red sauce. I was hurting inside, but I was hungry too.

"We should buy your mother a gift card from Romeo's," I told Steve. "Say thank you for taking care of the kids." I missed Snacks and Michael, but understood that Steve and his mother meant well and were only trying to help. Still, I think we might have been wrong. Selfishly, I needed them home, needed to hear them in the house, playing, fighting, asking to have something to eat. I needed them to help fill the hole that was growing inside me and to take away some of the ache that came with it.

"Dig in," Charlie said abruptly. I passed him a fresh napkin, digging out a cloth one after a cheap paper one shredded and disintegrated against his clammy forehead. The sight was funny enough, and he laughed it off. It wasn't hot in our house—not even warm, but Charlie tended to sweat and wheeze. And I thought sadly that his wife probably had more to concern herself with than just retiring. "Don't tell the missus, but I ordered extra parmesan cheese on the chicken. Got extra bread too."

"What and when?" Steve began, wasting no time. I was fine with a work discussion, having realized just how hungry I was after that initial bite of food. "What have you got and when do you need it by?"

"Was hoping to have less on our docket, but the cases seem to be piling up lately, and the missus and I have got a date to keep," Charlie answered.

"Do you really want to retire?" I asked, making light of Charlie's pending retirement date. Secretly, I was hoping he'd stay. I felt a twinge of selfishness and then wrestled with a familiar fear. Steve caught the tone in my voice, and in turn, I caught his glance and arched brow. I'd convinced myself that when Steve filled Charlie's shoes, taking over all the cases and the team, he would get lost in his new role and forget about going to law school. But what scared me more was that I knew Steve would love every minute of it.

"Now, now. You know the answer to that, don't you?" Charlie said, and winked. "But I think the wife might have something to say about that."

"Sorry she couldn't join us," Steve added, changing the subject.

"Appreciate that," Charlie answered. He patted my

arm, apologizing for Vickie's absence. "The missus couldn't break her appointment. That realtor is just a pain in my ass, but she'll stop by before the move."

"The cases?" Steve asked.

"Yes, yes," Charlie answered. "Where are you on the homeless man's case?" I stiffened. I hadn't realized their shop talk would include *my* work. Steve never looked up at me, preferring instead to dig into his food and move it around on his plate. He did the same whenever he didn't know what to say.

"Nothing solid yet, but I'm following up on what was found at the scene."

"The buttons?" Charlie asked, and I nearly choked on my food. I was certain they could hear the thumping in my chest. "Probably nothing, anyway. I bet he picked those up, meaning to add them to his collection of junk."

"Still, there's enough evidence to suggest otherwise—" Steve began but stopped when Charlie raised his hand.

"No need for details. I was hoping to close this one before moving on. So, you're going to keep the case open?"

There was a long pause then, and I could sense that Steve wanted to look at me. I froze, waiting. "I think we have to," he answered with his head down. "The case stays open with the investigation."

"Okay then," Charlie said, shaking his head, disappointed. "Wanted that one out of the way to free up time for the Bear investigation. By the way, looks like Todd Wilts was murdered. It's not official until the tox screen, though. Could have died from natural causes, but that doesn't seem likely."

The Bear investigation. Katie's case had a name, but more than that, they had included my mark in it, linking Todd Wilts to Sam and Katie. It was official. I felt a small part of me die.

Would they also include John's murder?

I felt sick inside, as if a spider's silk had been used to bind up my innards. I couldn't eat another bite. Whiskey. A shot of White Bear Whiskey came into my mind, along with the touch of the smooth burn it would have as it warmed my gut.

I did this, I said to myself. I began to tremble, tuning out the world. Steve noticed when I got up from the table. I could tell he was watching, concerned, as I went about cleaning up the kitchen, trying to vanish in the busywork.

This is practice too, I thought, and forced myself to listen to what they were saying.

Charlie went on to tell Steve that Jerry had been moved into the custody of the FBI. "The agency," he called it, as if it were a television show from the past. A sizable team had been pulled together to build a case around Jerry's testimony. Katie's murder, though, stayed within the local police department's jurisdiction. Todd Wilts had been included in the case, but they were still awaiting an autopsy report to confirm the cause of death.

Steve sat up and puffed out his chest with a sigh. The Bear case was his. Three murders—all connected to Sam Wilts. I always found jurisdiction confusing. A part of me wanted to see the case go to someone else in the department, but with Steve owning the case, I'd at least have some eyes on the investigation. I winced when I thought of the photos of John. It was just a matter of time before photos of Katie crossed Steve's desk.

"Feds won't take this case?" Steve asked, but then waved his question away like a fly. "Never mind. No jurisdiction."

"They're interested in what Jerry's got, but unless a murder takes place on federal property, it remains a local case. It's yours," Charlie said. "But take care when working with the 'agency'—they can be an ornery bunch and come back to muck things up for you."

"And Jerry?"

Charlie put his fork down and wiped his mouth. He glanced at me, wondering if it was okay to speak openly. I shrugged, telling him that I was fine.

"Jerry is now the property of three federal agencies

—not just one. Talk about your wild dogs fighting over a chunk of scrap meat," Charlie said, shaking his head. "I've got the DEA, the FBI, and the ATF up my ass, calling the station and wanting everything we've got in triplicate."

"Why so many?" I asked, having no idea how they related to Katie's murder.

"For starters, there's the illegal production and distribution of liquor. Jerry had Sam on that one, extorted a lot of unaccountable dollars too," Charlie answered.

"And it is likely that the bikers were trafficking more than just whiskey across state lines," Steve added. "I'm surprised the IRS hasn't called in yet."

"Give them time!" Charlie exclaimed, his eyes growing wide. He swiped a bead of sweat from his brow. "The IRS is smart. We won't see the likes of them, not just yet. They'll let the other agencies chew on things, do the heavy lifting before swooping in for their share."

I'd never been a fan of Jerry, but Katie loved him. To listen to Steve and Charlie discuss his fate left me feeling sorry for the guy. After all, he was the father of my best friend's children. I wanted to think that he'd just gotten lost while trying to find his balls.

"What's going to happen to him?" I asked, drying some plates. "I mean, he's got the twins."

Charlie cocked his head and offered his most casual cheeky expression. I gave an involuntary sigh. The news was bad. At once, I felt for their boys—Katie's boys. What would become of them? Charlie's pressed lips and fat dimple told me that Jerry would be going to prison.

"Turns out that Jerry's been taking a lot of requests, and not just from Sam. He's been using the mayor's name as his own, dishing out favors and shaking the bikers down like they were money trees," Charlie answered.

"I'll reach out to Jerry's sister," I said, my voice breaking. "Fill her in on what's going on and find out where the boys will be staying."

"He wasn't all bad," Steve added, his voice flat. "Sad to see a family destroyed just like that." Steve's words stung. Guilt tightened my chest.

Charlie pushed his plate of food away from him and produced a miniature notebook. The spiraled cover and leafy pages looked so tiny in his chubby hands. He flipped a few sheets—his writing scratched above the lines in big, curvy letters. "Almost forgot, I've got a lead for you. Might be small, but it's a place to start."

"Lead?" Steve said, interested. "Katie already?"

"Nope, not Katie," he answered. "Though, I'm sure

with Sam Wilts and his son's autopsy, we won't have far to go when closing that case."

"Lay it on me," Steve said, scrambling to grab his notebook.

"Do you remember the Sharon Sutherland case?" Charlie asked. "Young, pretty girl, beat to hell?"

"How could I forget?" Steve answered. "Technicality my ass. DA dropped the ball on that one. If Todd Wilts were still in prison, we might not be here talking about Katie."

Steve's face went red, and he shifted in his chair, unsure if his words had made me uncomfortable. I remembered him talking about the case and the problem with the DA. Only, Steve was careful never to use names—not at home, not when he needed to vent. That technicality was what had put Todd Wilts back on the streets and right in front of me. My mind raced to bring up the images Nerd had showed me. Beautiful, walnut-colored hair, sunny highlights. Young. She was just a baby.

Her name was Sharon.

"Turns out that we've talked to Sharon Sutherland's brother recently in connection with the homeless man's murder," Charlie said, the tone of his voice lifting optimistically.

Nerd?!

My blood ran cold. I wanted to scream, but gripped

a plate instead, straining to contain my shock. "His name is Brian Sutherland. Older brother. Maybe pay him a visit, ask a few more questions about the homeless guy as a guise and fish around about Todd Wilts. Weak and might be a stretch, but this could be a vengeance twist?"

"Vengeance? He didn't seem the type," I heard Steve say. "Probably just a coincidence. Nothing official until the tox—"

I threw the plate into the sink. Rage filled me as I pieced together what Nerd had done. He'd used me. The sound of shattering porcelain filled the kitchen.

Charlie clutched his chest, joking. "Easy there, might give me a heart attack before I get to do my retiring with the wife. Vickie would not be pleased."

"Babe?" Steve asked.

"I'm sorry. It's nothing. Just clumsy," I answered. "Dropped a plate." One of the plate's edges—sharp and unforgiving—had bounced, slicing open my hand. A flower bed of crimson blooms appeared on the broken ceramic. I stared, concentrating, as the bloody droplets lost form and ran into the surrounding wetness. My heartbeat found its way into my hand, pulsing a rapid clop that made me dizzy.

Take a breath, I demanded to myself. I quickly wrapped a kitchen towel around my hand. I grimaced at the sting and bit down on my lip.

"Looks to be a little more than nothing," Steve said, his voice directly behind me. I jumped when his hands grazed my sides. I swung around to face him and was already in full panic mode about to hyperventilate. "Stitches maybe. Are you sure you're okay? I mean, you look pale, babe . . ."

I gave him a vicious nod in place of any words. "Yes. Just need to get some air," I managed to say as I brushed past him. He took my arm, holding me until I turned back.

"You're sure?"

"I'm good," I answered. "Just want to get some air." I grabbed my coat and bag and gave both the men a wave before leaving.

"You take care of that hand," I heard Charlie say. "She'll be fine, Steve. Just needs some space."

Yes, I need some space.

That was the overall consensus, so I took it, practically running from our house. But I wasn't fine—not as Charlie stated. My mind raced and my heart thumped with fiery rage.

How much of what Nerd showed me was even real? Any of it? I thought back to how he had wanted Todd Wilts to suffer a slow and tortured death.

"She'll never have children," he'd said.

None of this was a coincidence. He'd set me up. Nerd set the whole thing up in a sick fucking game of twisted revenge, dropping me in the middle of it. Our business was a scam. Katie was dead because of *him*.

When I made it to Neshaminy Creek, I drove the car off to the thin shoulder on the bridge, turned off the motor, and opened the door. My foot slipped on the frost covering the metal grate. I grabbed the car's hood with my bloody hand, bracing myself as I made my way toward the bridge's railing. I did need air. That part was true.

The autumn season was over. Winter was here. The arctic air stung my lungs as I slowed my breathing. I clutched the old metal railing hard, choking the round metal. My anger was out of control. I stamped bloody prints, steamy smears, into the pale green and mottled rust. I followed the sound of flowing water, trickling as it disappeared beneath growing stretches of ice along the creek's banks. It wouldn't be long before the freeze traveled from one side to the other, preserving the evidence of my murders, holding them until the springtime thaw.

Would it be a passerby, a jogger maybe, or someone walking their dog who'd glimpse one of my clues, my liabilities, my evidence, putting me in prison for the rest of my life?

"I deserve to go to prison," I said. Then I screamed until my voice became hoarse. I heard someone scream back at me—a shrilling voice that echoed off the far hills.

“Fuck you!” I screamed. Then I whimpered, “Fuck me.”

What had I done? I took a mother away from her children.

“She’ll be missed—” I began to shout, but couldn’t finish the words. I screamed until my voice broke like the shattered dish, cutting into my throat with stabbing pain.

“I’m going to kill him,” I said solemnly. Any affection I had for Nerd was gone. He played me in his game of revenge. “Making up our plans, *my* plans, the business.” And I realized as I went on and on, arguing, reasoning, with nobody, I had trusted Nerd with my most intimate secrets. He broke my heart. This time, the damage was fatal.

29

LATE-AFTERNOON SUNLIGHT streaked through the library windows, its harsh rays cutting across the tables and books, making a faint shiver of dust loom in the light. Empty. "People don't read anymore," I heard in my head. I was suddenly thankful for that sad truth. The young librarian—Becky I think her name was, aloof, white headphone cords dangling from her ears, popping gum, her attention lost to her phone's screen—waved me by the counter without raising her head.

I wouldn't have stopped, anyway. I couldn't have stopped. I would have walked past anyone at the counter, eager to find my business partner. So I could kill him. I saw Nerd's head—or rather, just the top of his moppy hair. The rest of him was hidden behind the computer. I stopped, uncertain of what to do. A shudder ran through me as the twisting in my stomach grew tight.

"Not yet," I said, quietly hissing my words like a poison mist. "Not directly at him . . . surprise him."

The vast library gave me room to move around the computer table—flanking is what it's called. I took a path behind the ceiling-tall bookshelves, stepping quietly along the back wall. I looked until I found another exit—an emergency exit. I'd use that when leaving if I had to, removing any risk of passing Becky, not that I expected her to see or hear a thing. My legs felt rubbery—a nervous rubbery that I hadn't expected. There was no real reason to be afraid, but I was. I was terrified of what I was about to do.

"Simmer," I told myself, trying to channel my rage about what happened to Katie into a more controllable form of the rage I had felt on the bridge. "He's the reason she's dead."

I circled around the end of the computer table, sweat beading on every inch of me, trumpets blaring a roar in my head, my hand still pulsing from the glassy bite. Nerd moved. I froze. He rose from his seat, peered over the computer monitor, and looked toward the door.

Was he looking for me?

Except for the librarian, the library was sadly empty.

Before I could stop it, before I could control it, fury erupted, and my hands were sliding an encyclopedia off the shelf. A dank, green, leather-bound book. My hands gripped the spine and the bulky, closed pages. A weapon.

I ran at Nerd, my hands swinging it high and off to one side. I crashed the book down on him in a blur, like a blade of lightning touching the ground. Nerd's head rocked violently to one side—a sickening thud sounded, making me think I'd crushed his skull. He grunted and tumbled to the floor. I raised my hands for another hit, but realized I'd dropped the book, having underestimated the force of the impact. The encyclopedia had flung out of my hands and crashed onto the computer table, opening, spiraling, spitting out loose pages in a random flurry.

Nerd rolled onto his back, his eyes—and pupils—wide. I peered toward the front, but found the librarian still busy with her phone, oblivious to the commotion.

"Wait! Wait, please." Nerd managed to get out, throwing his hands up to block me, but I ignored his plea and straddled his body, shoving my fingers around his skinny neck. I was going to do this—my new kinship with murder was driving me. I would become the murderer I'd always wanted to be. "I can explain—"

"I don't want to hear it. Didn't you think I'd find out

who you were and figure out that you'd set me up?" I squeezed and at once his eyes blew open, wider than I thought possible. His face filled with terror. He looked like a child who'd been thrown into the deep end of a pool, unable to swim, realizing death was pulling on his ankles. He kicked and bucked, trying to throw me. I braced my legs around his middle, clutching, hanging on. I stared into his bulging eyes. Nerd's lips moved wildly, screaming silent words. His hands balled into delicate fists that batted at my arms. He made a feeble attempt, and for a second, I felt sorry for him.

Something was different this time. The way my fingers closed around his throat to strangle the life out of him, the purplish hue that came over his complexion, and his dying gaze that stayed fixed on me. Huge pools of tears welled up and dripped, cutting wet paths down the sides of his face. I was crying now too, suddenly feeling terrified that I was going to crush his neck, that I was going to finish what I'd started. It wasn't at all like the homeless man or like it had been with Todd Wilts. The electricity, the magic, the passion that came with those murders was missing. I was killing for personal reasons. That meant I was killing for the wrong reasons.

Nerd stopped fighting back. He stopped trying to talk. His mouth puckered in a grim wrinkle as he sucked emptily, starving for the air he couldn't have.

His arms dropped to his sides and his fingers crawled toward his backpack.

Was he reaching for a weapon?

Instinct kicked in, and I tightened my grip. His eyes disappeared, rolling up until they were all white. Thready red explosions appeared in them and turned into bloody pools. My heart sank, and I quickly let go. He gasped and rolled over onto his side, erupting in a violent series of coughs. My hands cramped, trembled, and shook. I glanced above the desk, peering through the computers to see where the librarian was. I could make out the white lines hanging from her ears as she swayed to her music. We were alone.

"Why?" I cried.

But he couldn't talk. He vomited onto the carpet and then rolled onto his back. He was quiet then—too quiet, and a dark fear hit me.

I killed him.

A gasp.

I tensed up, waiting.

Another gasp and a sudden fit of coughs made his skinny frame buck up and down again as he tried to breathe. When the coughing settled into a steady wheeze, other signs of life returned.

"Why?" he wheezed.

"Do you know what you did? My best friend is dead because of you!"

"I . . . how did you find out?" he asked, spitting and trying to prop himself up on his elbows.

"Do you really have to ask that, Brian Sutherland!?"

"I was so careful—careful so that nobody would know." His eyes remained stunned-looking from my attack, but slowly cleared. And when he began to shake his head, I knew that he understood the slip he'd made. "Your husband. The dead guy in the alley."

"Did you think that I wouldn't find out?" I asked, but I didn't wait to hear an answer. "Do you know what killing Todd Wilts started?"

"Do you think I care?" he answered abruptly, blubbering. He swiped at his nose.

The color in his face had started to return, giving me a sense of relief. But I could already see the rise of swelling on the skin around his neck. It'd bruise by tonight, but it was his eyes that really gave away what I tried to do. The color was there, but the whites were bleeding red—blown, hemorrhaging.

"Can I show you something?"

I hesitated and then asked, "You mean what's in your bag?" His gaze fell on it, and he clutched it to his chest like a security blanket.

"Got this for you," he answered, his voice sounding like a pouty child's. "Thought you could use it for our next hit." He took out a small gift and tossed it to me. A flash of neon purple and silver wrapping paper bumped from my one hand to the next as I tried to catch the gift.

"What makes you think there is *going* to be a next time?" I asked, putting his gift down. "My best friend was killed because of what we did. Don't you *get* that?"

Nerd shrugged and shook his head, fixing me with a look of disbelief. "How?" he asked, "How's that even possible?"

"Her husband," I answered, but suddenly felt the emotion choke my words. "Her husband was involved with them—the White Bear, Todd, and his father, Sam. What we did started a war."

Nerd continued to shake his head, struggling to believe what I told him. "That isn't what was supposed to happen."

"Yeah, I know, but it did. And now there are two little boys who will never—" I couldn't finish. I was done, both mentally and physically. I gave Nerd a hard look then, disappointment reeling inside me like a sickness. "How much of our arrangement was fake? The money?"

He shook his head, again. "I used it to buy the strychnine."

"There's no bank account full of Bitcoins, is there? And the job listings?"

"That part is not true," he answered, his voice breaking. I began to think that I'd damaged his vocal chords. "I mean at first I did set up the link to find someone, someone like you to do the hit on Wilts. But what you want to do, the business, I'm in. I'm all in."

"I don't know how I could ever trust you."

He pondered what I said, thinking hard, as if it were a trivia challenge. "How about I give you something?" I peered at the gift, and then saw him shake his head while getting back up in front of the computer. I sat down next to him and felt the event fall out of me, draining, taking any energy I might have had in reserve. I couldn't explain anymore, do anymore. Instead I watched as Nerd went to work on the computer.

He attacked the keyboard, his fingers tapping in a blur, the sound of his fingernails scraped against the keys loudly. A flurry of words appeared on the screen like accumulating snow, growing deeper, scrolling, until there were an abundance of sentences. He stretched his arms, continuing the volley of keystrokes; lips moving in a whisper, spouting the words, translating them into mechanical pushes that clicked beneath the keys. The snowfall became a blizzard and the sentences formed themselves into paragraphs and then filled a page. And when he was done, he flicked his hands at the screen and stood up to face me. His eyes were dark and wet, with a deep gray puffing beneath them. But I didn't know if I was looking at the result of exhaustion from the attack or the grief over his sister.

"That's my confession," he said gravely. "All of it. It spells out in complete detail how Todd Wilts was killed. There is evidence in that confession that only the DA, the coroner, and the killer could possibly know. I'm giving it to you. Digitally signed too—incriminates only me." He rummaged through his bag, came up with another flash drive, and copied the file containing his statement onto it, then handed it to me.

"I don't know if this is enough," I told him. "But for now, I think I'm going to need a little time to reconsider our arrangement." The words stung him. His lip trembled, and he dropped back into his seat, skipping his fingers over the keyboard and lifting his hand, telling me to wait.

"Please," he asked. "Please understand why." Images flew onto the screen that immediately made me gasp. It was his sister, but then it wasn't. What I saw was a gut-wrenching, terrible horror show that made me feel sick and want to turn away. A beautiful girl had been terribly disfigured—a wide ragged scar stretched from the corner of her mouth to her ear and then again from the other side in a sickening permanent smile. Her right eye was half-shut and clouded over with blindness while the other stayed open wide, but askew, like a stroke victim's. And her jaw had been broken and now closed misaligned. I could only imagine what she must have gone through. I felt for the girl and hated seeing her beauty destroyed. I shook my head, but it couldn't change how I felt. Not now. Not ever.

"Now do you understand? This is her, this is my sister. Today," Nerd said. "The person she was died that night. She'll never be the beautiful woman she was meant to be. The world will miss her. I *miss* her!" he finished as he broke down. I wanted to put my hand on his shoulder, but couldn't bring myself to do it. After all, I'd just tried to kill him.

I did the only thing I could think of. I left. And as I walked away, leaving the same way I had come in, I heard Nerd stand up. I paused, turning to look over my shoulder in time to see him pointing to the computer.

"If you change your mind!" he said, his voice sheepish, yet tense. "We've got something that will work. Partners. I'll be here."

I tugged at the air, giving him a short wave, discreet and meaningless. As I left the library, I felt emptier than I'd ever felt in my entire life.

30

WHEN I CLOSED the car door, my gut told me that I would see Nerd come running out of the library, waving his hands, pleading and begging to keep our business going. But I couldn't think of going on. Not yet, anyway. I was crushed, having been misled and having lost Katie. A desperate emptiness filled me like the silence filled the car. The only sound I heard was my own breathing and the crunch of upholstery as my seatbelt clicked home. A fluttery scurry came from above the car—the blackbirds swarming, I imagined, winding down before the evening began. I dared a glimpse at my rearview mirror and was thankful to see an empty road behind me. I stayed like that for a long time, not wanting to move, not wanting to do anything, hiding in motionless oblivion.

"Maybe I deserve this!" I exclaimed as I picked at the cut on my hand. The kitchen towel had already become stiff with the dried blood. "Eye for an eye—Katie for Todd, right?"

Could that really be how this worked? But I didn't want to believe that, couldn't believe that. Katie would be missed, but Todd Wilts deserved what he got. A part of me understood why Nerd did what he did. If it were Snacks? I would have done far worse and would have gladly used anyone dumb enough to get involved. I peered into the mirror again only to see the daylight turning into night. How long had I been sitting there? Long enough for shadows to have crept along the blacktop, becoming monstrously tall before fading with the disappearing sun. A streetlight overhead flickered, catching my eye, and turned on a faint glassy light that became brighter without notice, as if by magic. It was time to go home. Even the blackbirds swooped in and out of the alley a final time, settling down to roost in the evergreen bushes for the night.

Nerd remained in the library, but in my hand I found the gift he'd given me in place of my car keys. I wanted to throw it to the floor of the car, thinking it could be dangerous. It could be something he'd picked up to blow me into a thousand pieces. But that wasn't his style. He wanted our business and he wanted me as a partner—he needed me more than I needed him. I told myself that, but didn't entirely believe it.

With the tip of my finger, I needled the corner of the wrapping paper just enough to lift the edge and see what was beneath it. I narrowed my eyes, squinting as I tried to make out what I thought was velvet. Tearing the paper away revealed a black box—a ring box. I lifted the lid. There was a creak and then click as the top snapped open. A folded piece of paper fell from inside, landing in my lap. And beneath the note there was a ring, but it was unlike any ring I'd ever seen before. A sterling silver band, thick around the bottom and with a large oval-shaped stone on the top. Gaudy was the first word that came to my mind, and I hoped for Nerd's sake that this wasn't his way of being chivalrous.

I put the ring down to read the note. Handwritten and signed with the name "Nerd," the note went on to say that he'd found this antique in one of the red links. An odd place for a ring it seemed, but this was no ordinary ring. It dated back to the Cold War era, when the countries were in a never-ending game of Spy vs. Spy. This was an assassin's ring.

"Turn the stone," the note instructed. So I did, lifting the ring close enough to my face to see a small inscription engraved on the inside of the band. I turned the stone, instinctively thinking that clockwise made the most sense. The setting didn't move, and I wondered if Nerd was having some fun with me. Then I heard one soft tick. And then another. The stone easily slid, like the second hand of a clock, rotating around the face until it reached three o'clock. The shank of the ring popped, flicking open and spitting a tiny needle. I jumped, surprised by this sudden appearance. I had nearly stabbed my own hand. I laughed too, realizing at once that the assassin's ring was a syringe. An assassin's tool that I'd certainly like.

"Well, he knows my taste." I tried to laugh. "But where is the plunger?" I wondered, curious. I was actually not at all sure if that was what the other part was called. This ring could be useful—very useful—for dosing a hit's drink, sticking him or her in the shoulder with a polite pat, or giving a jab in the thigh during an accidental bump. My thoughts bounced around with ideas like a writer's muse creatively teasing an author working on the next novel. Turning the stone in the other direction loosened it, and I found that I could open the top. With the touch of a surgeon, I carefully lifted it. The tiniest hinge sang a squeaky chirp to me, as if it had been unused in nearly a century. Beneath the stone was a stainless-steel reservoir. Not huge, but large enough to hold a lethal dose of poison if it were potent enough.

"I call her Needle—very *Game of Thrones*, don't you

think?" Nerd went on to say in his note. And while only I vaguely understood the reference, I loved the name. Needle. "She is my gift to you for doing business together. Thank you for the opportunity."

I thought I'd been exhausted of all emotion for one lifetime, but the sentiment raised a feeling that I hadn't expected. That was the way it should be. We should have a finite amount of emotions that can be spent in one lifetime. That way, we could dispense with the saddest first and never be bothered by them again.

"Please dispose of this note properly."

I folded the note and put it back inside the box with the ring, then stuffed them both into my jacket. I had something new to add to my secret box. After all, there would be room now—I had the Killing Katie designs to fetch and burn. I'd cremate them, just like my friend would be in a few days.

"Thank you," I said aloud, starting the car. The evening fell from the sky, covering me in darkness as a few blurry stars began to show. I swallowed the dryness in my mouth, craving a taste of White Bear Whiskey. Maybe I wouldn't go back yet. Maybe I'd take a trip for a shot of the homegrown stuff.

31

THE SMELL OF fuel and exhaust. The sound of idling truck engines and of men chiding each other back and forth with sarcastic banter. I'd sweated enough this hot August night to tire while waiting, motionless. But I'd fallen asleep again, and now the man was above me, his smell filling the car. Their voices moaned in rhythm, coming to a peak. I hadn't made the belt loop yet but I held the buckle in my hands, tracing its winged form with my finger. My dad always liked belt buckles shaped like airplanes. "They're so hard to find," he'd said, telling us how he stopped at nearly every roadside stand while traveling for work.

"I'm going to come," I heard rain down from above me. The heavy buckle slipped from my small fingers as her voice lifted too, rising in pitch—she was getting close. I threaded the leather through the hinged loop as fast as I could, nervous urgency eating my insides like acid.

I can't miss it again. She'd be so mad.

I succeeded, throwing the noosed belt around his neck just as the first grunts sounded from his mouth.

"Swing," I whispered as I jerked the strap with all my weight, hanging, bobbing up and down as the sound of two lovers became one. When I peered up, I saw the balding man's dome glistening with sweat, his head twitching as he died.

And then *her* face was above me, eyes finding mine, her body collapsing onto his.

"Shush," Katie said, her finger to her lips, the bullet hole in her head festering with maggoty death.

"Katie!" I screamed, vaulting upward in bed, panting. I searched the fuzzy gray light, wondering which part of the dream I was in. When I shivered and felt a bead of sweat roll down to the small of my back, I knew that I was home.

"You okay, babe?" Steve asked, his voice groggy. "Amy?"

I shuddered and cradled my face in my hands and cried, trying to understand what the dreams meant.

And why now? Why had they started now?

There was so much detail—familiar, like a recent

memory—but then the details were gone again, lost in a sleepy haze.

Steve's hand encouraged me to lay back down, facing away from him so that he could wrap his arm around my middle. I eased into him, shaping my hips and legs to match his. We fell into one another and before I could stop it, I confessed the unthinkable.

"I killed a man."

There were no words—only the interruption of his chest rising and falling. He stayed still for what seemed forever, for what felt like an eternity.

"What did you just say?" he asked me, his voice having lifted out of the sleepy fog.

"I killed that man," I repeated. "The homeless man. The one you and Charlie were talking about." Steve remained still—his arm around me, his chest pressed firm against my back and his hot breath becoming heavy against my neck.

"I know," he answered, surprising me. "I've known since the night we drove to Romeo's."

"Then why didn't you say anything?" I asked, craning my head over my shoulder. "You could have—"

"Could have what?" he interrupted. "You're the mother of my children, my wife. What was I supposed to do?"

"But you never said anything."

He propped himself up on his elbow so that we

could face each other. “And say what?” He cupped my chin and softly caressed my cheek with his finger. “I did the only thing I thought was safe—nothing. Which is why the case is still open.”

“Steve, I’m so sorry that I put you in that position,” I told him, my words sincere as a pang of guilt hit me. For the first time, I thought of what could have happened to *him*. “It happened so fast, and then I . . . I just panicked and wanted to hide.”

Steve sat up then, and even in the darkness I could see that he was nearly nude. There was no badge, no golden shield, no mystical powers that harnessed a magic from the heavens. I wasn’t talking to a cop, I was talking to my husband.

“What happened?” My hands went to his neck. I held him as I brought myself to his lips and kissed him. The urge to kiss him was strong, the need to kiss him was stronger. And maybe deep down I thought that once I shared the truth with him, it would be the last time that we ever kissed. He put my hands in his and slipped them away from his neck until I was lying back down. “What happened?” he repeated.

“I was at the library; that part was true. And when I was on my way to my car, I heard this voice calling out for help. Crying almost. I thought someone had been hurt bad.”

“The homeless man,” Steve added. I nodded,

agreeing. "That's what the other girl said too. Only we never shared that part with the newspaper. It's a ruse, a trap that he used to lure his victims."

"Anyway, when I went to help him, he attacked me with a knife. Steve, he was going to rape me . . . and . . . and I think he would have killed me too."

"Babe," he said and brought me into his arms. "I'm sorry that happened to you. But you should have told me what happened that night, or even stayed at the scene and called the police."

"But I'm telling you now," I answered, pushing against his chest, separating us. But he was shaking his head and I could tell by the look on his face that there was more. "What is it?"

"Amy, it doesn't look like self-defense. Not anymore. It might have started out that way, but the wounds . . ." He stopped talking, and my mind flooded with pictures of the man's head leaning to one side, half of his neck cut open.

"I cut him," I said blankly. "When I had the opportunity, I shoved his head into the bricks and took his knife." By now, I was crying, but I didn't even know when I'd started. A rasp came into my chest that forced a shaky breath. Steve continued to waver, telling me it was all wrong without saying a word.

"You killed a man when you could have just run away," he said, his voice as choked up as it had been in the kitchen when he begged to have my blouse. "The buttons torn from your blouse—they were in his hand. They can put you at the scene. I've been sitting on them, but Charlie wants the crime lab to try and pull prints, pull something, anything."

My mind raced, searching for a way out. I felt like a mouse in a maze, but there was certainly no cheese reward waiting for me at the end. There was only life, protection from the cat chasing me. I couldn't get my mind to work fast enough. It felt like the world was closing in on me. I was suffocating.

"My fingerprints?" I said, asking. "I've never . . my fingerprints aren't on file . . ."

"The school," Steve said abruptly. More images swarmed in my mind, image of Snacks and fingerprinting the children in her school. I had been the first to volunteer, showing them that it was safe, that it was like a game.

"Tell me what to do," I begged, sounding desperate. But not because I was working him, because I *was* desperate.

"You can't come forward. It's too late for that now, and there is no way to explain it as self-defense, not with wounds like that."

"But it was!" I nearly yelled. Steve touched my mouth. It was three in the morning and the house was quiet. "Steve, he was going to rape me. Kill me."

"If you'd run or even cut him just enough to get away, then yes. But now?"

"What do *we* do?" I begged, but this time I paired him in with me, wanting to see if he was with me or not. It was a huge risk. He said nothing but continued to shake his head. "Steve? Babe?" A dark notion stirred, taking flight in my gut like the thousand blackbirds fleeing the coming night. Sadly, there was no *we* in this, after all.

Steve came forward, taking my face in his hands as he kissed me. "I don't know how much I can lie, how much I can hide. I'm not going to say this will pass, because, babe, I really just don't know." He began to mumble to himself then, spitting words about keeping the case open and how long it could stay open. There was a mishmash of other detective jargon that I would never even attempt to try and understand. The dark notion felt like a bullet slowly burrowing through me. I needed to scream.

Steve finally came back to me, his eyes clearer than before, as if an epiphany had been discovered like a gold nugget by a desperate miner. "We can do this. We can keep the case open. As long as it stays my case I can leave it alone. It will become another unsolved dust collector. Just don't *ever* tell me what happened to the knife. Eventually, we're going to have to find a way to close the investigation, though—

quietly too. I mean close it so that it stays closed forever."

My eyes welled up, and I clutched Steve, squeezing his body until he groaned uncomfortably. I hardly registered his plans, but I did hear one word. He said *we*.

32

"FLIP IT," STEVE said, pointing at the stove. My mind had wandered, thinking of Nerd and Katie and what I could do to fix things. Everything had fallen apart. There was a very good chance the plans for law school would become another one of our forgotten talks. But starting over without Nerd seemed daunting. Formidable, even. And I wasn't at all sure that I wanted to start over with anyone else. Without law school as an option, Steve was going to step into Charlie's shoes and never look back. "Babe. Flip Snacks's grilled cheese before it burns."

"Damn," I snapped as smoke drifted up, catching my eye with a sting. I choked the pan's handle and slid the spatula beneath the sandwich. Hot butter spat back and popped, flying out of the pan. "Sorry, I got it. My mind's elsewhere."

"You're going to your mother's today?" Steve asked, grabbing his coat to leave. But I didn't answer, choosing instead to ignore him as cheese oozed from between the bread and seared on the hot pan. I left the cheese to burn, letting the sound be my answer. He stopped and waited. I could already sense his vibe whenever it came to discussing my mother. "Amy, she's your mother. You should spend some time and talk to her about Katie—"

"She already knows about Katie," I interrupted. "I called her the morning after it happened."

"But you should go see her. I'm sure she'd appreciate it. Michael and Snacks can go with you."

"They just got home from *your* mother's yesterday," I added, feeling selfish, feeling justified. "Plus, I was just there." I kept my head down, eager to give the grilled cheese more attention than our conversation. But when I heard Steve drape his coat over the door handle and come back into the kitchen, I knew I'd already lost.

"For Katie and you, not just the kids," he said softly, holding me. He'd said *we* last night, and I was only now beginning to understand what that really meant. *We* knew about the homeless man. *We* knew there was incriminating evidence. And *we* knew that I'd murdered someone. Yet Steve was with *me* and wanted to protect our family.

But what if he knew about the rest? What if he knew who killed Todd Wilts and triggered the events that led to Katie's death?

I overheard Steve giving Charlie an updated status —he was planning to interview Nerd, bring him into the station, intimidate him. Would Nerd hold up? Would he tell Steve anything? I thought of the flash drive and of Nerd's confession. "Digitally signed," he'd said.

But what did that mean exactly? And could it actually help me if I needed it to?

"Earth to Amy. Better flip it again."

"Seems like I was just there," I added, turning the sandwich over one more time before taking it off the burner. My mouth watered at the smell of the butter and melted cheese and the toasted bread. I cooked it in extra butter, after all, just the way Snacks liked it. I'd been losing weight since Katie's death but would steal a bite before she dug into it.

"Babe, that was a few weeks ago."

"You keeping tabs on me?" I scolded, but shrugged it off jokingly. "It's sad being there, Steve. You should see it. All of Dad's things are boxed away. She even had his oak tree chopped down. Said it would open up the yard and help with the resale value."

Steve leaned over my shoulder, sneaking a bite of our baby girl's sandwich. He devoured a corner, and smiled.

"Damn, that's good. But hot!" he said, waving at his mouth. "I'm not taking sides, but your mom is probably right. I mean, she's got to be lonely and probably wants to find folks her own age. Maybe an over-sixty-five community?" And as he finished, he stole another bite.

"Babe!" I yelled, but eagerly joined him, eating up the other corner. "I can make her another one." We shared the rest of our daughter's sandwich, saying nothing about my confession. I'd been preparing to answer any of his questions, expecting him to have been in detective mode from the moment I heard the shower come on. Instead, I found Steve—the father of our children, the husband I married, the man who asked what music I liked and then scoffed when I had danced to a country tune. Maybe my confession had changed something, and maybe it changed everything.

God, I hope so.

What Steve was doing was illegal. I knew that. Exactly which laws were being broken, I didn't know.

Obstruction of justice, maybe? Or tampering with the evidence? What exactly could he be charged with? What if Charlie discovered Steve was sitting on my buttons, stalling the case until it was forgotten? And if we were both arrested, what then?

As I fed the last bite of grilled cheese to Steve, he parted his lips in a boyish expression, and a feeling of angst came to me. What I'd done, what I'd *selfishly* done, was risk having Michael and Snacks taken from us, taken away by child services in the event of being caught. We only needed to be suspected of something to have that agency pay us a visit. I wanted to say something to Steve, felt compelled to say something, but held onto my worries.

"Love you," Steve said, still chewing. "So you'll go? Take the kids?"

"Yes," I said, but without the endearing tone he'd wanted to hear. He stopped chewing and pouted his lips, staying like that until I kissed him good-bye.

"Good," he answered. "I bet that it'll do more for you than you know."

"Get out of here so I can make Snacks another sandwich," I said, nudging him.

The anxiety about visiting my mother made the time pass quickly, and before I knew it, she was greeting us at the door. There was love in her eyes for Snacks and Michael, and a flash of derision for me. I'd come to accept this as a part of our "normal."

I searched the lawn for the stump from the big oak tree but only found green—lots of green that had been stitched together. She'd had the stump removed and put new grass in its place. It looked sad like that.

He's all gone now, I thought sadly. It was as though

the roots of my father's life had been yanked out too, disappearing forever from this world.

"Water the roots, not the petals." I suddenly heard his voice in my head and bent over, tears coming to my eyes. "Understand, Amy? If you water the petals, what will happen?" my father asked me.

"They'll burn in the sunlight, Daddy," I'd answered him.

"That's right. So what do we do?"

"We only water the roots, not the petals."

"Good girl. Remember that. Make the roots good and strong—then they'll survive anything."

I cried, remembering the words we'd shared when he showed me how to tend his garden. And without warning, I felt my mother's hand on my back, comforting me. The emotion of missing my father was overwhelming and zapped what little strength I had. Michael and Snacks came to my side too.

"What is it?" my mother asked, but I couldn't get the words out and motioned to where the oak tree had been. "That old thing? Again?"

"It was the last of him," I said. "Of Daddy."

"Nonsense," she countered. "There is plenty of him right here. There will always be plenty of him." But I shook my head, disagreeing with her more out of rehearsed instinct than anything thoughtful.

"He's gone," I repeated sharply.

"He's *here*," she said, patting her hand on Snacks's little heart. "And *here*," she repeated, tapping Michael's heart. The kids smiled and nodded the way kids do when they're not quite sure about what grown-ups are saying.

"Uh-huh," I mumbled, understanding and drying my eyes.

"And," my mom said, tearing up with me, "he's here with *you* Amy, always will be." She laid her hand on my chest.

33

"THIS IS BITTER," I said, sipping and cringing but wanting to laugh at the sharp taste in my mouth. As my mother explained it, her international tea club was on a monthly exchange, trading and sharing the delights from their respective hometowns. And for this cold, wintery month, she had received a tidy little bag of Asian tea she couldn't remember the name of, let alone pronounce. "Mom, not sure what country that came from, but I swear that looks like pot."

"Amy!" she blurted and motioned to Snacks and Michael. Michael's head was down, but it lifted a moment and then dipped again, his attention locked on his phone. Snacks was adrift in a sea of couch pillows, rolling around on the floor. I waved off what I said, laughing. I really needed to laugh. And we rarely ever shared anything funny. The corner of her mouth curled as she fingered the plastic baggie, tugging on a leafy green bud. "Who knows? Could be good." She giggled and gulped a mouthful. When she cringed and shook her head wildly, we both laughed until we couldn't breathe. I needed that.

"Maybe you grabbed the wrong baggie?" I joked, trying to keep the humor going, keep our spirits up.

My mother swung her chin toward the wall of open moving boxes and said in a discouraging tone, "Your father collected so much stuff . . . it's been overwhelming. I loved the man but had no idea how much baggage he really had." We both let out a light laugh at the humor, but the sight of all the boxes made me sad. It wasn't the home I'd grown up in. Not anymore.

I dared another sip, partly curious and partly earnest, wondering if it *was* a bag of dope. Loose tea leaves floated high in my cup—a tall, slender cup. "Because that's how best to steep this particular type," my mother had said. A curled leaf slowly rolled open in the hot water like a young butterfly drying its papery wings before their first flight. Disappointing. I could tell by the shape that we were drinking nothing but tea. I decided to keep that to myself and slurped to avoid the heat. More leaves opened up and a few fell away, sinking toward the bottom, having a lazy swim in the hot water. I rubbed my eyelids, feeling the exhaustion of the last days catching up again. I was in a no-win race to try and stay ahead of my grief. One moment I'd be ahead in a sprint, and then the next I'd feel like I was coming in last with a dog biting at my heels.

"You look tired," my mother reminded me, though her tone was supportive—like it had been about the oak tree. "When is Katie's funeral? I called her parents to offer my condolences but they didn't pick up."

I shook my head and realized I hadn't heard from Jerry's sister or Katie's parents. "I'm not sure," I answered. "But I'd think it would be soon?"

"So sad. And such a nice family Katie had," my mom said. An immature pang of jealousy hit me.

Had I ever heard her say anything like that about me?

But this was Katie, this was expected. I tried to be better than my jealousy. My mother loved Katie like a daughter, and this had to be just as painful for her as it was for me. Her hands remained steady as she sipped the tea, but I could see the loss on her face and in the saddened way she smiled when trying to talk fondly about Katie.

"It's hard," I agreed and stood to go to her, to hug her. I knelt down and put my arms around my mother. I closed my eyes. "I know you loved Katie. It is sad."

"Thank you, Amy," she answered and broke from

my embrace. "Women in this family are strong. Have to show strength for them . . ." Mom motioned to the kids and then turned back to face her tea. The abruptness hurt, but that was something else I'd gotten used to over the years.

"There's no Internet here," Michael's voice chirped in my ear. I leaned away, irritated by the complaint. A quick scan of the room showed me the television, unplugged and sitting on the floor. Next to it was the old radio, packed up and taped. And then I found the faded wallpaper and the silhouette of old picture frames. The kids were going to bore quickly without anything to keep them occupied.

"Nonsense," my mother said. She stood and went to the stout moving box labeled books. She hunted through a pile of dingy black and brown and green hardbacks until she came upon what she was looking for. I recognized the book, and a warm recollection came to me. It was one of my father's favorite books. We'd read it together, page by page, cover to cover, every night for a month when I was just beginning to discover books. My mom gave me a look. "You remember this one: *Robinson Crusoe*."

"I loved that story," I answered.

My mother approached Michael, the old book in one hand, her wagging finger in the other. "There is no need for the Internet in this house," she said, twisting her wrist, joking with him. He glanced over at me with uncertainty, and I dipped my chin with a nod, encouraging him to take the book. My mom knelt, her knees popping as she did, and placed Michael's hand on the book's spine. "Your granddaddy loved this book. It was his oldest and it was his favorite, and it is time that you have it."

"To read?" he asked in a mock-amused tone, but with the innocence of not knowing what it held. I opened my eyes wide then, telling him to say thank you. "Thank you, Grandma."

"You're welcome," she said, stretching up to peck him on the forehead. "You're getting so tall. Gonna be a man soon. Now go on over to that chair. Your grandaddy liked to read there, saying how the light in that window was perfect for old pages." Michael reluctantly made his way to the chair. He begrudgingly slunk down beneath the window and opened to the first pages of *Robinson Crusoe*. Seeing him settle into the giant reading chair, his knees bent, the book pushed up to his chin, renewed some of my sentiment about the yard and what had become of the old oak tree.

My father is here, I told myself. *He's right over there.*

As if Michael heard me, he looked up, a reflection of sunlight off the pages brightening his handsome face. I tilted my head, telling him I loved him. He smiled and then went back to reading the book.

"And me, me, me?" Snacks insisted, having come up from squirreling around on the floor. "What's for me?"

I filled my mouth with more of the bitter tea, finding an odd liking for it after all. Stretching my arm behind me, I fished through one of the open moving boxes, but this one had no label, no designation written on the side of it.

My old toys? I wondered, hoping to find something to keep Snacks busy.

My hand fell blindly into a pit of leathery snakes. When I touched the familiar squarish buckle, a terrible, deathly cold filled me. I came to understand what I held in my hand. I didn't move. I didn't say a word. I let my fingers scream for me. I traced the outline of the belt buckle, finding a metal wing, and then on the other side, I traced the matching wing. I shook my head, telling myself that this couldn't be, that my dreams were just dreams, nightmares brought on by what I'd done to the homeless man.

"What is it, Amy?" my mother asked. "Did you find something for Snacks to play with?"

"Uh-uh," I answered, but the dryness in my mouth made my tongue feel thick, and I thought I was going to choke. I couldn't talk.

"I'm sure I have your toys somewhere. I remember packing them up for the Salvation Army."

I kept my arm in the box and fished out the belt buckle, resting it above the others. Behind the metal plate, I found the hinged ring and shoved my finger into it. I shut my eyes then, shuddering at the remembered nightmares of strangulation, sex, and murder.

"Make a loop," I whispered to myself and saw the memory of what my mother had showed me. "Backward and inside out, so the buckle faces me." The bitter tea was back in my mouth, coming up as I nearly vomited on the table.

"What's that, Amy? Speak up," my mother demanded. I jumped.

"It's nothing," I answered. "Still looking."

Then loop the tail around and fish it through the hinged ring, I heard in my head. I wanted to run away and hide. *The noose is ready*, I mouthed.

My phone rang, scaring me so badly I shrieked.

"Amy!" my mother shouted, clutching her chest. "You nearly scared me to death."

"Jumpy," I quickly answered. "Ringer is too loud," I added as I yanked my arm from the box, leaving the belt alone there, leaving it hidden and unseen.

Charlie's name showed on the small display, his cell phone number at the bottom. But Charlie rarely called me. When he did, it was almost always from his desk phone at the station. At once I forgot about what

I'd found—my nightmares of the men being killed replaced with the dread of why Charlie might be calling.

"Yeah, Charlie?" I answered. I heard the sounds of yelling men and the distant wail of sirens in the background.

"Amy," he answered, his voice breaking in the ruckus of noise and shouting voices.

"Charlie?" I repeated. My mind began to race with worry.

Did I hear something in his tone? Had he said my name differently than any time before? They were just supposed to interview Nerd today. That's all. Nerd wouldn't have hurt anyone. Would he?

"Amy! It's Steve." I placed my head in my hand, my elbow propped on the table, my other hand cupping the phone against my ear. "Hospital. On the way to Mercy General."

"What happened, Charlie?" I cried. "You tell me what happened!" My mother came to my side. Snacks followed. Michael was at the table then too, his brow furrowed, and I realized how I must sound to them.

"Amy . . ." I could hear Charlie's emotion through the phone, sense something bad had happened. "Kiddo, Steve's been shot." My world crumpled and disappeared with his words, leaving behind a vast blackness. My worst fears had come true. I could feel myself slip, but found strength in the hands on me and the eyes around me.

"Daddy's shot?" Michael asked. He must have heard Charlie's booming voice. "Is he?" He cried into my mother's arm while she braced him, holding him.

"What, Charlie?" I asked, my voice shaking. I heard what he said and shook my hand in the air, waving off my question. "Charlie! Is Steve . . . is he . . ."

"Hospital!" Charlie thankfully answered for me. I couldn't say the words in front of the kids, but I could see in Michael that he was asking the same. "But Amy, it's bad. There's a car at your house to pick you up."

"I can drive," I yelled back, lying to him. I had no idea if I could drive or not. "Listen, Charlie. I'm not home, okay? But I'm leaving now."

When I hung up the phone, Michael jumped into my arms, squeezing until I had to pull him off of me.

"Is Daddy going to die?" he asked in a voice I'd never heard. He collapsed into my shirt, knowing I couldn't answer him.

I knelt down, trying to be strong and put my son in front of me. I saw Steve in his young face, and the urge to cry became overwhelming. My breath shook, and he took hold of my shaky hands and then handed me the car keys.

"He's strong, okay? And he loves you guys very much," I said, hating that I didn't have anything better to say, anything more assuring. "Mom, can you watch—"

"Go!" She pulled Michael and Snacks to her as I fled the house.

I could drive, after all. I found a strange serenity in the eerie quiet of my car. I only vaguely knew where the hospital was, having passed it on my way to the White Bear. But if Steve had been interviewing Nerd and had been shot, they would be coming from the station.

Shouldn't they be at a different hospital?

"Were they at the library?" I questioned, but Mercy General was in the wrong direction.

And when I realized what must have happened, the familiar guilt of having caused Katie's death stabbed at my gut. Again. My body went cold and every emotion disappeared as the stony horror of my actions continued to unfold. Steve hadn't been at the station interviewing Nerd. Steve and Charlie had gone to the White Bear.

"Amy, what have you done?"

34

CHARLIE TOOK ME into his arms, where I stayed until I could catch my breath. The run from the parking garage and then through the labyrinth of hospital halls had left me winded. For a while, I didn't know what to search for. Every wall, every floor, and even the ceiling looked exactly the same. And then I found colorful bands along the walls, giving some direction. I followed the rainbow, turning corner after corner, as colors peeled away one at a time until I was left with just three. From there, a map told me to follow the purple band. I tried running, tried lifting my heavy feet from the emotional quicksand that dragged me down. I found Charlie by the emergency room, swimming in a sea of police uniforms.

Sudden jolts of crying were of no help either. It was as if Charlie had some allowance for crying.

"Let it out, kiddo," he said. And I did.

When I pushed my emotions down, I searched his face for hope. I searched for anything that would tell me Steve was alive and fine. I wanted him to say that it was a simple wound, a superficial wound, the kind they would be laughing about at the station tomorrow. *In one hole and out the other*, I could hear Steve joke. *Like air whistling through your ears*, someone would add. I needed to hear one of those jokes now, but Charlie's eyes told a different story, a grim story. The faint glimmer of hope I was holding onto began to slip. My legs turned to jelly.

Charlie blinked and squeezed his eyes slowly with a short shake of his head, telling me that it didn't look good.

"No!" I yelled, throwing a feeble punch against his chest. "No, Charlie. You tell me it was nothing. You tell me a joke about how silly Steve felt for getting shot."

"I wish I could, Amy," Charlie began. He didn't call me kiddo, I noticed. My heart sank. "He's strong, though. He's in surgery . . . strongest guy at our station."

"Where was he shot?" I heard myself ask. I knew I was slipping into a preservation mode. I'd seen it happen to the other wives. First there is the initial shock. And then the reality of your worst nightmare finally arriving, finally buckling you in for a horror ride. And last, there was the sanctuary of nothingness. All emotions shut down and you entered a surreal world where short nods and a shake of your head replace the use of words. I saw the waiting room behind Charlie where I was to take my place and began to make my way there, completing the transition to becoming a wife-in-waiting. "I need to sit. Is that okay, Charlie? Can I sit?"

"Yes! Please, please," he answered and crouched down to sit with me. His legs made noises as he sat—the pain of it registered on his face with a brief wince. "Are you thirsty? Can I get you something to drink?"

I'd forgotten about drinking. In this mode, there was always a cup of water or coffee on offer. But it wasn't for drinking, it was for taking small sips, enough to wet the back of your dry throat. After all, a drink meant the possibility of having to use the bathroom later—and the last thing a wife-in-waiting was going to do was miss the doctor calling on her.

"Sure," I said. "Maybe some water. Thank you."

"Baker!" Charlie yelled in my ear, causing me to flinch. He patted my shoulder, apologizing, and then added, "Sorry, dear. Baker, how about some water?" A young man in a fresh-looking uniform disappeared from the corner of my vision, following Charlie's request.

"What happened? Where was he shot?" I asked again. Charlie pressed against the back of his chair, sliding over the seat. Then he raised his hand to take a radio call. Scratchy voices clicked on, spelling out a count of how many were dead, how many were in custody. The words rambled on in a familiar radio voice, and my ears went numb to the content until I heard the name Sam Wilts. Hearing that name twisted my stomach, confirming my fears that they'd gone to the White Bear. "Charlie! What about Sam Wilts? Was he involved in this? I thought Steve went to interview that girl's brother?"

Charlie raised his hand and patiently offered a set of instructions, responding to the drone of radio voices. When he was done he clicked off the speaker, turning the black knob until the chipped line of paint reached the number zero.

"We never made it to the Sutherland boy's interview. A call came in about a disturbance at the White Bear."

"A disturbance?" I asked, interrupting him, but heard the annoyance in my voice. "You mean a fight. It's a bar. People fight. That's a call for uniformed patrol, not for you and certainly not for Steve."

"Amy, please," Charlie answered. He motioned to

the younger man approaching with bottles of water. "Thank you, Baker. Why don't you go back to the station and start writing up your report?"

"Ma'am," the young man said. I braced myself, shifting in my seat, gripping my chest. His was going to be the first of many, I suspected. Many with empty faces and premature condolences, while my hope slowly withered away. His leather holster and shined shoes creaked as he shifted uncomfortably in front of me. "I'm so sorry that I caused this."

"Baker!" Charlie snapped, raising his voice. "The report. Get to it, now!"

I flinched again, blinking rapidly, trying to digest what the young man had confessed. But by the time I could ask, Charlie had shooed him away. I could only watch his freshly pressed uniform shrink away into a rising tide of doctors and orderlies and nurses and other cops.

"What's he talking about?"

"It's what may or may not have started the shooting."

"What are you not saying, Charlie?" I asked, hearing the pleading in my voice. He was being purposefully vague. He was being a cop when I needed a friend.

"We received word that Sam Wilts was holed up at

the Bear. We had a warrant to serve him, needed to bring him in for questioning about your friend Katie."

"And?"

"Couple of uniforms were already there, reporting on the disturbance call. But Sam wasn't alone. He had a half-dozen guys with him, guarding him. Steve talked Sam into coming out and went to the front to escort him. I don't know for sure how, but a shot was fired. I'm not saying who pulled the trigger, but Baker thinks that maybe he got anxious. An accidental—"

"And Steve got caught in the cross fire," I finished for him. I began to weep and hated myself for doing so. If I started crying, I knew I wouldn't be able to stop. "Charlie . . . Charlie, can you tell me how bad it is?"

But he didn't answer. From the corner of my eye, I saw his lips tremble and a tear wet his cheek. I lost it then and shoved my face into my hands. Charlie's bear-size hand lay warmly on my back, coaxing the tears to come forward, but they were endless. I was at that place I swore I would never be—slipping into a state of head nods and hopeful smiles, and all I could think of was how I would have to tell the kids our world was ending.

35

I MADE THE calls. All of them. Steve's mother began packing, cutting her trip to Florida short, before I could finish telling her what had happened. I only needed to mention the word "hospital" and Steve's name. The words sounded impossibly unreal coming from my mouth, like someone on television. I called my mother then, and she told me not to worry about Michael and Snacks, that she'd keep them busy. I heard Michael in the background, begging to take the phone. A shuffling of hands and plastic clanging came through my phone and then I heard the sound of Michael's voice.

"He's in surgery, honey."

"Did you get to see him yet?"

"No, Michael. I won't be able to see him until he's in recovery."

"Mom?"

"What is it, baby?"

"I'm scared for Daddy."

"I am too, baby. You hold onto Snacks . . . give her some hugs and love from me. Love you."

How many hours had passed? I'd found the clock on the wall and appreciated the sight of the old-fashioned hands, but couldn't remember where they had pointed when I first got here. *It was eleven in the morning,* I thought, counting the hours from our morning at my mother's. *My phone,* I thought. *The time I'd gotten Charlie's call would be on my phone. But did it matter?* The second hand swung around the circle, mindlessly passing the numbers without a care of what lie ahead or behind it.

"It's all a big circle," I heard myself mutter. Charlie leaned in toward me, thinking he had missed something I said. I waved him off, telling him to ignore me.

"All one circle," I continued. John and Todd Wilts and then Katie and now Sam; they were part of the circle too. Only they didn't make it around to the other side of the clock like the sweeping second hand.

My mind wandered as Charlie got up, gently squeezing my shoulder before leaving. He'd left before, stayed away for hours. I was sure of it. *Needed at the station*, he'd said. *But I'll be back.* Time seemed to disappear into a blur of unfamiliar faces. Then I saw John's wife. The look in her eyes was more telling than anything I'd heard. She pierced my heart with what she didn't say. I cried into her shoulder for as long as she could stand to be there. I was grateful that she came. I know how hard that must have been.

In his place, a steady stream of uniformed officers and detectives came and went like a tidal flow. Rising and then ebbing, the tide always thoughtful, telling me how strong Steve was, how much of a friend he'd been when they were new to the force. And the wives and friends too, my hand cramping from the squeezes, my cheek sore from the brushes of stubble. And always the same words: "He'll pull through—you just wait and see." I hated when someone said that. I hated that single statement most of all. Of course I'd wait.

What else was I going to do?

After a while, I could no longer distinguish the faces from one another or the voices of those speaking to me. My senses had become numb, had gone on autopilot. I nodded, shook hands, leaned forward for a supportive kiss on the cheek. The bottle of water I held onto was a third gone. Dozens of tiny sips kept my throat wet. I'd grown terribly thirsty, having refused the idea of the bathroom for fear of missing the doctor.

"Mrs. Sholes?" I heard, and then I felt someone sit

down next to me. The smells of the hospital became stronger, fresher. "Mrs. Sholes, I'm Dr. Aahana Lu."

"Yes! Yes, Doctor. How is Steve? How is my husband?"

The doctor paused. Her caregiving eyes seemed to search deep into mine, as if seeking out the strength I'd need to hear what she had to say. The younger doctor was stunning—striking golden eyes and short brown hair. When she spoke to me, I heard a slight accent in her voice that sounded like a melody. She picked up my hand in hers. She had warm, delicate fingers that I couldn't help realizing had been inside my husband's body just moments before, working to save his life. She squeezed reassuringly and nodded, telling me he would make it. I dipped my head forward, pleading to learn more.

"He's a fighter and should make a good recovery. The next forty-eight hours are going to tell us more."

My arms were around the doctor's neck then. Sobs came to me and stole anything I could have said. She rose from the chair and led me toward an ominous-looking set of double doors. I stretched my neck, craning to see through the small opening slinking between the panels. I'd done the same a thousand times during Steve's surgery, waiting. I saw fluffs of white, equipment on wheels, and the occasional eyeball peering back at me, searching the waiting room. Patients and doctors and all kinds of hospital staff came and went without pause, slapping the large square button on the wall or choosing to muscle their way through the swinging doors.

Doctor Lu took my elbow and guided me to the doors. I hesitated, afraid to finally pass to the other side.

"It's okay," she assured me. "Just through these doors."

I tried to swallow, but my mouth was too dry. Passing the threshold felt like I was crossing over into some forbidden sanctum where the healing came as a judgment of good or bad, saved or unsaved.

Steve is a good person, I told myself. *Steve was saved.* And that's all that mattered to me.

We passed through the doors, which opened up onto a deeper hospital room. What I found inside was a world filled with anything but waiting—it held the opposite of the waiting room's hushed and anxious pacing. Hospital scrubs and lab coats hung from shoulders, the colors of white and green and blue moved around quickly on Croc-covered feet. We only had to stand there as a swarm adapted and moved around us. It was like a magnetic field that repelled and received the bodies at the same time.

I heard the sound of respirators and saw yellow and green winking lights atop equipment bursting with round dials and clear tubing that passed through black-pleated bags that inflated and fell like a bellows. And then I saw even more men and women gathered around a central counter, clamoring with one another, shuffling clipboards and shuttling bags of medicine and blood back and forth, anxious to go, their feet moving in place. Along both walls there were curtained stalls, some with lights glowing behind them and darkness behind others.

Steve's behind one of those, I told myself. I felt a twinge in my chest.

"This is recovery?" I asked, searching the few open stalls, hoping to see something familiar, something that told me Steve was alive in there. His shoes, maybe, or socks? But I only saw gurneys holding legs and feet that I didn't recognize. "He'd hate it if his feet were sticking out like that—especially if they're uncovered." I wasn't sure why I told the doctor that, but it was true. Steve hated it when his feet were uncovered.

"I would too," she said, smiling. "And yes, this is recovery. Would you like to see your husband?"

"Yes," I answered. "Yes, very much."

"Okay, but we'll want you to keep it short. He's awake, very groggy, but he has been asking for you."

"You said Steve would make a *good* recovery," I began. "You didn't say a *full* recovery."

She paused in front of one stall. The curtain was

closed, but the faint light of machines bled through. "You have a very strong husband and I expect he'll do well."

"What is it?" I asked, wanting to scream: exhaustion was getting to me. The doctor raised her hand, trying to calm me.

"Your husband was shot twice," she answered, pointing to her side. "The first bullet entered his side. It hit a rib, which probably saved his life."

"And?" I asked, impatiently. "The other bullet?"

"The second bullet entered here," she said, pointing to her thigh. "The injury to his leg was substantial."

"How substantial?" I asked, hating that my voice shook.

She cocked her head, her lips becoming thin, and answered in a voice that sounded less confident. "Depending on his recovery, he may never regain the full use of his leg." Images flared in my mind of Steve wearing a brace that wrapped his thigh and knee and ankle in long, steely bands pinched together with knobby bolts.

"How bad?" I asked. A tear pricked my eye and emotion stuck in my throat. "Will he be able to walk his little girl down the aisle?" The doctor offered her arm and let me lean on it to steady the shaking.

"Yes," she said, her smile promising. "And he'll be able to dance with his daughter too."

"I'm so sorry for crying again," I said, but she waved it off. "Can I see him?"

"Shhh," she told me. "We're in the no-apology zone. You can cry and say anything you want back here."

I laughed at that, my nose runny as I swiped at it impatiently. "Might need some more tissues."

"Yes, we've got plenty of those," she answered, her accent sounding stronger the more we talked. "Here he is. We just removed the respirator, so his voice is going to be a little hoarse."

She pulled the curtain back, sliding it on rings above us. I cringed at the scraping sound—like fingernails on a chalkboard to me. I let out a soft gasp, stepping back unintentionally. The sight behind the curtain briefly overwhelmed me—needly eyes pierced the dark, and tubes ran back and forth, hanging from bags filled with clear and yellow and wine-red fluids. But then I saw what I needed to see and everything else faded into the background. I saw my husband's outstretched hand, fingers moving, motioning to me. I followed his arm past the snaking myriad of hospital tape, over the thin fabric of his gown, and to his eyes. He warmed me with a tired smile. I shook my head, collapsing at his hand, taking his into mine, bringing it to my face.

"Babe, what did you do?"

"Come here," he begged. I heard the rings sliding on metal as the light from the main room vanished behind the curtain. "Come on up here."

"Do you think it's okay?" I asked, unsure of what to do but knowing what I wanted to do. I moved without waiting for him to answer—quietly, safely, taking care not to crimp a hose or pull on a wire. When I found his face with mine, our lips touched. I wanted to yell at him, tell him how scared I was, but I said nothing.

He looked at me then like he had on the night we met—as if I were the only woman he'd ever seen. "You're so beautiful," he said, taking me back to that evening. And like before, the moment lifted me. I hated him for making me love him so much. "How about a dance to some country music?"

"I'll lead," I joked. Wet cut into my eyes and his face blurred. "On account you'll be hobbling awhile."

"Long road," he said, agreeing. He strained his neck to see the cushions of bandages around his right leg. "Come up closer."

"At least we *have* a road," I told him, tapping my open hand on his face, shaking my head, showing him how angry I was. "I need you, Steve. I need you with me."

I glanced beneath the paisley curtain to see if we were alone. Shadows moved, hovered, and moved on. We were alone. I crawled farther onto the hospital bed, careful not to set off one of the machines. I laid my hand on his chest. The smell of antiseptic and bandages made my nose twitch, but I found Steve in there too. I snuggled against him. His chest rose and fell, a steady tempo to close my eyes to. I draped my arm around him, joining the rhythm of his breathing.

"I love you, babe," I told him, sounding terrified. Sounding resentful. "I'm sorry, but I can't do this again."

"I know," he answered grimly. "Amy, I think I'm done." He began to cry then, a painful, quiet sob.

"We'll figure it out," I told him as I dried his eyes.

36

I DIDN'T KNOW the time—or the day—when I finally made it back to my mother's house. The minutes had become hours and the hours begat an entire day. All of it a blur. The sky hinted to me that it was the afternoon—lunchtime—the smells of steamy salted water and macaroni and cheese came to me when I entered my mother's kitchen. I said nothing, just put my arms around my kids, kissing their heads and cheeks and necks until they couldn't take it anymore. I assured them with my smile that everything would be okay.

"Oh, thank God," I heard my mother say. "We hadn't heard anything and I wasn't sure what was going on."

"He's good," I said, turning to give my mother a short hug. As expected, it stayed thankfully brief. I knelt at the small kitchen table, bracing Michael's shoulder. His eyes filled with questions. "Daddy is going to be fine."

"He's okay?" Michael asked. "All okay or just some okay?"

I squeezed my lips tight, wondering how much to share. "Your daddy was shot... twice."

"How . . . how bad is it?" Michael asked, his chin quivering.

"One bullet here," I said, tapping the side of Michael's chest. "But that bullet hit his rib and didn't do anything bad."

"And the other one?"

"Where's Daddy?" Snacks interrupted. Her words sounded wet and sloshy; she was busy scooping mac and cheese onto her spoon. "Momma, where's Daddy at?"

"He's been shot, you dope!" Michael yelled.

"Hey now," my mother said, rubbing his shoulders. But he was hurting, I could see it in his face. He slid his chair back from the table just far enough to escape, and ran off into the other room.

"What?" I asked, raising my hands to my face, feeling an exhausted flush.

"It's a lot, Amy. Nothing you did," I heard Mom say.

"I know," I answered from the side of my mouth, lying. How *could* I know? Steve had never been shot before. I put my hand to Snacks's back, rubbing her little warm body until I got the smile I needed. She'd already forgotten what she asked. She lifted her nearly empty bowl and asked for more, showing us a sloppy grin.

"Go talk to him," Mom instructed. "Go see your son. Snacks will help me clean up in here. Maybe do some more drawing too."

"Drawing, you say?" I repeated, lifting my voice in surprise. Snacks nodded. "Thank you, Mom." And before I left to see Michael, I did something that was unexpected: I hugged her again.

"Now, now," she said, comforting me. And as she patted my arm and said soft, quiet words, it seemed as though all the years of fighting fell out of us, disappearing from who we were.

I went to Michael, clearing my damp eyes as I entered the room. Crouched in a ball, he was sitting as far back in my father's old chair as he could. Michael was hiding behind the old *Robinson Crusoe* book, but he peered up as I approached.

"You're a fast reader," I told him, seeing that he already managed to read a third of the book. "A lot faster than me."

"It's an easy read," he said plainly, making me laugh. "It's a fourth-grader's book."

I could hear the defensiveness in his tone. He

needed to be angry at someone for what happened to his father, and that was okay. I could be that person for him if I had to be.

"Daddy is going to be okay," I said, tilting the book away from his face so that he could see me. I stared into his eyes. Teary streaks claimed his cheeks, and I quickly wiped one away. The book fell from the chair, and Michael was in my arms before I could say another word.

"It's my fault," he confessed.

"What? Why would you say that?" I asked, shaking my head.

"'Cause! I'm always telling him how cool I think it is that he's a detective. You know—a cop!"

I pushed his shoulders around until we were face-to-face, and said, "Your father was a cop long before you and Snacks came along. Understand?" He lightly bumped his head against mine, trying to nod.

"I understand," he said as a loud, clamoring noise erupted from the kitchen. The sound of a pan spiraling like a coin, teetering on the kitchen's hard floor.

"Mom!"

Silence.

Snacks's giggly laughter.

I stood up and began making my way toward the kitchen, but I stopped in the dining room when my mom spoke out.

"We're fine in here. Snacks dropped the pan is all."

"Okay," I answered as I braced my hand on one of the moving boxes along the wall. A tangle of leather and buckles filled the box. And on the top of the snake pile, I found the belt and buckle I had set aside just before receiving the call from Charlie. I peered over at Michael. He'd found his way back to the pages of *Robinson Crusoe*. The kitchen was silent again, save for the patter and shuffle of tiny feet—Snacks running around, playing.

My fingers twitched. I tried to swallow, tried to lick my dry lips as I carefully touched the belt buckle. The metal was cold but it burned my fingers as I traced the wings.

How many men?

At once, I could see all of them. It was as if some magical barricade had been lifted from my mind. There hadn't been just one or two. I saw a dozen faces, maybe two dozen. I wanted to pull my hand from the moving box, but I couldn't force myself. I grabbed the belt, whipping it out of the thick cardboard box. I wrapped the leather around my fist. The leathery smell and creak of it brought even more faces to my mind. Men of all shapes and sizes, men of all different ages. They had come to our station wagon, seduced by my mother's promise for sex like sailors following the alluring call of a mythical siren on a dangerous ocean reef.

And then I relived the travels between towns and mountains, the endless stretches of single-lane roads. I saw the darkest passes, lit only by our headlights. I saw faraway stars—tiny pins of light peering down, judging us. When we were far enough from a truck stop, we'd pull over on some obscure, desolate back road where nobody ever came. She'd open the car door and the taste of road dust would fill my mouth. She'd motion for me to take the man's feet. I'd get out, taking hold of cold ankles, dead skin always feeling like paper. My mother would push as I pulled, dragging him from the car. Some of the men slid off the front seat easily while others got stuck and made noises, cracking as if their bones were breaking. We'd roll the dead men off the edge of the road, off the edge of nowhere. Then we'd go home.

Rigor mortis, I said to myself, finally understanding what the sounds were. *I remembered thinking that their ghosts were trying to talk to me, threatening to haunt me for what I'd done.*

My mind began to swim with the understanding that I'd been a murderer all of my life. The homeless man hadn't been my first after all.

Just how many had there been!?

Snacks ran from the kitchen, playing chase with

her grandma, laughing hysterically before tumbling hard into my legs. I threw my hands into the air, jumping with a screech. She laughed harder and then motioned to me as if she had a secret to share. Instinctively, I bent over, closer to her, the smell of macaroni and cheese rising to my nose. My baby girl raised one hand and pressed a finger to her lips.

"Shush," she teased. I stumbled backward at the sight, falling to my bottom. Michael came to help me just as my mother caught up to Snacks. I watched, frozen, as my daughter turned to my mother, and they both motioned to one another with their fingers pressed over their lips.

Shush.

I saw my nightmare, my mother looking at me from the front seat of our old car, her finger pressed against her lips, motioning for me to kill her lover. I screamed. Michael shook me, trying to wake me from the horror. He jolted me into knowing the truth of what I had been reliving at night.

"You taught me this!" I screamed, getting back to my feet, shaking the belt at my mother.

Snacks ran back to me. "Shush," she repeated.

My insides burst with revulsion and then rage. I threw my hand high above my head, the leather belt wrapped around my fist, threatening to strike my baby.

"Mom!" Michael screamed, jumping between us,

blocking me. His eyes were filled with terror. "What are you doing?"

Every part of me began to crumble, to collapse, to dissolve into a maddening decay of horrific memories. And now I had brought that all upon Snacks and Michael. In all my life, I'd never struck my babies, never even considered it.

"Oh my God!" I cried as I pulled my arms down to my sides.

"Mom, what are you doing?" Michael begged, staring with eyes wide, guarding his baby sister against my assault.

"Michael! Hurry! Get your things. Get everything. We're leaving. Now!"

"Amy . . ." My mother tried to console me, coming to me with her arms raised. "I did it for you. All of them. They were for *you*." Her face wore a pitiful expression, pleading for forgiveness. But then I saw a change in her eyes as her lips thinned into a sneer. She became the woman from the car, the woman who murdered those men.

"You're a fucking crazy woman," I screamed at her. "How . . . how could you teach me to do those things? I was only seven!" Michael was back at my side, crying, his face lit up with fear, reflecting the sudden chaos that had filled my mother's home. He had no idea why we were fighting. He had no idea why I'd almost struck his baby sister.

I soon had Snacks in my arms. I ran to the door with Michael clutching my shirt, pulling on it as he stumbled but kept pace. I glanced at the empty walls, at the stacks of moving boxes, passing them to leave the home I'd been raised in. And I was leaving the woman who'd brought me into her world of murder, making me a part of it, turning me.

"Amy!" my mother yelled with insistence and urgency in her tone. I passed Snacks to Michael and told him to go to the car.

"Get in the car and lock the doors!" I instructed. "And don't unlock the door for anyone but me."

Michael said nothing, just swiped at his face to clear his eyes. He picked up Snacks and then ran to the car.

"Amy, look at me!"

I still held the belt. I squeezed my hand into a tight fist. The old leather sang to me a nursery rhyme of pitchy creaks. "What?" I asked, turning around.

My mother held her finger to her lips and teased: "Shush." But unlike in my nightmares, this time she laughed. I took the belt into both of my hands, wanting to do to her what she had me do to all those men. But then she said something that stopped me cold.

"Amy, I only did it because you told me to."

37

I RAN FROM my mother's house, tears distorting and stretching the view in front of me. Michael opened the car door and I tumbled inside, hugging the steering wheel as I searched for my keys. Michael was at my side, fishing out the car's ignition key from the jumble on the ring when I heard my mother's laughter. She'd come to the doorway. She was staring out at us, a small, insignificant family on the run from the monster-maker she was. At least, I thought that's who we were running from. *I* did those things.

Was I running from the memory? Was I running from what I'd become?

"Amy, you come back when you've found your senses," she hollered after me. Her tone was motherly, even grandmotherly—as if nothing had ever happened. And maybe in her sick, twisted mind, nothing had been wrong with killing all those men. "I'll send you a letter with my new address. And you can keep that trophy. I've got more." I peered down at my hand. The belt was looped into a noose, and the ends of it wrapped around my knuckles like a kerchief the buckle draped, hanging, swaying back and forth. I threw the belt to the floor of the car, the ghost of men trapped in the noose haunting me.

Please just let me get the car moving, I begged myself. *Get the kids home.*

"What's going on, Mom?" Michael asked, the terror still on his face, his cheeks stained with fresh tears. "Why are you and Grandma fighting? Is it Dad?"

"Oh baby, your daddy is fine," I assured him. "This is an old fight. A very old fight." When the car's steering wheel was firmly in my hands, I dared one last look at the house I'd grown up in. In a flash, images came to me of my mother and I leaving. My small hand in hers, leading me down the path to our old station wagon. The sky covered in a soft pink blanket and the sun piercing red on the horizon.

"When your Daddy is away . . ." she'd sung, staring down at me with a haunting grin.

"The woman will play!" I'd finish for her, trying to sing along.

My stomach lurched with the memory—more painful this time. It doubled me over as a cold sheen of nauseating sweat covered my skin. I opened the car door, fell over onto my side, and vomited.

"Mom!" Michael cried, pawing at the back of my jacket, trying to lift me. "Should I call Da—who can I call?"

"I'm okay, baby," I told him, clearing my throat. I spat at the ground, spat at my old home and the curse she had set upon me. "All good now."

"Please, Mom. Please tell me what's wrong."

I shook my head, wondering how to explain something so impossible to a young boy. "I can't, Michael. It's just one of those sad things that happen between grown-ups."

When I turned around to face the backseat, Snacks gave me a long, wary stare and then turned away. She never had reason to look away before. Not before today. I stretched my hand, cupping her tiny knee, squeezing it playfully to jog a giggle. She twisted her head and crossed her arms, her usual reaction when she didn't get her way.

"Baby girl," I pleaded. "I'm sorry that I raised my hand. It was a reaction, you know, like jumping when you see a bug."

"I'm no bug!" she exclaimed.

"I know, honey. I know you're not a bug," I tried to reason. "It was a mistake and I'm sorry."

"Don't you like that game?"

"What game, baby?"

Snacks looked at me then, bringing her hand to her mouth: *Shush*. I squeezed my eyes shut, revolted by the sight.

Shaking my head, I said in a voice that shook, "No. No, I don't like that game."

"But Grandma says you played it all the time with her."

"Well, I don't play that game anymore."

"Can we go home?" she asked, already losing interest in what was being said. She'd be fine and hopefully would bury the memory. I just wished I'd buried some of mine a little deeper.

38

I DIDN'T SEE my mother again until the day of Katie's funeral. Without Steve to lean on, I walked from my car alone, having chosen to drive by myself. I preferred the company of one on this day when I had to bury my best friend. I braced myself when I stepped up onto the grass, expecting my heels to sink in, but the winter had seized hold of all life, laying it dormant until spring, hardening the ground like stone. Winter birds took flight along the evergreens lining the cemetery, and I realized Katie's grave wasn't far from John's. I glanced around, searching for tented mounds of freshly dug grave sites, wondering if Todd or Sam Wilts might be buried nearby. Sam had died days after the shootout with my husband, and his son's death was deemed a murder. But his murder hadn't been connected to Katie; I wondered if it ever would be. I stopped to close my coat but instead decided to welcome the winter air, let it take hold until my teeth began to chatter. I wanted to feel cold. Deserved it. I was convinced that my heart was as stony as the ground Katie would be laid in soon. If she'd known who I really was or what I'd done . . .

The memories of when I'd swung from the leather belt were sporadic. Some were fleeting, while others stuck and wouldn't go away—those were the ones that scared me. The few when the men fought back, escaping from my mother. I remembered one man who had lurched up when I tried to close the belt on his throat. He'd let out a horrendous noise and vaulted forward, sending my body crashing into the car door while my mother flew off him and into the windshield. That man could have turned around and killed me then, killed both of us, but having the strap around his neck spooked him. He took the noosed belt and hurled it at me, holding on to the buckle but whipping the strap over my head. I heard his hands fumbling with the door handle, jerking it until the door squealed open in a lurch. He escaped that night, running across the pavement, his cock still hard and glistening by the pale light of a streetlamp. My mother tried to send me to fetch the belt that had fallen from his hand when he tumbled, but I was afraid to leave the car, certain that he'd come back.

"Go or we'll lose it," she scolded. "You want to use it again, don't you?"

I clutched my chest, remembering what I said. "Yes, Momma. Yes, I want to use it again."

And now, as I stood at my friend's grave, I wondered what my mother would have to say for herself. She stood opposite me, perched in black, a dark, lacy veil covering her eyes. She made the sign of the cross and then touched Katie's casket before fixing me with a look of contentment. There was no mistaking what I was seeing. She looked happier than I had seen her in years, as if our past had happened just yesterday. I closed my eyes to focus on the ceremony, kept them closed with Katie on my mind. I was here for *her*. I wasn't here for my mother, or myself. I was here for my best friend.

"I'll miss you, Katie," I whispered, placing my hand onto her casket. Katie's body would be lowered into the ground soon. The thought of her being gone put a hole so deep inside me that I didn't think it could ever be filled.

"Thank you for coming," I heard Jerry say. I nodded in his direction. Katie's boys stayed sitting by the grave, their eyes on the casket. Two large men were perched directly behind them. They looked like bodyguards and wore sunglasses, but I was certain they each held a badge inside their jackets. "Please tell Steve that I wish him well."

"I will," I answered as I offered my condolences—a formality, but in my gut I felt that this would probably be the last time I would ever talk to Jerry. As if to confirm what I was thinking, the taller bodyguard spoke into his wrist, whispering about the funeral ending. He tapped Jerry's shoulder.

"Time to go, sir," he said, his voice guttural and reserved.

"Just give me a minute, would you?" Jerry begged, raising his hands to show his palms. "I just want more time with my boys."

"We have to go, sir," the man said, raising his voice and drawing curious glances. Clouds of cold breath appeared as folks turned around, only to turn back to their cars.

"I've got them, Jerry," Katie's mother said, coming to their side and pulling them closer to her. The boys said little, just cried softly and reached for their father, who'd already moved to leave. "You take care, Jerry."

I sensed my mother behind me before I heard her voice. "So sad," she said and cautiously touched my arm. "So sad to see a family broken apart like that."

"What is it, Mom?" I asked. I heard her shift around, shuffling as though trying to find something to say.

"Amy, I'm sorry. Really, I am. What happened all those years ago was my fault."

I swung around, sickened and appalled. But more than that, I was afraid. "I was just a kid. This doesn't go away with an 'I'm sorry'!" I had heard enough. I stepped around her. My mother gripped my arm, jerking me back. "What are you doing?"

"Listen to me," she pleaded. "This is important. You have to know who we are. This is who Snacks will be!"

"No. No, you're wrong!" I shouted, looking at her like some monstrous vampire and not caring who heard me. By now the graveyard had thinned to only a few curious onlookers anyway. "You're wrong about that!"

"I think she has a secret box too," my mother said. I cupped my mouth as the air rushed into my lungs in a gasp. My knees went weak, causing me to stumble. My most intimate of secrets were known to someone else.

But how?

Her eyes widened, surprised. "Oh, you didn't know? I've known about your little secret box since your earliest designs. You weren't exactly quiet about it, Amy."

"How . . . how?" I stuttered, but then realized a squeaky floorboard would easily draw a curious eye. "Snacks! What about my baby?"

"She told me that she had a secret too," my mother

explained. I clenched my fists and jaw, squeezing them in anguish at what I feared my mother was going to say next. "And then she showed me."

My mother handed me a rolled-up piece of construction paper. I unfurled it, and found myself looking at a small design that had been drawn in crayon. I shook my head as a burning took over my face and my body flushed with heat. It was a Killing Katie–type design. But Snacks was much younger than I had been when I started drawing mine. I tried to make out an innocent shape in my baby girl's crayon scribbles—a rabbit or tree or anything else—but there was no mistaking that it depicted a sharp blade and knife handle and a pool of puddled blood, which she had filled with a waxy red. A twisting erupted inside me when I saw the poorly written name of my baby girl on the sheet. She was too young to write her whole name, but she knew a few letters. In the corner, she had scratched a big letter *S* with a short scribble after it. A pang of jealousy came then, but I wasn't sure of what hurt me more—that Snacks had opened up to my mother or that my mother knew about my secret box.

"You're wrong," I insisted, deciding she had encouraged Snacks. "You did this! You drew this with her. This is not from my girl. This is your fucking sickness."

"It's *ours*," she argued, squeezing my arm with a heavy pinch. "Just like it is going to be hers!"

I swung my arm, crashing my open hand against her cheek with a swift crack. My mother fell back, catching herself in a shuffle of clumsy footsteps. I was crying hard. I folded my arms around myself as if to guard against her vileness.

"Just stay away from us!" I said. "You're not welcome in my house or in our lives."

"Amy!" she cried out in a wail. Her voice shaking, pleading.

"Not my baby girl!" I heard myself screaming back to her. "Not my baby girl!"

39

WEEKS HAD PASSED since Katie's death. Her children had moved in with her mother and father. At least they would be together. Jerry had been passed from federal agency to agency like a bone in a circle of dogs, trying to offer testimony in exchange for a reduction in his sentence. That is, less time in prison—though I thought it was still likely he would die in there. And my best friend? Her body, unmoving and cold, remained in the ground. It made me sad to think of her like that, to think of her beauty withering away into dusty nothingness.

For some reason, I'd gone out of my way to drive by Katie's home during my trips to the hospital. Maybe I was punishing myself, wanting to witness the end of a family. Yellow police tape still hung from the porch columns, abandoned, tattered, the ends shredded and whipping in the breeze. The curtains Katie and I had picked out disappeared, leaving the windows dark and lifeless. And the brass porch lights we'd installed—thinking we didn't need an electrician, just a pair of pliers and a bottle of wine—had been ripped out, leaving behind a tangle of wires like nerves from a severed limb.

Eventually, Katie's home was emptied, gutted, and boarded up. But the ending came with a foreclosure sign, hung from a square post, stabbed into the ground with one wrenching blow as if to make sure the family was really dead. I teared up a few times at that, catching my breath in a shudder. I would have to drive away soon after. Seeing what had become of my best friend's home was nearly as hard as seeing her body in the casket. A tornado had come, hit them head on, and sent the pieces of their lives in every direction. I couldn't stand the idea of being the cause, of being the tornado. Jerry may have stirred things up, but it was Todd's death that had moved Katie's family into Sam's path.

A month after being shot, Steve finally came home. And what a day it was. His mother joined me and the kids as we filled the foyer with a hundred balloons—all shapes and sizes and colors—the sound of them squeaking, a few of them popping, the sudden lift of our voices filling the house with shrieks. We added long, curly streamers to the colorful montage and hung a shiny *Welcome Home* banner across his office door. Michael had picked that one out, insisting on the electric blue and silvery colors.

Steve's leg would never fully recover, we learned. I quickly sensed the sadness of what he'd be losing. My husband was alive. My husband was home. But my husband would never be the same person. That last fact stung, and I could only hope that what we had could survive it.

"Charlie isn't going to Florida," Steve said, stuffing his mouth with cake. I leaned against him, taking him in: his smell, his vibe, his presence. I realized how much I had missed having him home. I rubbed his leg, tenderly and softly, hoping that the massage would help ease the chronic pain.

"Nerve damage," Doctor Lu had told us. "It's the nerve damage that is causing the pain."

He winced. I yanked my hand back, cringing.

"Easy," he pleaded, sighing impatiently.

I shook my head, "I'm sorry. Would a heating pad feel better?" I asked, carefully feeling around the bandage on his thigh.

"I like what you're doing. Just softer."

"So Charlie is staying on?" I asked, unsure if I wanted to hear the answer.

Steve nodded. There was reluctance in the motion.

Regret and disappointment too. "He's going to stay on for another two years. It's already a done deal."

"How do you feel about that?" I asked and then wished I hadn't. But I found that, more and more, I didn't quite know what to say to him. The disappointment rolled off him like a wave.

It's the depression, I told myself. I'd read an encyclopedia's worth of material online about recovery's challenges, hoping to be the best wife I could be for him.

Steve chomped on another bite of his cake, choosing not to answer. Too soon, I supposed. I didn't push it. He offered the fork, brushing my lips with the chocolate. Teasing. I licked at the icing playfully until the grim look on his face disappeared.

"I'll be riding the desk for a long time. A very long time—but with an occasional distraction like that, I think I can deal with it."

We were alone in his office. I shut the door, hoping to have him to myself for at least an hour. I bit at his fork, licking it again and said in a breathy voice, "Been a while. Do you feel up to it?"

His furrowed brow lifted and he leaned in, kissing me. I moaned, hungry for more than cake. I slipped my tongue into his mouth as I unbuttoned his pants. We made love that afternoon—for the first time in what felt like forever—taking our time, rediscovering, easing back into a familiar rhythm. And in my mind, I kept my thoughts on my husband and pushed away the wreckage of my actions. Sure, I still wanted my peanut butter and chocolate, but I wanted my husband more.

The first winter snows came with the whiskers of Steve's unkempt beard. I begged him to cut the scraggly mess, insisted he shave it. But he decided to keep it, calling it his "recovery beard." He spent months in and out of physical therapy. When he began to drive again, he came home after one of his sessions and sat me down. I pulled a chair out from the table, my heartbeat aching in my chest as the chair legs scratched against the floor. I expected him to tell me that he knew everything, that he knew what I had done and that he blamed me for getting shot. I held my breath. He pinched at the straggle of whiskers—brown whiskers, peppered with a bristle of untamed gray—his hand disappeared into his coat, fumbling for a moment before revealing law school pamphlets. He dropped them on the table, slid them in front of me, and looked proud for following through. I tucked my finger beneath the first, lifting it open. I didn't know what to say, and I think he was at a loss for words too. His lips peeked through his heavy beard, smiling broadly. He nodded as if to say that he'd made up his mind, that he was going to go back to school.

"We just need to figure out how to pay for it," he said. "But I found one. I found a school that would work out perfectly for us."

"Thank you!" I answered, planting kisses all over his face, even the itchy parts that I didn't care for very much.

Steve eventually rode the desk job, just as he said he would, going back to work once the doctors gave their okays. He took on new cases, investigating in ways that he'd never thought of before. A small cyber crime division had opened up under Charlie, and Steve jumped at the chance to try something new. I had my reservations, though, knowing how good Nerd was and how much better others were than Steve when it came to swimming in the deep end of the Web. I thought of the red and yellow links, and what the click of a mouse button really meant. I wondered if Steve could ever unknowingly bump into Nerd. But the new position let Steve keep his detective's shield, and it kept him safe. And what was even better, the homeless man's case remained his—albeit unsolved. My buttons were safely hidden away in an evidence room that only Steve knew about.

. . .

Early one afternoon, I found myself on the bridge over Neshaminy Creek again. I decided to get out of the car. With the world at work, the kids in school, and the bridge empty, I had the creek to myself. Springtime was in the air, buds had started to show on the thinnest branches, and the tall piles of plowed snow had grown dark and begun to shrink. Soon they would be a memory, forgotten until the first snow of the coming year.

Gripping the rail, following the sound of passing water, I looked to where my bloody handprint had been stamped the day Katie was killed. Instinctively, I searched around me, making sure I was alone before picking up a pack of loose ice to clean the blood that was no longer there. I thought of Katie then, as the ice melted in the heat of my palm. A drop of water caught the sunlight, the shine skipping into my eyes.

I missed talking to my friend. But there was something else I missed. It took me a minute to understand what else it was—my mother. We hadn't talked since the day of Katie's funeral. She had listened to my demand that she stay away from my home and my family. Steve was suspicious of our falling out, and pried me with questions, but I talked around them and then fixed him just the right look, telling him to back off.

My mother did give me something that day—forewarning. I watch Snacks every day now, hoping that she'll not fall under the same curse as I did, as my mother did. But the only drawings she shares with me are of scribbly trees and stars and the sun and the moon. And on occasion, a cow jumping too.

Who knows how many other women from our line were murderers? Vampires are real—I remind myself of that constantly. There are some days when I don't have to remember. There are some days I'm no longer the mother and wife I want to be. A hunger pang will come, followed by another, and soon my dreams are filled with new designs.

Water rushed beneath me, spouting white foam over jutting boulders, sinking others beneath a heavy flow. Once a year the tranquility of Neshaminy Creek is disturbed by the flood of feeder steams during the spring thaw that rises over the banks and makes rapids run. I searched the stony bank and the sandy mounds, looking for any hint of my trophies. By now, my evidence had surely been washed out to a bigger river and then caught up by currents that joined other rivers, deeper, faster. And eventually to the ocean, disappearing forever.

. . .

When I made it to town, I decided to park in front of the alley—*my* alley. My fears, my reservations had been lessened by Steve taking the case. I brought out Nerd's gift to me. A huge ring, I could only fit Needle on my thumb, and it was there that I put it. I kept the poison reservoir empty, deciding to pretend I was an assassin, keeping the dreamy thought of filling it as a new fantasy.

"But that doesn't mean I can't be someone else for a while?" I asked no one in particular. Then I spied an open chair at a new hairdresser a street over from Romeo's. I pushed Needle back on my thumb and made my way to the salon. Mr. C's the window announced in bold gold-and-silver lettering that glinted in the light. A bell jingled, bouncing back and forth as the door closed behind me.

"Well, don't you look ready for a change?" a short man said, his Latin accent sounding effeminate, his grin leading me to grin back.

"You're open?" I asked, feeling insecure while he eyed me from head to toe.

"We are. I'm Carlos—the *C* in Mr. C," he said proudly as he rocked on the balls of his feet. "What can I do for you, baby?"

I pointed to the sample hairdo pictures on the wall, and he began to go through each one, talking up which would work with my bone structure. Between his lisp and the way he stood—one foot perpendicular to the other—he was a living stereotype. I could never have made his mannerisms up.

"I like number seventeen," I told him. He cupped his chin and shifted to his other foot, sending one pointed shoe out. He tilted his head.

"That won't work for you, baby," he exclaimed. I wasn't sure if I should be embarrassed or ashamed. He came over to me, reaching his hands up, pausing to ask for my permission. I nodded, and he dove his fingers into my hair. He smelled strongly of a cologne that tickled my nose.

"What you want, baby?" he asked, stepping back.

Had he given up on me already?

My eyes wandered up to the sexy hairdos again, avoiding number seventeen, but I couldn't find anything I liked.

"Oh, don't bore yourself with those, honey," he instructed, waving them off. "Those pictures are for the tittiest girly girls who only want what their man wants, anyway. Girl, tell me: what do *you* want?"

His words were inviting. His tone warm. I liked him, and wished Katie was with me. She would have liked him too. No. She would have *loved* him. I fixed him a smile, trying to show some confidence. Then I joked, "I want you to give me back eight years."

"Ahhh," he said and nodded his head, circling me,

studying me. “You want your sexy back.” He motioned me toward his chair and winked when he brought out a pair of scissors.

“I do!” I answered excitedly. “I want my sexy back.”

“And baby, your man is gonna love this.”

I nodded eagerly, plopping down to get comfortable. I sat in his hairdressing chair for the next hour and stared back at us in an oval mirror. I watched him use his comb and scissors like an artist, trimming, combing, and shaping, taking away who I was one hair at a time. He brought out someone I had never seen before, but had known my entire life.

I spun Needle on my thumb as I left, liking the feel of the thick metal against my skin, the feel of death touching me. I was growing more comfortable wearing it, having put my friendship ring where it belonged—in the ground with Katie so it could stay together with hers forever. A breeze rushed over the skin of my bare neck, giving me a chill. I hurried inside the library, not remembering when I had last worn my hair so short. The skirt I was wearing didn’t help, but I had wanted to go for leggy and beautiful today, uncertain of where my free afternoon was going to take me. And now I had the hairdo to match.

I waved to the older librarian as her eyes appeared above her glasses. She did a double take and then smiled, recognizing me. When she stretched to get up from her chair, I stopped her and gave a short wave, telling her to stay.

"I'm just here for a few minutes."

"Good to see you again," she said and motioned to her hair. "Love what you've done." Hearing her compliment warmed me.

"Thank you."

The library smelled the same, looked the same, felt the same—but was completely different somehow. I found Nerd at the computers and, like the librarian, he did a double take when he saw me. I circled around the tables, keeping some space between us, unsure of what I wanted to say or do.

Nerd saw the ring on my thumb and gave an approving nod. I moved around the table toward him. He slowly leaned in the opposite direction, his gaze wandering with me, staying cautious of my moves like an abused child forever afraid of what's behind them.

"I was sorry to hear about your husband," he said, breaking the silence. "Is he . . ?"

"He's fine," I answered, lifting the corner of my mouth, hoping to see him do the same. He pitched his head and thinned his lips, happy to hear the news.

Nerd raised his hands then, showing me his palms. "Just so you know, I didn't have anything to do with it."

"I know," I told him as I motioned to a chair for permission to sit down. He lowered his hands and pointed to the chair with a shrug. My hand wandered over the keyboard. I brushed my fingers between the keys, pressing one and then another, teasing them as if I had something to say. "Anything good come up lately?"

His ears perked up but he furrowed his brow cautiously. "Amy . . ." he began flatly. "What do you want?"

"I thought maybe we could just look," I answered. I waited to see his reaction.

He stayed calm, eyes cautious and fixed on me, but then they wandered back to what had begun to scroll by on his screen. Bright green text flew upward, rising until he clicked his mouse, stopping it long enough to read a few lines. His lips moved without making any noise.

"Just look?" he finally said, asking while he studied his screen.

"Maybe do more than look. But no promises," I said. "Just wanted to see what you thought of the idea. Finish what we started?"

He considered what I proposed and then answered, "Maybe I've found someone else already."

I sat up, suddenly feeling both surprised and hurt at the same time. I'd never considered that he would have found someone else to work with. I never considered that he'd even look for someone else.

"Oh. Good for you!" I tried to sound as if it didn't matter to me, to sound as though it wasn't a big deal.

"Amy! Seriously, are you interested?"

"I'm interested!" I nearly shouted, showing my enthusiasm, deciding it didn't matter.

"By the way, I love the new look. It's you. It's very you."

The hours of the day ticked by. I ate alone at Romeo's, all the while imaging Katie sitting across from me.

No more sadness, I told myself, forcing back a memory of when we were young.

The sun had dipped out of the sky and the crisp moonlight made me realize how late it was.

A drink. I was going to celebrate the end of this fine day with a drink. Katie would have approved. A shot of White Bear would have been my first choice, but from what I'd seen during my last drive out there, I thought it likely that the Feds would still have that place closed up.

I got in the car and started driving, crossing a bridge into a part of town I hadn't visited since Steve and I were first dating. I passed our old movie theater, liking that it was still open, still had a line of teens waiting to buy popcorn and see the latest flicks. Their faces were filled with the nervousness of first dates and the eagerness of first kisses, and on some, I saw the hope of a little more.

I found the bar Steve and his friends frequented, the sports bar that nearly ended who we were, who we'd eventually become. The name had changed, and the outside wore a younger look, catering to a dance crowd more than to a sports scene. I parked my car and colored my lips and cheeks using the makeup I'd applied for my visit to the White Bear.

Just a shot, I told myself, hoping they might carry a bottle of White Bear Whiskey. *Maybe two.*

In place of sports commentators came the jarring thump of hard dance music, which thrummed against my body as sharp lights bounced off the walls and ceiling, skating over the tops of dancers jumping up and down. I made my way through a sea of sweaty faces, naked shoulders, and hard abs. Long hair whipped around as hands pawed at my arms and back, the dance crowd absorbing me into their pulsing, amorphic beat. Eager fingers pulled on my hands, inviting me to join them. I rocked my head and motioned that I'd be back, thankful that I had enough of a look to be accepted, to pass the test.

"Shot of White Bear?" I asked, dropping twenty dollars on the bar. I sat down on a round stool, catching my partial reflection in the mirror behind the bottles of liquor. I looked hot. I looked hotter than expected. "Well, Mr. C., you put *ten* years back. Congratulations."

"What was that?" the bartender asked, bending over to hear me better. Tall and cute, sandy blond hair swept to one side, high cheek bones ridged above dimples. "Whiskey, got it. Rocks or neat?"

"White Bear, neat. If you've got it."

He dipped below the bar, glass bottles tolling like bells as he searched. "You're in luck. Last bottle," he answered, reappearing. "And from the sounds of it, last bottle for a long time. With all the news coverage, we've been going through this stuff."

He cracked the cap of the round bottle, set the glass in front of me, and poured my drink. The smell came next, rising to my nose, strong enough that I could taste it. I reached for the glass, but just then another hand touched mine. Slender fingers, painted nails *—and three tattooed hearts between the thumb and forefinger.*

"Can I try?" I heard in my ear, the smell of perfume reaching my nose.

"Aren't you a bit . . . forward?" I asked, then turned to face a woman who was chasing youth, just like me. Beautiful. Her wavy red hair revealed to me a truth only fantasies are made of. I couldn't believe my luck. But then again, maybe somewhere in the deepest recesses of my murderous mind I thought there was a chance that I'd run into Little Miss Three Hearts here. "Skank," I believe my old friend had called her. Even after a decade and a change from a sports bar into a disco, she was still hanging out in the same sad spot. Here she was, within reach of my lips, touching my hand, clearly wanting to do more with me than drink my whiskey.

"I've never gotten anywhere without being a little forward," she answered, lifting my drink and sipping it with her tongue on the glass. "Anyone ever tell you how hot you are? Your husband say that to you, lately?" I wanted to laugh when she asked me that, wondering if she'd even remember straddling my husband's lap.

"He has," I answered, calmly. And then I quickly added, "But we have an understanding."

"Nice," she said, raising her brow. "Bring him around next time."

Her hand moved to mine again, soft and tender. It touched Needle, touched death.

I thought back to how we were going to pay for law school. I thought back to Nerd and the open offer I had made him.

"Things must be different this time," I had said softly. "Careful this time. No mistakes."

"Right, no mistakes," she answered, thinking I was talking to her. "I love your ring."

I watched as she played with the large stone,

waiting to see if she would twist the gem, rotate it, release Needle's syringe. For law school and for Steve, I decided that I needed to become who I was supposed to be. But first, I just needed a little practice.

Sometimes you have to kill a few to save a life.

THANK YOU

Thank you for reading the first book in my series, *Affair with Murder*. Want to read more? Pick up book two, *Painful Truths*, and don't forget to tell me what you think about it!

If you enjoyed reading *Killing Katie*, I would appreciate it if you would help others enjoy my book. How can you help? Tell your friends and family about the great book you just read. Reviews are a great help too. Post online and let me know that you wrote a review so that I have an opportunity to thank you.

Want to read some of my other books and keep in touch? Click my newsletter link, or navigate to https://brspangler.com/sign-up to subscribe and stay informed.

NEWSLETTER

Subscribed members of my newsletter get more than just announcements.

Want to know when the next book will be published? Or how about some FREE stuff? Click the newsletter link, or navigate to https://brspangler.com/sign-up/ to subscribe so that you know when I've posted some freebies or hit the publish button on something new.

What's in it for you when you sign up?

- A chance to win a new Kindle or an Amazon gift card.
- Short stories and free eBooks.
- Signed paperbacks.

And it isn't just about free stuff. I'm always looking for readers and opinions on cover designs and book formatting. There is no better way to work the finer details of a story than to have a few dozen eyes giving me feedback. I tend to reach out to a sizable group, so don't be surprised if you receive an email from me inviting you to help.

Also connect with me online:
Facebook—facebook.com/brspangler
Twitter—@BR_Spangler
Web—brspangler.com

ALSO BY B.R. SPANGLER

Detective Casey White Series

Detective Casey White Series—An absolutely unputdownable crime thriller with twists and turns that will have you racing through the pages. Fans of Kendra Elliot, Rachel Caine and Robert Dugoni will be completely hooked.

Sheriff Jericho Flynn Series

Deadly Tide—A totally gripping crime thriller with unexpected twists and turns. Fans of Gregg Olsen and Lisa Regan will love this book.

Affair with Murder Series

An Affair with Murder—Murder is easy. The consequences are deadly. A heart-pounding Murder and Serial Killer series that will hook you from the start.

A Contemporary Fiction

An Order of Coffee and Tears—Friendships, romance, secrets, and forgiveness come together in this terrific cozy mystery.

Supernatural Suspense

Superman's Cape—A grim and suspenseful tale of a boy lost in a forest that holds all of his fears.

Short Stories

Naked Moon—For one young traveler, a naked moon may mean the difference between life and death.

Some Sci-Fi, Dystopian Thrillers, and Anthologies

From the Caustic *Series—An Apocalyptic and Dystopian series:*

Fallen—Book One

Endure—Book Two

Deceit—Book Three

Reveal—Book Four

From Hugh Howey's World of Wool

Silo Saga: Lottery—What happens when you have one too many mouths to feed?

For more, visit my site and subscribe to my newsletter.

https://brspangler.com/

WHO ARE YOU? WHO ARE YOU?
I'M A WALRUS!
Brian Johnson—*The Breakfast Club*

Who am I?

I'm a resident of Virginia. I live there with my family, along with five cats—sometimes more—two birds, a lizard, and the funniest hamster on the East Coast.

Although I live in Virginia, my heart is still in Philadelphia, Pennsylvania, where I was raised. And I hope that, one day, I'll be able to call Philadelphia home again.

Growing up, I liked to read short stories, but struggled with the words. You see, I had a secret, a sad little secret. Ashamed and embarrassed, I was the little kid in the back row of the schoolroom quietly moving my lips along with the class while everyone read aloud. I couldn't read. I couldn't write. I hoped nobody would notice, but they did. They always did.

By the time I reached the fourth grade, my secret wasn't a secret anymore. The teachers knew something was wrong. *Dyslexia*. Maybe that's why I liked science fiction so much? All those crazy-looking glyphs on the screen, glowing, flashing.

The fix? Back to the third grade for me, and then

special classes three days a week. But it worked. Once I started reading, I never stopped. Stephen King, Piers Anthony, Dean Koontz, and even the Judy Blume books my sisters discarded.

I'm still one of the slowest readers I know, but school was never a problem again. I finally graduated from the third grade, and then kept on going until I finished my master's.

These days, I work as an engineer and spend my nights writing, editing, and thinking up the next great story.

Happy reading,
B.R. Spangler

https://brspangler.com/